KT-389-214

Norman Russell was born in Lancashire but has lived most of his life in Liverpool. After graduating from Jesus College, Oxford, he served a term in the army and was later awarded the degree of Doctor of Philosophy. He now writes full time.

DEPTHS OF DECEIT

In 1894, renowned archaeologist Professor Roderick Ainsworth unearths an ancient Roman temple of Mithras, in London's Clerkenwell, and his career is set to be crowned with a knighthood. Then a young analytical chemist is murdered in the temple, and circumstances suggest a ritual murder. And on the same day, a prosperous manufacturer is found slaughtered at Carshalton . . . Again, evidence points to ritual sacrifice. Detective Inspector Box of Scotland Yard and Sergeant Knollys probe into the professional lives of Roderick Ainsworth and his deadly rival, Sir Charles Wayneflete — and uncover the dreadful truth about the Mithras murders . . .

Books by Norman Russell
Published by The House of Ulverscroft:

THE DRIED-UP MAN
THE DARK KINGDOM
THE HANSA PROTOCOL
WEB OF DISCORD
THE AQUILA PROJECT

NORMAN RUSSELL

DEPTHS OF DECEIT

Complete and Unabridged

ULVERSCROFT
Leicester

First published in Great Britain in 2008 by
Robert Hale Limited
London

First Large Print Edition
published 2009
by arrangement with
Robert Hale Limited
London

British Library CIP Data

Russell, Norman
  Depths of deceit.—Large print ed.—
  Ulverscroft large print series: adventure & suspense
  1. Box, Arnold (Fictitious character)—Fiction
  2. Police—England—London—History—
  19th century—Fiction 3. Excavations (Archaeology)
  —England—London—History—19th century—
  Fiction 4. Blood accusation—Fiction 5. Walbrook
  Mithraeum site (London, England)—Fiction
  6. Detective and mystery stories 7. Large type books
  I. Title
  823.9′2 [F]

  ISBN 978–1–84782–519–3

Published by
F. A. Thorpe (Publishing)
Anstey, Leicestershire

Set by Words & Graphics Ltd.
Anstey, Leicestershire
Printed and bound in Great Britain by
T. J. International Ltd., Padstow, Cornwall

This book is printed on acid-free paper

Contents

1

The Man with the Honeyed Tongue

Detective Inspector Arnold Box and Sergeant Jack Knollys emerged from the cool and shady premises of Mr Mackinnon, the Clerkenwell Stipendiary Magistrate, and were immediately assailed by the hot, sultry heat of the August day. The sun blazed on its throne in a cloudless sky, even though the morning held a promise — or threat — of thunder to come. The water-carts had been out soon after nine o'clock, but the wide sprays of water had done little to make the pavements any cooler underfoot.

It wasn't often that Box came out to Clerkenwell, but that day, Tuesday, 14 August 1894, it had been necessary to hand over personally two dossiers of evidence concerning a fraud case, the preliminary hearing of which the magistrate was due to hear the next morning.

As they began to walk out of Pear Tree Court, where Mr Mackinnon lived, a uniformed police constable hurrying along the opposite pavement caught sight of them, and they heard him utter a little cry of satisfaction. The man looked positively boiled in his heavy serge uniform, and, as he crossed the road to greet them, they saw that his round red face was glistening with perspiration. Box could see the gleaming silver identity badges on his collar: G15. This man was one of Superintendent Hunt's 480 constables in Finsbury Division, working out of King's Cross Road.

'Mr Box, sir,' said the constable, saluting, 'I'm glad to have caught you. Sergeant French knew you'd be here just about this time, because you were entered in the day book as coming on to our patch this morning. He'd be obliged if you'd come and see a dead body that's been found in the old heathen temple next door to Priory Gardens.'

'Sergeant French?' said Box, raising his hat to acknowledge the constable's salute. 'Oh, yes, I remember. He and I worked together two years ago on that Shoreditch throat-slitting business. Have you got a name, Constable, or do you prefer to be called G 15?'

'PC Gully, sir. Will you come? They only discovered this body three-quarters of an hour ago — '

'You don't stand on ceremony, do you, PC Gully?' said Box, smiling. 'Let me introduce

Detective Sergeant Knollys. Now, I know you're one of Mr Hunt's gallant band of men from 'G', but are you a local man? Do you know your way around Clerkenwell?'

'Yes, sir. I was born in Clerkenwell, near Hatton Wall. Will you — ?'

'Yes, yes, I'll come. Don't worry about it. Now this heathen temple: is that the archaeological dig that was reported in all the papers in June?'

'Yes, sir. The 'Mithraeum' they call it, or some such name. I don't know what that means, but it's Roman, so Sergeant French tells me.'

'The Mithraeum — yes, I remember seeing some engravings of it in *The Illustrated London News*. It was excavated by a man called Professor Ainsworth, as I recall. And this body — it's not some old skeleton, is it? I'm rather busy this morning. Sergeant Knollys and I want to get back to King James's Rents before one o'clock.'

'No, sir, it's not a skeleton. It's the body of a young man freshly killed. Perhaps it was an accident, or maybe it was murder. I don't know, sir. But Sergeant French would like you to come and take a look.'

'A murder? I thought Clerkenwell was a genteel kind of place — at least in parts.'

'It doesn't happen often, sir,' said PC Gully

3

defensively. 'Murder, I mean. There are some very nice people living in Clerkenwell.'

The three police officers turned left into Farringdon Lane. PC Gully stole a sly glance at Box, and thought to himself: you'd think a famous Scotland Yard detective would be taller. He couldn't be more than five foot seven. Still, he looked very smart and dapper in that double-breasted fawn overcoat and the brown curly-brimmed bowler. The trim moustache suited him, too. How old was he? About thirty-five? He'd been one of the youngest inspectors in the Metropolitan Police at the time of his promotion, so he'd heard.

And that sergeant — Sergeant Knollys — was a giant of a man by contrast. He must be nearing six foot four — talk about the long and short of it!

They turned abruptly out of Farringdon Lane and into Priory Gate Street. Halfway along the street, and set back several feet from the carriageway between a piano emporium and a stationer's shop, a muddy platform constructed of stout planks had been built across the pavement. A wooden gate let into crude palings gave access to a roughly levelled area covered in rubble, in which stood a number of builder's huts, marooned among heaps of excavated soil and stone. Tall, gaunt buildings of sooty brick rose to the rear and the left of the site, while to the right could be glimpsed an attractive miniature park.

'Remind me, Constable,' said Box, 'there's a name, isn't there, for this little island of tumbledown buildings.'

'It used to be called the Rat Run in the old days, sir, on account of the vicious folk who lived in the dark little courts and alleys between here and Baker's Row. Most of it was thrown down in the eighties, and the whole area's due to be cleared by 1897. That's how they discovered the underground heathen temple, sir, after they demolished a couple of empty courts in '93.'

A small crowd had gathered at the entrance to the site, and two constables were busily engaged in keeping the bolder members of the throng from clambering over the muddy boards to see what was amiss. As Constable Gully helped Box and Knollys over the planks and down into the excavation site, the inspector could hear the comments of the onlookers, who, despite the rather gruff warnings of the constables to keep their distance, refused to disperse.

'There's been an accident . . . Someone's been killed . . . Murdered, most likely . . . It's not that famous professor, is it?

Ainsworth, he's called. He's the one who dug up that heathen place . . . Maybe the old Romans put a curse on it. You hear some funny things . . . '

A rough wooden canopy had been raised over a yawning gap in the earth, and from the lip of this murky pit Box saw a flight of wooden steps leading down into the darkness.

'Mind how you go, sir, and you, Sergeant,' PC Gully warned them. 'Those steps are a bit slippery, and they'll take you down twelve feet into the bowels of the earth.'

Arnold Box stooped down, and, followed by Knollys, carefully descended from the bright sunlight of the street into the engulfing shade of the Mithraeum.

★　★　★

An emotionless, almost tranquil face, a halo of fair curls topped with some kind of leathern cap, and then a lithe body, the knee of the left leg pressed into the back of a writhing white bull; the left hand of the owner of the tranquil face pulled back the bull's head, while the right hand, grasping a sickle, cut the beast's throat . . .

All this Arnold Box saw in a haze of sepia, and umber, sienna, and pallid green as he stepped down on to the stone floor of the subterranean chamber. Then, as his eyes grew accustomed to the shade, he saw that he was staring at a brilliant painting, rendered on plaster-covered stone, part of a structure resembling the reredos of a church, which rose some ten feet to the vaulted roof of the crypt. A great shaft of sunlight penetrated the chamber from the wide opening, bathing the reredos in a strong and steady glow, which was why Box had been so suddenly mesmerized by the image of the man with the sickle.

'Good morning, Inspector Box, sir. It's very kind of you to come. I'm over here, in this aisle.'

Instantly the spell of the pagan image was broken. Box moved cautiously in front of the reredos until he came in sight of Sergeant French. The sunlight glinted off the silver buttons of his uniform jacket. He was kneeling in a gloomy aisle beside the huddled form of a young man, and as Box crouched down, French opened the door of a dark lantern.

'How are you, Sergeant French?' asked Box. 'This is Detective Sergeant Knollys, my colleague from King James's Rents.'

The two sergeants nodded to each other, and then Knollys moved away, apparently on an investigation of his own. Box knelt down beside the sergeant, and looked at the body of the young man. What had he been doing in this pagan shrine? He was wearing a dark broadcloth suit, and well-polished shoes. No more than twenty-eight or thirty, thought Box. His arms were stretched out awkwardly at his sides.

'His fingers are stained with chemicals,' he said. 'Perhaps he was a photographer. There's a gold signet ring on the third finger of his left hand.'

The dead man's head lay partly concealed by what seemed to be a fallen slab of stone. Sergeant French tipped the lantern on its side, so that it illuminated the ceiling of the vault. Box could see the space where the fatal block of stone had once been fixed.

'At first sight, Sergeant,' said Box, 'it looks like an accident. This young man was probably here on legitimate business of some kind, and died instantly when that block of stone suddenly fell on him. When was the body discovered?'

'Not more than an hour ago, sir. One of the workmen came down from the sheds to look for something that he needed, and found him. Constable Gully was here within minutes, and sent a man round to fetch me from the local station.'

Arnold Box sighed. French was a good

man, but he had a very hazy concept of time. Box slipped his watch from his waistcoat pocket, flipped open the lid, and looked at the dial.

'Sergeant French,' he said, 'it's exactly half past ten. What time was it when the body was found? What time was it when you arrived? It's no good telling me that PC Gully arrived 'within minutes'.'

'I'm sorry, sir. I've logged all the times here, in my notebook. Let me see — the body was discovered at twelve minutes past nine. Gully, who was out on his beat, arrived here at twenty past, and I was here before the half-hour had struck.'

'Good. And why did you send for me, Sergeant French? Surely this is a case that 'G' can handle without assistance from Scotland Yard?'

'Asking your pardon, Mr Box, but I don't think it was an accident. There's something weird and horrible about this business. Would you lie on your side, sir, and take a peek under that stone slab?'

As Box moved to do as the sergeant advised, his eyes were drawn momentarily to the tranquil pagan man in the leathern cap. A silent witness . . . What abominations had that figure seen enacted in this hot, oppressive vault over tens of centuries?

Sacrifices, perhaps. Wresting his eyes away from the pagan figure, Box lay on his side, and directing the beam of the dark lantern, looked under the fatal slab of stone.

He saw at once that something was wrong. The slab was, in fact, leaning against the wall of the aisle, so that the dead man's head was untouched by it. Poor young fellow! His abundant fair hair was clotted with congealing blood. His blue eyes were still open, gazing incuriously at Box from only inches away. His features retained an expression of sudden surprise. In the cramped area beneath the fallen stone, Box's sensitive nose could detect the first faint signs of dissolution.

What was this? A clear yellow liquid had escaped from the dead man's mouth. It formed a sticky patch, no bigger than a penny, on the pavement of the vault. As though in answer to an unspoken question, Sergeant French said, 'It's honey.'

'*Honey?*'

'Yes, sir. That's one reason why I sent PC Gully to find you in Pear Tree Court. There he lies, Mr Box, apparently killed in an accident — an 'accident' which in my opinion was faked — and with his mouth full of honey. I wouldn't touch him until you arrived, sir. I've sent another constable for the police hearse. We'll have to move him out of

10

this dark corner soon, and get him to Clerkenwell Mortuary. This hot weather . . . '

'How long do you think he's been dead, Sergeant? Did you send for a doctor?'

'I did, sir, but nobody's come, so far. I reckon he's been dead for about three hours, Mr Box, which puts his death at about seven this morning. I'm usually correct at making these estimates when there's no doctor at the scene.'

'From the present state of the body, Sergeant,' said Box, 'I'm inclined to agree with you. Seven o'clock sounds about right to me.'

Arnold Box stood up, and dusted the knees of his trousers.

'And you're quite right about this not being an accident. That honey . . . It's a very sinister detail, Sergeant. As for that stone slab, I thought at first that it had been placed deliberately over the body to suggest an accident, but whoever did this deed wasn't concerned to conceal the fact of murder. The honey in the mouth shows that. What we must do now is get him out of that dark corner, so that we can look at him properly, and perhaps find out who he was. Sergeant Knollys — Where is he? Where are you, Sergeant?'

Box's professional interest was now fully

aroused. For the first time since he had descended the steps, he was no longer conscious of the pervasive image of the bull slayer in the leathern cap. Sergeant Knollys, who had ventured further into the area of the temple behind the reredos, appeared out of the darkness.

'There are some massive baulks of timber rising to the ceiling at the back of this chamber, sir,' he said. 'I expect they've been put there to support the roof.'

'Perhaps, Sergeant,' said Box, 'But never mind the beams for the moment. I want you to take this poor young man's shoulders, draw his body very gently out of that aisle, and lay him out decently in this patch of sunlight on the floor. Careful, now! Watch his head! That's it. Now, let's have a closer look at the back of his skull.'

Box knelt down beside the body, and carefully drew his fingers down the eyelids, closing the blue eyes. The two sergeants watched him in silence as he raised the dead man's head, and drew it forward towards his chest. It seemed an age before he gently laid the body down once more on the flags.

'Well, Officers,' he said, 'this man wasn't killed by a slab of stone falling on him from the ceiling. There's a long wound in the back of his head, caused by some kind of sharp instrument — it might have been an adze, or a cleaver of some sort. The blow penetrated the skull. That was the cause of death. Struck from behind, by someone standing a little to his right. So it's murder, as we suspected, Sergeant French. Now, it's time to find out who the murdered man was. As this is your patch, Sergeant, I think the honours lie with you.'

Arnold Box watched the uniformed sergeant as he began a careful search of the dead man's clothing. They'd worked together once before, on a bloody murder in Shoreditch. French was a narrow-faced, slow-breathing man of fifty, with steady grey eyes. He had removed his helmet to reveal his sparse grey hair, brushed back neatly from his forehead. French had retrieved the dead man's wallet from an inside pocket of his coat. He removed a calling card, and held it near his eyes.

'His name's Gregory Walsh,' said French. ''Gregory Walsh, B.Sc., Assayer and Sampler'. That's what it says on this card. He lived at 5 Hayward's Court, off St John Street, EC. That's not very far to walk from here. So now we know who he is.'

Box looked doubtful.

'We know his name, Sergeant French, and where he lived. But we don't really know *who*

13

he is, do we? Is he married or single? Rich or poor? What does he assay? What does he sample? No, it's early days yet. Incidentally, does your inspector know that you've asked me to come down here? I very much want to be associated with this case, but I can't act without your inspector's permission.'

'I've not contacted him yet, sir, but he's a man who likes his officers to use their initiative. As soon as we've got the body out of this foul place I'll go and see him. Until then, Mr Box, I regard you as being in charge here.'

From somewhere in the roadway beyond the gaping entrance to the Mithraeum, the sound of a handbell was heard. At the same time there came an excited murmur from the crowd. PC Gully appeared in the opening, and announced that the police hearse had just turned into Priory Gate Street.

'Sergeant French,' said Box, 'I know you'd intended to convey the body to Clerkenwell Mortuary. Instead, would you tell the drivers to take it straight away to Horseferry Road? They've more facilities there, and someone I know is duty surgeon there today. It's a long drag out from here, I know — '

'Say no more, sir,' said French. 'Is there anything else you want me to do?'

'I'd like you to lend me PC Gully for half

14

an hour, if you will. He's a local man, he tells me, and I'd like Sergeant Knollys and me to be given a little tour of this block of buildings before we return to Whitehall.'

'Have him by all means, Mr Box. Ah! Here's the stretcher party at last. Now we can get the poor young man decently covered and taken out of this infernal heat.'

★　★　★

When the three policemen emerged blinking into the light, they saw that the persistent crowd of onlookers had moved further up the street to form a reception committee for the police hearse, which had just turned out of Farringdon Lane into Priory Gate Street. Box and Knollys followed PC Gully, who conducted them swiftly in the opposite direction. They passed the stationer's shop, which was closed and shuttered, and then turned left into a narrow shop-lined street. There were no pavements, and the cobbles were uncomfortable underfoot.

'This is Catherine Lane, sir,' said PC Gully. 'As you can see, it's got a number of jewellers' shops, and one or two optician's premises. This place here, on your right, is Mr Gold's workshop. He's a wholesale jeweller. Next door to him we have this grand-looking place, sir, with its fancy redbrick front, and a clock in a kind of gable up there, above the gutters. Hatchard's Furniture Repository, it used to be. It's been closed for years. And just further on — '

'Just a minute, Constable,' Box interrupted. 'Hold your horses, will you? As I see it, this Catherine Lane is one side of a rough square. The first side we saw was Priory Gate Street, with the archaeological site, and the stationer's next door to it. This Catherine Lane forms the second side of the square, and you're going to take us along the remaining two sides. Am I right?'

'Yes, sir. It's like a square, this whole block.'

'And this Hatchard's Furniture Repository — it looks in very good repair, but you say it's been closed for years. Curious, that, don't you think?'

'It *is* looked after, sir, I'll admit that. But I remember it being closed while I was still a boy. It's locked, barred and bolted, and quite empty inside. You can see through some of the windows at the back if you jump up and down, and look through the bars. We used to dare each other to climb up on to the roof when I was a boy. There are skylights up there.'

'Dear me!' said Box. 'I'm sorry to hear that

you had a disreputable past, PC Gully. So it's been empty for years?'

'It has, sir,' said Gully, smiling in spite of himself. 'And we only dared each other. We never actually climbed up there. Now here, beside Hatchard's you'll see this narrow back crack, which is called Miller's Alley. This is by way of being the third side of your square, Mr Box.'

They followed Gully along a narrow path between the windowless flank of the furniture repository and another dismal blind wall to their left. Miller's Alley was strewn with the detritus of decay: pieces of blackened brick, the charred remnants of mischievous fires, the yellowing bones and fragments of offal discarded there by some rogue butcher. Rank grass grew long between the uneven flags.

'And this is Miller's Court, Inspector,' said PC Gully as they emerged from the alley into a mean courtyard flanked on two sides by derelict slum dwellings. Roofless, and with the window sashes long plundered for kindling wood, the airless cottages looked like the skeletons of human dwellings.

'I wonder who Miller was, sir?' asked Sergeant Knollys. It was the first time that he had spoken since he and Box had joined PC Gully on their tour of the area, and the constable jumped in surprise. For a sinister,

17

scar-faced giant of a man, he thought, Mr Box's sergeant spoke very well. He could almost have been mistaken for a gentleman.

'Miller? I expect he was another of those slum landlords who threw up these courts in the forties,' Box replied. 'Can you imagine having to live here? Miller's Court . . . Wasn't this one of the cholera courts, Constable?'

'It was, sir, back in the early sixties. There were still people living here when I was a boy — desperate folk, they were. But it'll all be gone and forgotten by '97.'

Facing the ruined cottages the back wall of Hatchard's Furniture Repository rose towards the sky. A rear entrance was closed by stout doors containing three mortise locks. The remaining wall of the enclosed court was topped by a line of broken glass cemented into the brickwork. Beyond this wall lay the archaeological site in Priory Gate Street.

Arnold Box glanced up at the hot sky above them. Not a cloud was to be seen, but suddenly there came a rumble of thunder. A single dark cloud appeared from over the rim of Hatchard's roof, and Box felt a few drops of rain fall on to his upturned face.

'I don't like the feel of this place at all, Sergeant,' said Box, turning towards Knollys. 'Locked, barred and bolted — it's what my old pa calls a bag of mystery. Constable, can you show us the fourth side of the square?'

'You'll have to come through one of these ruined cottages, sir,' said Gully. 'Mind how you go! The floors are firm enough, but there's a lot of rubbish lying about.'

PC Gully selected a dwelling on the left side of the court, and led Box and Knollys through the doorless entrance. Tramps had lit fires in the building, and what remained of the staircase had been burned into a mound of fine ash. They emerged through a gap in the rear wall into a thin strip of beaten clay bounded by a sturdy wooden fence.

'This is your fourth side of the square, Inspector Box,' said PC Gully. 'Beyond this fence lies Priory Gardens, the little park laid out in 'ninety. Very soon now, Miller's Court will be thrown down, and the gardens extended across the site.'

'What about Hatchard's Furniture Repository?'

'Well, sir, that'll stay where it is. So will all the shops and little factories along Catherine Lane. It was just that warren of slum houses called the Rat Run that was to be demolished, so I've been told.'

'Well, thank you, Constable,' said Box. 'This little tour of yours has given me a lot to think about. Incidentally, why is it called Catherine Lane? Who was this Catherine?'

'Centuries ago, sir, there used to be a church facing on to the lane, and it was called St Catherine's. And it was just near the steps leading up to Hatchard's that the famous treasure was found in 1887. The Clerkenwell Treasure.'

'The Clerkenwell Treasure? I seem to remember reading something about that in the paper, Constable. So it was discovered in Catherine Lane?'

'Yes, sir. It was in a specially made cavity beneath the porch of the old church, and it had been lost for centuries, so they said. And the funny thing is, sir, that it was found by this same Professor Ainsworth who discovered the Mithraeum last year — just a couple of streets away from here.'

2

At King James's Rents

When Box and Knollys had taken formal leave of Sergeant French and PC Gully, they walked down Leather Lane and into Holborn Circus, where they hailed an omnibus that would take them to Whitehall. Despite a further episode of thunder spots, Box assured Knollys that it was not going to rain that day. They mounted to the empty upper deck.

'The sky's all wrong for rain, Sergeant,' said Box as they settled themselves on one of the wooden-slatted seats. 'And besides, it would be stifling inside on a day like this. All that straw, and hot bodies. Did you know, Sergeant, that in this great metropolis of ours, nine hundred tons of horse-droppings are deposited on the carriageways every day?'

'No, I didn't know that, sir,' said Knollys, 'but I can well imagine it. It's certainly very olfactory today.'

'Olfactory? What does that mean? Did you invent it?'

'It means smelly, sir. It's in the dictionary.'

Box took his notebook from a pocket, and

21

rapidly flicked through the pages.

'Let's forget all about horse-droppings, pagan gods and temples, Jack,' he said, 'and concentrate on the murdered man, Mr Gregory Walsh, B.Sc., Assayer and Sampler, whose home is at 5 Hayward's Court. Or maybe it's his business premises. Now, we can leave it to 'G' to inform the next of kin, and prepare them for a visit from you, tomorrow. Find out what he was doing at the Mithraeum. Funny name, isn't it? Sounds like a music hall. See if you can establish any connection between Walsh and this professor — what's his name? Ainsworth. We'll have to talk to the professor, too, before many more days have elapsed.'

The iron tyres of the horse-omnibus screeched as they passed over the cobbles at the junction of Fetter Lane and Fleet Street. Above the all-pervading ring of traffic, they would both hear the menacing roll of thunder.

'What will you do, sir?' asked Knollys.

'Me? Well, the first thing I'll do when we get back to the Rents is see if PC Mackenzie's in his telegraph cabin, and get him to send a wire to young Dr Donald Miller, who's on duty at Horseferry Road Mortuary today. I want him to perform an immediate postmortem. You remember Dr Miller, don't you? He came out to Corunna Lands last year, to examine the body of poor PC Lane. I'll call on Miller early this evening, and hear what he has to tell us.'

They had reached the Strand, and the traffic was becoming very dense. The sky was rapidly blackening, and the hot air of the August day was turning humid.

'And another thing, Jack,' said Box. 'I'm going to send Sergeant Kenwright to go through that Mithraeum with a fine-tooth comb. And while he's there, he can make drawings of that stone reredos, and any other little detail that takes his fancy. You know how good he is at that sort of thing, and — Ah! Whitehall, at last!'

As Box and Knollys rose from their seats, there came a flash of sheet lightning, followed by a terrifying clap of thunder. The heavens opened, and in seconds both men were soaked to the skin. Clattering down the open staircase, they jumped off the moving vehicle into Whitehall.

As they hurried down the little narrow street called Great Scotland Yard, Arnold Box could see the old entrance to 'A' Division, where, until four years earlier, members of the public had come when they'd wanted to 'see a policeman'. It was in actual fact the back entrance to Number 4, Whitehall Place, the old office of the Metropolitan Police Commissioners.

Three years earlier, the Metropolitan Police had removed themselves, lock, stock and barrel, from their festering collection of cramped old houses in Whitehall Place and its environs, and had taken up residence in the gleaming new fairy palace on the Embankment, known as New Scotland Yard.

Some officers, though, had been left behind, including Detective Inspector Box and a dozen others, shepherded by Superintendent Mackharness, an elderly and often irascible veteran of the Crimean War. It was, they had been told, only a temporary measure, but already the original dozen exiles had swollen to over thirty.

Leaving the gleaming wet pavements of Whitehall Place, Box and Knollys picked their way over the slippery cobbles that would take them to their headquarters at 2 King James's Rents. The leaden atmosphere of the hot August day had caused a pall of blue smoke, blown down from a hundred chimney stacks. It covered the battered old building, which was one of the later annexes acquired by the Criminal Investigation Department in one of its frenzies of expansion out of Whitehall Place.

King James's Rents, with its labyrinth of

24

connecting rooms on two floors, was reputed to be as old as Whitehall. It got its name from the fact that it had provided lodging for the Scottish courtiers who had arrived in London with James I. That canny monarch had charged them rent for the privilege. The rear portion of the Rents, a former carriage-maker's establishment, had been acquired in 1845.

Box and Knollys entered the vestibule of 2 King James's Rents. The scrubbed wooden floorboards were wet with the drippings from countless regulation cloaks. Ahead of them were the glazed swing doors of Box's office, a room into which daylight never penetrated with any conviction, and where the gas mantle burned and spluttered for most of the day and night.

'Box, come up here, if you please. I shan't keep you more than ten minutes.'

Superintendent Mackharness was standing at the top of the steep stairs that led to his dim, mildewed office on the first floor. He must have seen them crossing the cobbles from Whitehall Place. Leaving Knollys to enter their office, Box hurried up the stairs in obedience to his master's summons.

Arnold Box regarded his superior officer with a judicious mixture of affection and apprehension. Mackharness was well over sixty, and afflicted by occasional bouts of sciatica, which had given him a more or less permanent limp. His yellowish face was adorned with neatly trimmed mutton chop whiskers. He was a tidy man, dressed in a black civilian frock coat, which made him look rather like an elderly clerk in a counting-house. Box thought that he deserved better accommodation than the gloomy, lop-sided chamber, smelling of stale gas and mildew, that he was obliged to occupy.

'Sit down in that chair, will you, Box,' said Mackharness, 'and listen carefully to what I have to say. You look very damp — positively bedraggled. You're usually a smart man, Box — well done! — so after this interview, you'd better tidy yourself up a bit. Put a comb through your hair, and so forth. Now, what was it I wanted to say? Oh, yes. I've had a communication from an Inspector Perrivale, out at Carshalton. I don't know him, but he writes very succinctly and well. A man was found murdered there this morning, so he tells me, a man called Abraham Barnes. I have his letter here . . . Yes, here it is.

'Abraham Barnes, Esquire, principal of the Royal Albert Cement Works. Apparently he was semi-retired, and his factory was run by a resident manager. This Barnes was sixty-four. He lived with his wife and unmarried daughter in a house called Wellington Lodge, built in the grounds of his works. He was found in the conservatory of this house, and Inspector Perrivale says he was killed by a blow with a sharp instrument to the back of the skull.'

Mackharness put the letter down on his ornate desk, and smiled rather grimly.

'Perrivale says that this Abraham Barnes was a popular man, esteemed by all, and with no enemies. Well, we've heard that kind of thing before. It means little or nothing. Go down there, will you, Box, and see what it's all about?'

'Why does Mr Perrivale want a Scotland Yard man, sir? Does he say?'

'He says that there were peculiar and sinister aspects to the murder that are beyond his capacities as an investigator. Very honest of him, I must say. Our uniformed friends are usually most unwilling to make any such admission! Go down there first thing tomorrow morning. There are frequent trains from London Bridge Station.'

It was very hot in Mackharness's office, and the room seemed to be pervaded by the combined odours of mildew, chimney smoke, and snuff. One of the sash windows had been raised a few inches, and had wedged itself stuck at a drunken angle between the frames.

The superintendent handed Box the folder containing Inspector Perrivale's letter, and then sat back in his chair.

'How did you get on in Clerkenwell this morning?' he asked.

Box described in detail his summons to the Mithraeum in Priory Gate Street, and his brief investigation of the murder of Gregory Walsh.

'Assayer and Sampler?' said Mackharness after a few moments' deliberation. 'That suggests that he was a chemist of some sort — perhaps an analytical chemist. Now I wonder what a man like that would be doing in an old Roman vault? Pursue the case by all means, Box, but see if you can clear up this business at Carshalton first. I'd be interested to hear what Perrivale considers to be 'sinister aspects'.'

'I'll go first thing tomorrow, sir,' said Box. 'But for the rest of today I'd like to pursue some leads connected with this business of the Mithraeum.'

Superintendent Mackharness did not seem to hear him. His eyes were narrowed, as though he was recalling some incident in his own past. Presently he spoke again.

'This Mithraeum, Box, will have been concerned with the worship of an old Roman god called Mithras. I remember doing him at school. We did them all: Zeus, Apollo, Minerva . . . And then we had Hercules, and Perseus, and Aeneas, and the story of Troy. Did you do any of those things at school?'

'No, sir.'

'You were lucky. We did it all in Greek and Latin, Box, from little tattered books with missing covers, and if you dared glance out of the window, you'd see people going about their lawful occasions, their heads mercifully free of all this stuff . . . '

'It sounds awful, sir.'

'It was. And then I attained my sixteenth year, and rushed off to the Curragh to join the Royal Irish Rangers. No Latin or Greek there! Now, what was I saying? Oh, yes. Go out to Carshalton tomorrow, and find out what's amiss. I think that's all, Box. Good afternoon.'

⋆   ⋆   ⋆

When Box left Mr Mackharness's office, he made his way along a narrow windowless passage, at the end of which an iron spiral staircase took him up to the telegraph cabin, a small room that had been built upwards through the roof of 2 King James's Rents. There was no landing: you stood on the top step of the spiral staircase, and pushed open

29

the narrow door. The telegrapher, PC Mackenzie, was sitting at his single telegraph engine, reading a newspaper. He sprang to his feet as Box, still standing on the staircase, half leaned into the bright little room. Through the large window he could just see the telegraph wire stretching from its insulator across the roofs of Whitehall.

'Constable,' said Box, 'I want you to send a wire to Dr Miller at the Horseferry Road Mortuary. Ready? 'Miller — please perform immediate post-mortem on the body of Gregory Walsh. Will call after six this evening. Box. King James's Rents'.'

'Do you want a reply, sir?'

'No, thank you. Just send the wire, Constable. I'm quite certain that Dr Miller will oblige me.'

Box closed the door of the cabin, descended the iron staircase, and threaded his way along the maze of passages that would take him back to the first-floor landing. In the fairy palace on the Embankment, he mused, men similar to himself would be hurrying along spacious tiled corridors, lit by the electric light; it was humiliating to know that parts of King James's Rents were still illuminated by candles and oil lamps.

When Box gained the ground floor, he

pushed open the swing doors of his office. It was a spacious, high-ceilinged room, but very little natural light penetrated into it from the vestibule of the Rents. A rackety two-burner gas-mantle suspended from the soot-stained ceiling hissed and spluttered. On that particular day, the wooden floor had been freshly scrubbed, and the place smelt of carbolic.

Sergeant Knollys was standing in front of the fireplace, peering at some of the notices that had been gummed to the big flyblown mirror rising above the mantelpiece. Or was he, in fact, ruefully examining the livid scar which ran across his face from below the right eye to the left corner of his mouth? That scar was a relic of an encounter with a gang of vengeful thugs, who had used a length of sharpened iron railing to break his right arm and a number of ribs before disfiguring him for life. Such was a policeman's lot.

Sergeant Knollys turned as Box entered the office, and sat down at a chair drawn up to the big office table. Box slid out of his overcoat, and sat down opposite him. He flourished the folder that the superintendent had given him.

'Mr Mackharness wants me to go out to Carshalton tomorrow,' he said. 'A certain Mr Abraham Barnes, cement manufacturer, was murdered there early this morning, apparently under mysterious circumstances. I suppose I'll be there all morning. It's a nuisance, really, Sergeant. I want to start looking more closely at this Mithraeum business.'

'Carshalton? It's a very nice little place, sir,' said Knollys. 'We used to go down there by train from Croydon when I was a boy. It was on the line to Epsom. Barnes . . . Yes, I remember. Barnes's cement factory was next door to the old flour mill at Hackbridge.'

'Well, that's where I'll be going tomorrow morning, Jack. I'll go by myself, because I've other work I want you to do. Later today I'll walk into Westminster, and visit Dr Miller at Horseferry Road Mortuary. I've telegraphed him to let him know I'm coming. He'll have performed the autopsy on Gregory Walsh by then, and I'll bring the results, and all poor young Walsh's effects, back with me.'

'And what do you want me to do, sir?' asked Knollys.

'Well, I'm telling you, aren't I? I want you to call on the bereaved family in Hayward's Court, Clerkenwell. You can take all Walsh's things with you in a valise. Try to find out why he went to the Mithraeum this morning. See if you can establish any connection between him and this Professor Ainsworth, the man who discovered not only the heathen temple, but the Clerkenwell Treasure. I must go and see that treasure, Sergeant. I wonder where it is? Mr Mackharness will know — '

'It's in the South Kensington Museum, sir.'

'Is it really? I'll make a mental note of that.'

'And I've looked up this Professor Ainsworth, sir. Roderick Ainsworth. He lives at a place called Ardleigh Manor, out at Epsom. He's a moneyed man, by all accounts, connected with a shipbuilding concern up north.'

'Well done, Sergeant. Does he have a Town address?'

'No, sir, but he's a member of the Athenaeum. We could always contact him there.'

'Well, never mind Professor Ainsworth now. We'll meet here first thing tomorrow, Jack, and I'll give you the results of the post-mortem, and all Walsh's things for you to take out to Old St Pancras Road. Is there any chance of a cup of tea? Where's Sergeant Kenwright?'

As though in answer to Box's questions, there came a stirring in the narrow, tunnel-like passage joining the office to what Mr Mackharness called the 'drill hall', a long, whitewashed room at the rear of the building. Presently a burly, uniformed police constable, an impressive figure with a flowing spade beard, emerged into the office. He was carrying a tin tray, on which reposed two mugs of steaming tea, and a saucer of broken biscuits.

'Ah! Sergeant Kenwright! As always, you're just in the nick of time. Sit down there, will you, while I tell you what happened to Sergeant Knollys and me this morning.'

As Box sipped his tea, he told the sergeant all about the summons to the Mithraeum, and what he and Knollys had found there.

'I want you to go out to Clerkenwell, Sergeant Kenwright,' said Box, 'and take that art box of yours with you. You can take a cab if you like, or go on the omnibus. I want you to do some measurements in that crypt — its dimensions, and the dimensions of the big reredos I told you about. But more than that, I want you to make careful drawings of those pagan figures, and of anything else that you think is important. I want to know as much as I can about that Mithraeum, Sergeant, and we can start by having your collection of plans and drawings pinned up on boards in the drill hall for our contemplation. Go out there tomorrow morning.'

'Very good, sir,' said Kenwright, rising from the table. 'I'll put some things together straight away.'

He saluted Box, and moved away down the

tunnel. How lucky he was to have landed up there, at the Rents! Two years ago, as a beat constable, he had contracted rheumatic fever and had nearly died. When he was still convalescent, his divisional superintendent had arranged for him to be transferred to King James's Rents, for the performance of light duties.

There, he had discovered new talents, which had been put to such good use in the dramatic cases of Sir William Porteous, and the sinister business of the Hansa Protocol, that he had been promoted to sergeant. He hoped devoutly that he would not be returned at some time to the divisions. It was lovely at the Rents.

★   ★   ★

In the dim, panelled smoking-room of the Scottish Lyceum Club, where he was staying, Professor Roderick Ainsworth, LLD, MA, blew out the match with which he had lit his cigar, dropped it into the ashtray, and leaned back in his deep leather armchair. It was good to be in Edinburgh again, with the prospect of a capacity audience for his forthcoming lecture at the Royal Caledonian Institution. 'Mithras in the Shadow of St Paul's: How London's ancient Temple of Mithras was discovered'. He'd give the same lecture again, suitably retitled, at the Exeter Hall in London on the twentieth.

His friend David Mackay was holding forth on one of his deliberately mischievous hobby-horses. The others sitting round the table regarded him with amused resignation. David was getting fat. He didn't exercise enough, and he ate too much. They had all enjoyed a rather late luncheon, but David Mackay had turned his enjoyment into something approaching devotion!

'So you still maintain, Ainsworth,' he was saying, 'that the Romans never penetrated to any great effect into Scotland? Or, rather, what we now call Scotland? Surely old Wayne-flete maintained that they'd established a fortress of sorts near Newbie Mains, on the Solway Firth, just south of Annan? He wrote a paper about it, some years ago, in which he showed engravings of some fragments of tile — '

'Wayneflete's a charlatan! I know that you're just teasing me, Mackay, but it's true. And it's no good waving that confounded pamphlet of his at me: I told you that I've come up to Scotland without my reading glasses. I don't know *where* they are. Now, what was I saying? Oh, yes.'

Ainsworth put his cigar into the ashtray, and allowed it to go out.

'Wayneflete', he continued, 'knows very well that those bits of tile came from somewhere else. They're suspiciously like those that you can see on the damaged tessellated pavement at Crowton Magna in Dorset. I wouldn't put it past Sir Charles Wayneflete to have pocketed a few bits of that pavement when he was down there in '84, and then dropped them through a hole in his pocket when he visited Newbie Mains. Don't tell him I said so, though. He may sue me for slander!'

Everybody laughed, and began talking of other matters.

Roderick Ainsworth closed his eyes, and listened to his friends talking among themselves — the genial and mischievous Mackay, the learned Sillitoe, Murdoch Stuart — another practical archaeologist — and the others, all scholars of note, and all unequivocal admirers of himself. Yes, it was good to be in Scotland once again. As a young man he had often travelled up from Newcastle, where the family's shipyard had been established for a couple of lifetimes, and savoured the brilliant intellectual life of Scotland's capital, 'the modern Athens'.

Wayneflete . . . It was generally accepted that Wayneflete was his academic rival, but to regard him in that light was a vexing travesty

of the truth. He, Ainsworth, was a professional academic, Cordwainers' Professor of
Antiquities in the University of London. His
discovery of the Clerkenwell Treasure in 1887
had confirmed his status as an investigative
scholar of the first rank. And, then, of course,
his uncovering of the Mithraeum at Clerkenwell had been a triumph, kindling the public's
imagination, and making him overnight a
popular figure in the lecture halls.

As to Wayneflete . . . The man was a
dabbler, who had never mastered any
academic discipline. Was he really a charlatan? Well, perhaps that was too strong an
accusation. Sir Charles Wayneflete, Baronet,
was a titled amateur, jack of all trades and
master of none. He lived beyond his income
in a crumbling town mansion in Lowndes
Square, eccentric and reclusive, tended now
by an elderly housekeeper, who was said to
bully him.

It was ludicrous to see Wayneflete as a rival
in any sense of the word. But there was no
doubt whatever that he was a dangerous man,
whose mind held some obscure and threaten-
ing secrets. He was, too, consumed by
jealousy — jealousy of *him*, Ainsworth.
Wayneflete was a man to despise, but never to
ignore.

'And how is your family faring, Ainsworth?'

38

Roderick Ainsworth immediately opened his tired eyes and gave his full attention to Murdoch Sillitoe, who had asked the question.

'My family? They're in fine fettle, Sillitoe, thank you. Zena's sculpting gets better and better. It's all massive stuff, you know, big bronze affairs. They're calling her the second Rodin. And Margery — my daughter — is developing into a pianist of concert standard. She can play all that finger-breaking stuff by Chopin — rattles it off, you know, as though she's been doing it all her life. And that other fellow with the shock of white hair — she can play him, too. Liszt.'

'Isn't that the chap who died a few years ago?' asked David Mackay. 'Funny-looking fellow, who wore a floppy hat? Fancy being able to play *him*! Or do I mean Wagner?'

Professor Ainsworth hauled himself out of his comfortable leather chair. He smiled at the assembled company. How good it was to see them all again.

'Gentlemen,' he said, 'although it's only half-past three, I must retire to my room and sleep for a couple of hours. I'm absolutely exhausted. I will appear once more in the land of the living at six o'clock, consume a cold collation of chicken in aspic with a single glass of chilled hock, and then sally forth to the Royal Caledonian Institution. Till then *au revoir*!'

3

The Sign of the Raven

When Box arrived later that day at Horseferry Road Police Mortuary, he found Dr Donald Miller waiting for him in a chilly, white-tiled room leading directly from a grim chamber where some dozen sheeted corpses lay waiting for professional attention. Dr Miller looked tired, but his boyish, clean-shaven face held an expression of bright eagerness that Box knew to be typical of him. A house surgeon at Charing Cross Hospital, he had been appointed a police surgeon, at Box's suggestion, in the previous year. He was twenty-six years old.

'I've done your man for you, Mr Box,' he said, rising from a table where he had been seated. 'It was a bit difficult at such short notice, as I had another gentleman open on the table at the time, but I fitted him in quite nicely. Would you like a cup of coffee?'

'I would, Doctor,' said Box, shivering. 'This place always depresses me: it's all these tiles, and the sound of running water in those sinks of yours. Even on a day like this the place is

40

as cold as the tomb — well, you know what I mean.'

Young Dr Miller laughed, and busied himself with a percolator that stood over a little spirit lamp in a fume cupboard. Presently, he presented Box with a very acceptable cup of hot coffee, and invited him to sit down at the table. Pulling a sheet of paper towards him, he began to speak in the formal, stilted manner that belonged to his profession.

'Today, I conducted a post-mortem examination on the body of one Gregory Walsh, a man aged about twenty-five. I found the subject to have been a healthy young man, entirely free from illness, or from sinister lesions of any kind. The tips of his index fingers and thumbs were stained with chemicals, probably incident upon his profession of assayer and sampler. Beneath the fingernail of his right index finger I found a deposit of a dried crimson material, perhaps dried paint, which I have placed aside for analysis.

'Gregory Walsh met his death as the result of a blow to the back of the head, inflicted with an instrument in the nature of an adze or cleaver. Death would have been instantaneous. It was not possible for me to ascertain with certainty the time of death, but one can

41

safely assume that it was not long before the discovery of the body. In the mouth — '

Dr Miller's voice faltered, and he threw down his written report on to the table.

'Mr Box,' he whispered, 'I found that his mouth was filled with honey. There was none in his throat, or in his stomach. That honey had been *spooned* into his mouth by his murderer . . . Having felled the poor young fellow with a single savage blow, he found the time to spoon honey into his mouth. Presumably, he'd brought a jar of the stuff in his pocket for the purpose. Can you make any sense of that?'

'Not yet, Doctor,' muttered Box. 'But I will.'

Miller put his report into a manila envelope, sealed it, and handed it to Box. 'His clothes and effects are in the next room. Do you want to see them now?'

'Yes, please,' said Box, finishing his coffee. 'Perhaps you'd like to stay while I examine them? Or maybe you want to get back to your silent guests?'

'They can wait awhile, Inspector. In any case, they're not all my subjects!'

Young Dr Miller preceded Box into another tiled room, where Gregory Walsh's effects had been laid out carefully on a couple of trestle tables.

'I'll examine the contents of his pockets first, Dr Miller, and then look at the clothes. This is a very nice silver watch, with an inscription engraved on the back. 'To Gregory, on the occasion of his 21st birthday, 7 March 1889. From Father and Mother'. So he was, in fact, twenty-six. One leather watch-guard. One plain signet ring. Coins, retrieved from pockets: one sovereign, two half-crowns, four shillings, and one and sevenpence in copper. One plain handkerchief, stained with — now what is it? Coloured dust of some sort — some kind of red powder.'

Box produced a small hand-lens from his pocket, and examined the handkerchief closely. It had evidently been freshly laundered and ironed, but its centre was crumpled, where the red powder had formed a long, narrow stain, some two inches long. In two other parts the red stains were in the form of shapeless patches. Box put away his lens, and turned to Donald Miller. At the same time, he removed his own handkerchief from his trousers pocket.

'Poor Mr Gregory Walsh,' he said, 'had stained his right hand with some kind of coloured powder, which he proceeded to wipe off with his handkerchief, like this. That long stain in the centre was caused by his close wiping of his index finger. The other, fainter, stains were made as he cleared the powder from the palm of his hand. You mentioned that you had found a deposit of crimson powder beneath the fingernail of his right index finger.'

'It sounds to me that he was scraping paint off some surface unknown. Does it suggest anything to you, Inspector?'

'Not directly, Dr Miller. But it gives me food for thought. Let me flesh out these meagre facts into a little story. Mr Gregory Walsh, assayer and sampler, left his house very early this morning, and in his pocket reposed a clean handkerchief. At some time before seven o'clock, he went down into the Mithraeum in Clerkenwell, and performed some action or other which deposited a coloured powder beneath a fingernail, and on to the index finger and palm of his right hand.'

'Perhaps he was scraping something with an instrument — there was a spatula in his pocket. It's there on the table, beside his wallet. He may have used his fingernail as an extra instrument.'

'Quite possibly,' said Box. 'Whatever he did, he saw that he had stained his hand, and in the natural way of things he took out his handkerchief and used it to wipe away the offending stains. And then he replaced his handkerchief in his pocket. He was taking his time, you see. Perhaps his assailant was somebody whom he knew, and who had met him at the archaeological site. Or perhaps his killer was there before Walsh arrived, hiding in the gloom behind that reredos, in which case, he could have been either someone known to Walsh, or a complete stranger.'

'Bravo, Mr Box! You're painting a very convincing picture of what must have happened.'

'Well, it's a strong possibility. And then, Doctor, the assailant struck Gregory Walsh down, remaining on the scene long enough to spoon honey into the corpse's mouth . . . Incidentally, were you able to preserve any of that honey?'

'Yes, Inspector, it's in a small jar, and sealed with my official seal. I also preserved tissue samples from the major organs, although, as I told you, the unfortunate Mr Walsh had been in perfect health.'

The dead man's wallet contained a small photograph of a young lady, upon the back of which was written: 'To Greg, with love from Thelma'. There were also three of the dead man's business cards, a five-pound note carefully folded, and the cancelled halves of two tickets for seats in the stalls of the

45

Alhambra, Leicester Square, stamped with a date in July.

'What do you make of that, Dr Miller?' asked Box. He was inviting the young police surgeon to go a little beyond his own medical expertise.

'Gregory Walsh was engaged to a pretty girl called Thelma. He took her to the music hall last July. Of course, he might be married to this Thelma. I expect you'll find out.'

'I expect I will,' Box replied, smiling. 'Now, what else have we got? There's the spatula; yes, you can see faint traces of paint on the blade. Evidently, he wiped that, too. And what's this? It looks like some kind of talisman.'

Box had picked up a small disc, made of some blue material, perhaps lapis lazuli. On one side was engraved the figure of a rampant lion, with the Roman numeral IV beneath it. The other side of the disc showed an image of a seated figure, its head adorned with a garland. Beneath this image was engraved the words: *Diu Pater*.

As Box held the disc, something shifted in his mind, and the scientific certainties represented by the tiled room of the forensic mortuary became suddenly dimmed as a shudder of superstitious dread passed through his frame. He angrily threw down the

46

token on the trestle table.

If Dr Miller had noticed this untypical reaction, he did not betray the fact. '*Diu Pater* is a very ancient spelling for Jupiter,' he offered. 'The father of the gods, you know.'

'And what, I wonder, did a nice, down-to-earth young man want with a thing like that in his pocket?' asked Box, more to himself than to Miller. 'Well, we'll look into that later. Now, what's this? Here's a tin case, containing a pair of spectacles.'

'They're reading glasses. Quite strong, of their type.'

Box opened the case, and looked briefly at the gleaming lenses in their neat gold frames. Then he read the name of the optician, displayed on a little printed label in the lid of the case:

Reuben Greensands, Optician.
14 Catherine Lane, EC.

'Greensands . . . I noticed a few optician's shops when I was in Catherine Lane this morning. I suppose one of them belongs to this man Greensands. It's odd, though . . . '

'What's odd, Mr Box?'

'Well, if Walsh had started work on examining the reredos close up, why hadn't he put on his reading glasses? It's just one of

47

those little things, Doctor, that require some kind of explanation.'

* * *

Arnold Box had not visited Carshalton, a thriving little Surrey town a few miles distant from Croydon, since boyhood. It was much as he remembered it, with large houses belonging to wealthy merchants and financiers, a town centre which still had the appearance and feel of a country village, the man-made Lower Pond with its elegant Portland stone bridge, and a memorably beautiful park. As Sergeant Knollys had observed, it was 'a very nice little place'.

Enquiry at the railway station had taken him out to a suburb called Hackbridge, where a number of mills and small factories lined the bank of the River Wandle. Box knew that he had located the Royal Albert Cement Works when he saw a smart uniformed inspector standing in the road in front of a solid, four-square granite house, which was separated by a tall privet hedge from a busy works yard.

'Inspector Perrivale? I'm Detective Inspector Box of Scotland Yard.'

'Pleased to meet you, Mr Box,' said the inspector. He was a man who exuded an aura of responsibility and rectitude. He had a narrow, serious face, and a fair clipped moustache. His uniform was immaculate.

'This is a very peculiar business, Mr Box,' he said. 'It's quite beyond what we can cope with down here. I hoped it would be you they sent, because it was you who solved that Lord Jocelyn Peto business up at Croydon last year.'

As Perrivale talked, he led Box through an arched gate that brought them to the rear of the house. Behind a small back garden the cement works stretched in an array of irregular buildings down to the river. Despite the murder of the proprietor, the hands had still reported for work. The ground, the men, and most of the buildings, were covered with a fine white powder.

'This is Wellington House, Mr Box,' said Perrivale, 'and it was here, in the conservatory, that the body of Mr Abraham Barnes was discovered yesterday morning. He had been murdered — killed with a single blow to the back of the head, delivered with a sharp instrument, according to the local doctor here.'

'Could the blow have been inflicted with an adze, or hatchet?'

'Why, yes, Mr Box. In fact, that's what Dr Lowrie suggested. Do you want to interview the family first, or examine the scene of the crime?'

'I'd like to look at the scene of the crime, if it's all the same with you, Mr Perrivale,' Box replied.

The conservatory was a fanciful creation in cast-iron and glass, built out into the front garden of Wellington House. Perrivale opened a glazed door which was reached from the garden path, and the two men entered the site of Barnes's murder.

Box looked around him. There were plenty of potted ferns, some of them wilting in the heat, a few exotic blooms in brass tubs, but not much else. The place had been built for show, rather than as a centre for someone passionately interested in horticulture. There was a white-painted table of wrought iron, and two similar chairs, one of them overturned. Someone had drawn an outline in chalk to indicate where the body had lain on the elaborately tiled floor. A clever idea, that.

'Mr Perrivale,' said Box, 'I was told that you found peculiar and sinister aspects to this murder. Would you mind telling me what those aspects were?'

To Box's surprise, the Surrey inspector blushed, as though with shame, but when he spoke, Box realized that the man's face was suffused not with shame, but anger.

'Mr Box, I was summoned here by Mr Barnes's resident manager, a man called Harper. The police station is only a stone's-throw from here. He led me into this conservatory from the garden, where the door stood open. I saw poor Abraham Barnes lying on his back in a pool of blood. It's all been mopped up since. There he lay, where you see the chalk-marks drawn by my sergeant before we had the body removed to the mortuary.'

'What did you do when you started to examine the body?'

'I put my hands around the dead man's neck, and pulled him upright. I was able to see the wound in the back of his head. After that, I turned him right over on to his front, so that I could examine the wound more closely. And then, from his mouth . . . '

The inspector stopped to compose himself. The initial rage that had suffused his honest face had still not abated. Box hazarded a guess.

'You found that his mouth had been filled with honey?'

Perrivale looked at him as though he was mad.

'*Honey*? In God's name, man, what are you talking about?' he cried. 'I turned him over to look more closely at the head wound,

51

and *a stream of quicksilver flowed from his mouth on to the tiled floor.*'

'Quicksilver? That's another name for mercury, isn't it?'

'Yes, I suppose so. Who could have done such a wicked thing? What's the point of it? Here was a man who killed his victim with a savage blow, turned him on his back — unless, of course, he fell down on to his back — and poured a bottle of quicksilver down his throat. It stayed down in his stomach, or at the back of his throat, perhaps, until I turned him over, and then it flowed out on to the tiles.'

It was very humid in the conservatory. For a moment it seemed to Box like a savage jungle, and beyond the overgrown palms he fancied that he could see the shadow of a pagan face in a leathern cap, and hear the dying bellows of a sacrificed bull . . . Not honey this time, but mercury. It was insane.

'After that,' Perrivale continued, 'I sent my sergeant to fetch our local doctor, who arrived about twenty minutes later. He examined the body, and concluded that poor Barnes must have been killed between three and four in the morning.'

'Was Mr Barnes in his nightgown?'

'No, Mr Box, he was fully dressed. Later, I found that his bed had not been slept in.

Without wishing to be indelicate, I must mention the fact that Mr Barnes and Mrs Barnes occupied separate rooms. The fact that his bed hadn't been slept in makes me think that he was keeping a rendezvous with someone he knew.'

'That sounds more than likely, Mr Perrivale,' said Box. 'Did you find anything odd in Mr Barnes's pockets?'

'Now, what made you ask that, Mr Box? As a matter of fact, I did. And I still have it here, in my own pocket.'

Inspector Perrivale placed something in Box's hand. It was a lapis lazuli token, the size of a halfpenny. On one side was depicted a carved representation of a bird, and underneath it the word *Corax*. On the reverse was a familiar seated figure, adorned with a garland, beneath which was engraved the words *Diu Pater*. Jupiter. It looked very much as though the obscene mysteries of Mithras had not confined themselves to Clerkenwell. They were here, in the attractive little Anglo-Saxon town of Carshalton.

'There's nothing more of interest here, Mr Perrivale,' said Box. 'This murder may be connected with a similar case I'm investigating in Clerkenwell. In both cases, a token with the words *Diu Pater* written on it was found on the body, and something had been put into the victim's mouth. In this case it was mercury; in the other, it was honey.'

'It's certainly no coincidence, Mr Box. If you ask me, there's an insane killer on the loose. You know the kind of thing I mean. Someone with a twisted concept of justice, imagining wrongs to be righted by arcane rituals — a mad brain in a killer's body — '

'Or it might be the work of someone who's very sane, very cunning, and very wicked. I'd like to speak to the family, now, Mr Perrivale.'

'They know you're here, Mr Box, and they've assembled in the drawing-room. There's the widow, Mrs Laura Barnes, and Mr Barnes's unmarried daughter, Hetty. It was poor Hetty who found the body. Oh, and Mr James Harper is there. He's the resident manager of the works. He's only just come in from the yard.'

Perrivale led Box out of the conservatory and into the main house. It was a gloomy kind of place, thought Box. It was quite luxuriously furnished in the heavy styles of the 1870s, but there was a faded air about it, and the costly wallpaper was stained and peeling in places. The works buildings at the back of the house, too, had looked in need of repair and refurbishment. Maybe the late Mr Barnes had been tight-fisted. Or maybe he was on the brink of Queer Street.

They walked along a dim passage and emerged into a wide hallway. Perrivale knocked on a door to his left, and ushered Box into the drawing-room of Wellington House.

Three people stood before the fireplace, a handsome woman, with well-coiffured blonde hair, an older, thinner woman with a pale, tear-stained face, and a good-looking man of thirty or so. They turned to face the door when it opened, and created the illusion that they were three figures in a wax tableau: the elegant daughter, the grieving widow, and the loyal employee.

'Inspector Box,' said Perrivale, 'let me present Mrs Barnes, Miss Barnes, and Mr James Harper.'

The thin-faced tearful woman suddenly broke ranks, rushed forward, and seized Box's hand. Fresh tears gushed from her swollen eyes.

'You must bring them to justice, Mr Box!' she cried in anguish. 'What fiends could have done such a terrible thing? They poured quicksilver down his throat!'

'Hetty!' The single word, uttered with chilling authority by the handsome younger woman, told Box that he had confused the identity of the two ladies in the family. The tearful mourner still holding his hand was

Abraham Barnes's daughter. It was the younger blonde woman who had been the cement manufacturer's wife.

Hetty suddenly released Box's hand, and rejoined the others in front of the fireplace. She appeared both confused and humiliated. Mrs Barnes threw her a look of unconcealed dislike. Box saw immediately what he had to do.

'Ladies,' he said, 'and you, Mr Harper, I'm sure that my colleague Inspector Perrivale has already asked all the questions that needed answers, and he and I will consult together later. At the moment, though, I want to interview each of you again, as my kind of questions will be different from those asked by Inspector Perrivale.

'Miss Barnes,' he said, turning towards the still tearful daughter of the house, 'I'd like to hear from you how you came to discover your father's body yesterday — There, now, miss, there's no need to take on so! You must try to be brave. The more I know, the quicker I'll be able to bring your father's murderer to justice.'

Box found his eyes drawn involuntarily to a full-length portrait hanging above the fireplace. It showed a proud, heavily moustached but balding man in his late fifties, his hands clutching his lapels, his dark eyes glaring balefully from his pale face. This, surely, was the late Mr Abraham Barnes. The handsome young Mrs Laura Barnes must have been his second wife.

'Take Inspector Box into your father's office, Hetty,' said Mrs Barnes. Her voice now held unconcealed contempt for the other woman. 'James and I will remain here until we're called for. Mr Perrivale, will you stay with us?'

The faded Miss Henrietta Barnes made no reply to her stepmother's command, but she obeyed it nonetheless. Leaving the room, she led Box across the hall and into a small office near the main door of the house. It contained a roll-top desk bulging with papers and bundles of letters, a small round table, and a few upright chairs. Box opened his notebook, and put it down on the table.

'Now, Miss Barnes,' he said, 'tell me exactly what happened yesterday morning which, as you know, was the fourteenth of August.'

'My alarm-clock woke me as usual at six,' said Hetty nervously. 'After I had washed and dressed, I came downstairs. My stepmother, I knew, was already stirring, but it was too early for her to be down. Mary, our maid, had made a cup of tea for me in the kitchen, and while I drank it we chatted about various things — '

'What did you chat about, Miss Barnes? I need to know everything, you see.'

'Well, we talked about the forthcoming marriage of the vicar's younger daughter. We were both excited about it, because she was going to marry a foreigner, a man she met on holiday last year in Florence. We wondered whether she'd go out with him to live in Italy, or stay here. Oh, dear, it was such a normal, happy morning!' Hetty produced a handkerchief from her sleeve, and began to dab her eyes.

'What happened next?' asked Box gently.

'When I'd finished the tea, I filled the watering-can at the sink and made my way into the conservatory. It was a favourite place of my mother's, and I try to keep the plants alive in her memory. I'm not much interested in plants myself. Neither is Laura — Mrs Barnes.

'I stepped over the threshold, and there was Papa, lying on his back, with his head in a pool of blood. He was fully dressed, in his day clothes. The garden door was wide open. The world seemed to stop turning. I just clutched the watering-can and stared down at him. I knew he was dead. And that's all.'

'What time was it when you discovered your Papa's body?'

'It would have been about a quarter to

58

seven. Suddenly I seemed to come back to life. I screamed, and Mary came running out of the kitchen to see what was the matter. I told her to run out into the works, and fetch Mr Harper in. Then I ran upstairs to break the news to Laura.'

Box scribbled rapidly in his notebook, and then looked at the young woman sitting opposite him. How old was she? No more than thirty-five, but she dressed like a woman twenty years older than that. She rose at six, while young Mrs Barnes luxuriated in bed. She chatted to the maid, no doubt, because the maid was her only friend. Miss Henrietta Barnes was evidently treated as a skivvy.

'You did very well, Miss Barnes,' said Box. 'Did you by any chance touch your father's body?'

'Oh, no!' The horror in Hetty's voice was all too genuine.

'And you sent for Mr Harper . . . Surely he must be an early riser if he was out at the works before seven?'

'James Harper is always out of the house before six o'clock. He's a very conscientious man, who works very hard.'

'Do you like Mr James Harper?' It was a curious question, and totally unexpected. Hetty blushed. She looked suddenly both confused and resentful.

'I neither like nor dislike him. He works hard, but he's fickle and changeable. You can see how handsome he is, and Laura — well, I'll say no more. In fact, I think I've said more than I should. If that's all, Mr Box, I'll go, now.'

4

The Power of the Press

After Hetty Barnes had left the office, Arnold Box sat for a while in thought. He had sensed the tension in the family as soon as he had seen them, standing in front of the drawing-room fireplace like so many waxworks. There had been no feeling of unity in the face of a common ordeal. And now the daughter of the house had hinted at what he'd already suspected: the handsome works manager and the attractive young widow had already come to some kind of understanding.

Had that understanding between Laura Barnes and the works manager included murder? Had Abraham Barnes been lured to the conservatory at an early hour by Harper, and then slaughtered? It was possible. But then, what about the mercury, and the pagan amulet? He would have to tread very carefully.

The door was flung open, and Mrs Laura Barnes came into the room. Dry eyed, and in full control of herself, she exuded an air of invincible triumph. Without waiting for Box to say a word, she launched into speech.

'I don't know what that mewling cat has said to you, Mr Box, but now I'm going to tell you a few home truths. It's time that somebody cleared the air. Abraham Barnes, my late husband, was a mean, grasping hypocrite. Mr Perrivale will have told you that Abraham Barnes was a pillar of the community, without an enemy in the world. True, he was an elder in the Methodist Church, and one of the vice-chairmen of the Board of Guardians. But he was a penny-pincher, although he could always find money for whisky and cigars, which he'd consume alone in this vile den of his. Oh, yes: plenty of money for drink.'

'You mean — '

'Why don't you listen to what I'm saying? He drove his first wife to the grave by his meanness and his little cruelties. That fool Hetty adored him in spite of it all, and look at her now — a dried-up spinster, with no prospect of marriage. 'Poor Papa!' she cries. Well, 'poor Papa' can't help her now, and very soon she'll have to strike out for herself.'

Mrs Barnes seemed to be working herself into a passion. Her face flushed with anger, and she glanced around the stuffy little office as though wondering how best to commence its demolition.

'And the business, which is basically sound, is being run on a shoe-string. Nothing's invested back into the plant. James — Mr Harper — had pleaded with him to release money from the family trusts to shore up the works before it collapses. But no. My husband had all but retired. He wasn't interested. So here's what I'm going to do. After I've buried Abraham, and the will's been proven, I'm going to marry James Harper, and together we'll develop this business until it's a leader in this particular trade. I expect that Abraham has left Hetty a small competence, so she can make her own way in the world as she thinks best. This is *my* house now, Mr Box, and *my* works, and in a few months' time, James Harper will be *my* husband!'

Box brought his fist down angrily on to the table. Mrs Barnes's flow of words ceased.

'Do you understand, madam,' he cried, 'that your husband has been murdered? Your family arrangements are none of my concern, but you may be quite sure that I will track down and seize your husband's killer without favour, and without fear.'

Laura Barnes had turned pale, and for the first time since his arrival at Wellington House Box saw tears standing in the woman's eyes. She suddenly sat down opposite him at the table.

'I married him for his money,' she whispered, 'and when he was found dead yesterday, I was terrified in case poor James or myself were accused. I was only twenty-six when I married him. It was awful! But I'm sorry that he's dead, and I hope you'll catch the killer, and hang him. Do you want to question James — Mr Harper?'

'I do. Please ask him to come here, now. Was your late husband interested in archaeology? Did he read any books about Roman religion?'

Laura Barnes looked at Box as though he had lost his senses. For a brief moment, she forgot her seething resentments, and her frightened attempt to apologize for her heartlessness.

'Roman religion? I told you he was a Methodist. He didn't hold with Roman Catholics. And as for archaeology — well, the only thing my husband was interested in was cement!'

When Mrs Barnes had gone, Box swiftly examined the murdered man's desk. There were many receipts, all stamped as paid, and a number of carelessly arranged business letters, mainly requests for the supply of what seemed to Box to be enormous quantities of cement.

In one pigeon-hole of the roll-top desk

Box found four small brown manila envelopes, each of which was secured at the flap by a paper-clip. Each envelope contained what looked to Box like dark, coarse sand. Possibly, they were samples of mortar scraped from between bricks. Each envelope was numbered, and inscribed with a few words in a neat copperplate hand. Opening a fresh page in his notebook, Box copied the inscriptions.

1. Definitely Ancient Roman. Lime, Sand, Water.
2. Modern, i.e. this century. Bonner has trade analysis.
3. Definitely Ancient Roman, Lime, Sand, Water.
4. Not Roman. Probably 17th century.

So, Mrs Laura Barnes, thought Box, you weren't entirely right about your husband's interests. He knew something about the ancient Romans, if it was only about what they put in their mortar.

He carefully resealed the envelopes with the paperclips, and slipped them into the inside pocket of his coat. But what was this? Really, poor old Barnes had been very untidy! Two notes, pinned together, one evidently the projected answer to the other.

Barnes (the first note ran), can I trouble you to get these four done? I'm nearly there, and these four, if they show what I think they'll show, will be the final proof. — CW.

The second note was written in the same neat copperplate hand as the inscriptions on the four envelopes.

Bonner, in Garrick Flags, did these for me. He has the full analyses. Bonner charged me a guinea, which I paid. — Abraham Barnes.

'Garrick Flags?' said Box, aloud. 'I know where that is: just off St Martin's Lane. Perhaps a call on this person called Bonner would be in order. I'd better take those notes, as well as the samples. I'm beginning to think — '

He stopped speaking as a discreet tap on the door announced the coming of Mr James Harper.

'Inspector Box,' said Harper smoothly, and without preamble, 'I'm sure you'll make allowances for poor Laura. She doesn't mean half she says, you know. It's her excitable nature. We neither of us had anything to do with poor Abraham's death.

It's a tragedy, that's what it is.'

Box looked at the handsome young man standing awkwardly in front of him. He was obviously nervous, and seemed to be making an effort not to lick his dry lips.

'And how do you know what Mrs Barnes has been saying to me, Mr Harper? Did she tell you, just now? If so, it wasn't a very wise thing for her to do.'

'What? No, she said nothing. But I know how she reacts when she's upset. I don't want you thinking that either of us killed Abraham Barnes, that's all. You're an experienced man, Mr Box. It's a madman you're looking for, not a respectable widow and a hardworking manager.'

Box closed his notebook and stood up. He looked at the handsome young man with unconcealed distaste. Those two, James and Laura, deserved each other. They were both ruthless and heartless. God help the wretched stepdaughter once Laura came into the property!

'I *am* an experienced man, Mr Harper,' said Box, 'and so I don't need you to tell me who to suspect. Mr Perrivale has called me in to help him, and I can assure you that between us we'll apprehend the murderer — or murderers — of Mr Abraham Barnes. It's only a matter of time.'

* * *

It was quiet in Carshalton High Street, where the homely but attractive buildings seemed to be dozing in the strong August sun. The road was dry and dusty, reminding Box that he was getting very thirsty. His interviews concluded, he had parted from Inspector Perrivale at the front gate of Wellington House, before setting out on foot for the town centre.

He had suggested to Perrivale that the murder of Abraham Barnes was part of a crime that had its origins in London. Nevertheless, it would be a good idea if he watched Mrs Barnes and the manager Harper closely. Neither of them would have batted an eyelid about committing murder if it had suited them.

Nestling in the shadow of a fine church with a square tower Box found The Coach and Horses, a very comfortable and restful public house. He walked into the public bar, and asked the man behind the bar for a glass of India Pale Ale. Slipping on to a bar stool, he extracted his cigar case from an inside pocket. Soon, he was puffing away at a thin cheroot.

The ale proved to be very cool and refreshing. Box recalled the countless occasions when he and his sergeant, Jack Knollys, had downed similar glasses in his favourite public house, the King Lud in Ludgate Circus. He wished that Jack was with him now: he'd got into the habit of testing out his sometimes wild theories on his thoughtful sergeant.

Suddenly, a cheerily powerful voice broke in upon his thoughts.

'Is that the great Inspector Box? Well, what brings you down here to Carshalton this fine morning? Bring your drink round here, into the snug, and talk to me.'

The voice came from a little room leading off the public bar. Box knew that voice. It belonged to Billy Fiske, chief reporter of *The Graphic*, an old ally of his, with whom it was possible to strike discreet little bargains beneficial to them both. What on earth was Billy Fiske doing in Carshalton?

Box picked up his glass, and walked into the snug. Yes, there he was, sitting at a corner table, upon which he had placed a couple of books, his spring-bound notebook, and a copy of the previous day's *Graphic*. A pint glass of dark mild ale stood at his elbow, together with a plate containing the remains of a cold beef pie. As always, Fiske was flamboyantly dressed. For his visit to Carshalton he had chosen a capacious light blue overcoat, which he wore open to reveal his sage-green suit. A high-crowned hat lay on the table beside his notebook.

'Sit down there, Mr Box,' said Fiske, pointing to a chair opposite him at the table, 'and tell me to what we owe this honour? It's not like you to stray so far afield.'

'You cheeky man!' Box laughed, and accepted the indicated chair. 'If Fiske of *The Graphic*'s in Carshalton today, then he must have been trailing Box of the Yard. What are you up to, Billy?'

'Me? I'm just looking up a bit of local history for an article I'm writing.' He picked up a slim book from the table, and turned over a few pages. 'Did you know that, in ancient times, Carshalton stood on one of the lesser-known Roman roads? Apparently it was a staging-post for the legions on their way south. Or north. I can't quite make out which.'

'No, Billy, I didn't know that. But I *do* know that you've followed me down here for nefarious purposes of your own. Are you going to tell me what you're up to?'

The famous reporter threw Box a shrewd glance, swallowed a mouthful of mild, and carefully wiped his jet-black moustache with a handkerchief. He picked up another book from the table, and waved it vaguely in Box's direction.

'Did you know,' he said, 'that there was a big Roman fort buried under the ground just south of Cripplegate? Did you know that there's a first-century Roman bath within a stone's-throw of St Paul's? Did you know that there's a Roman Mithraeum in Clerkenwell? Did you — ?'

'Strewth! What are you up to, you devious man? You're up to something — '

'Listen, Mr Box,' said Fiske, throwing the book down. 'You were called out to investigate a murder at the Roman ruins in Priory Gate Street yesterday. Well, I was out and about in Clerkenwell, because that's how I work: hovering around places where things are likely to happen. So when you'd gone, I went and found my own sources of information, and got the whole story out of them.'

'What sources?'

Billy Fiske smiled, and laid an index finger on the side of his nose. He gave Box a knowing wink.

'The toilers and labourers of this great nation, Mr Box, the workmen sweltering in those huts beside the excavation. Covered in dust, they were, and dried up with the heat. Well, I sent over the way to the Harvester, for a gallon of beer. The dry toilers were ever so grateful, Mr Box. They told me all about the

71

poor young man with his head bashed in, and they told me about the honey — oh, yes, they told me about that. And they told me about the token, and what had been engraved on it. Very interesting, that was. Apparently a constable left on duty there had shared a can of tea with them earlier, and told them the whole story.'

'And so — '

'And so I came down here early this morning. Somebody in King James's Rents told me that you were going to Carshalton — no, don't ask me who it was, because I won't tell you. I got here two hours before you did, Arnold, and made my way out to the Royal Albert Cement Works. Plenty of dry toilers there! I went equipped with a bag of half-crowns, and came away knowing everything about poor Mr Barnes, flighty Mrs Barnes, pathetic Miss Barnes, and ambitious Mr Harper.'

Billy Fiske finished his beer, and set the glass down on the table.

'And I learnt all about the mercury in the dead man's mouth, and the little token with the word *corax* engraved on it. That's Latin for raven. Intriguing, isn't it?'

Arnold Box retrieved the token from his waistcoat pocket, and laid it in front of the reporter.

'There it is, Billy. It's almost identical in shape and size to the one we found in the dead man's pocket in Clerkenwell. What are you up to? I can't quite fathom what you're going to do.'

'Well, you see, Arnold,' said Fiske, 'from a reporter's point of view two dead men with their heads knocked in are not very newsworthy. Sad, yes, but not big news. But if I weave a sinister tale of slaughter-sites near Roman encampments, or scenes of murder lying on Roman roads, and then link those two murders to ancient rituals of the god Mithras, involving esoteric sacrifices, secret societies, and rumours of hidden vice — well, then I've got a really satisfactory story. *The Graphic* will love it. It's sensation that sells our kind of paper.'

'But it's all tosh, Billy — '

'Yes, I know it is, but you can see the use of it, can't you? That's why you let me see that token just now. Some account of the Clerkenwell murder has appeared in all today's morning papers, as you'd expect, but to us gentlemen of the press it's just another murder. But once someone like me turns these two murders into a press sensation, then people will want to come forward with stories of what they saw, or what they heard; and other parties will try to hide their connection with either of the dead men, and make their suspicious motives only too obvious in doing so.'

'You're a clever, man, Billy,' said Box. 'I've never thought otherwise. I'm inclined to give you a free rein on this matter. I'm catching the two-seventeen to Victoria, so I can't stay to talk further. It's a peculiar affair altogether. First honey, and now mercury — I'm going to need all the help I can get to make head or tail of this business.'

★   ★   ★

In the ground-floor study of his house in Lowndes Square, Sir Charles Wayneflete waited for his chess opponent to make a move. Josh Baverstock always took his time, stroking his chin intelligently with his left hand, while his right hovered over the pieces on the board. Such gestures apparently compensated for his lack of skill. Poor Josh! He was as much an old crock as he was himself, but they'd both been dashing young fellows forty years ago. In this modern world of fair-weather friends and declining incomes, Josh was as true as steel.

Josh's evening clothes were decidedly rusty, and stained with snuff, and there was no doubt that his laundress had begun to neglect his linen. His own housekeeper, Mrs Craddock, had only last week remarked on the fact in her no-nonsense, practical way. 'Major Baverstock's being neglected, sir,' she'd said. 'You should tell him to do something about it. It's not right for a gentleman to be treated like that.'

Old Josh scowled at the board, and ventured a remark.

'You shan't get the better of me tonight, Charles,' said Baverstock. 'I'm going to checkmate you for once, no matter how long it takes.'

Wayneflete recalled the occasion when he had bought that set of chess men. It had been in Vienna, in 1856. They were carved from malachite, and had belonged to a seventeenth-century bishop of Cologne. A pity that the original board had been lost. That's why he'd got the whole set cheap.

Major Baverstock made his move, and sat back in his chair, squinting defiantly at his friend from bright old eyes hooded by white bushy brows. Sir Charles leaned forward in his chair, and conducted a series of moves which first removed his opponent's queen from the board, and then imprisoned his king in a gaol from which there was no hope of escape.

'Check,' said Sir Charles Wayneflete, 'and also mate!'

He listened to his friend's rueful laughter as he rose stiffly to pour them both a glass of port. Poor old Josh! He was hopeless at chess, but insisted on playing once or twice a week. He lived in a suite of rented rooms in a street off Cadogan Square, and came over by cab.

'I read in the paper today that they'd found the murdered corpse of a young man in that Mithraeum place of Ainsworth's,' said Josh, gratefully accepting his glass of port. 'What do you make of it?'

'You can't have a murdered corpse, Josh: it's a contradiction in terms. I did read something about it in the *Morning Post*. I expect it was some poor fellow who ran down into the place to escape an assailant, and was cornered there. Still, it's Ainsworth's affair, not mine. Much good may it do him!'

'A man who lives next door to me in Cadogan Square says that the dead man was an analytical chemist.'

'Really? Well, that's very interesting. I expect his death was some private affair. Nothing to do with Ainsworth, obviously. In any case, he's up in Edinburgh at the moment, making a public spectacle of himself with one of his never-ending lectures on the 'Clerkenwell Mithraeum', as he likes to call that crypt of his in Priory Gate Street.'

'Why, what would *you* call it?' asked Major

76

Baverstock. There was a sudden shrewd light in his eyes that Wayneflete didn't much care for. Josh had always been a bit of a mind-reader.

He smiled and shook his head, at the same time retrieving his friend's empty glass, and going over to the decanters which reposed on top of a bookcase beneath an old faded mirror. He was not a vain man, but he could not help comparing his own smart appearance with that of his old friend. Mrs Craddock bullied him — he admitted that — but she was an excellent housekeeper. Times were not as affluent as they had been, and a stroke two years earlier had made him a virtual recluse, more or less confined to the house; but they managed very well.

He looked at his own frail, narrow face, with its fringe of white whiskers. His eyes looked steadily back at him, as much as to say, 'Well done, Charles, you're telling lies very convincingly tonight!' He didn't know that young man personally — what was his name? Gregory Walsh — but he knew where he'd come from, and who must have sent him. And now he was dead. He also knew why that had been inevitable — poor young Walsh was no match for his elders and betters . . .

How much did Ainsworth know about

Walsh and his mission? Best not to enquire. Best to pretend ignorance of the whole frightening business, because in ignorance lay safety. Say nothing. Still, the haunting question would remain to torment him: How much does Ainsworth know?

The door opened, and Mrs Craddock entered. Thin and grim, she looked at the two men, baronet and retired army officer, as though they were two little boys.

'Sir,' she said, 'it's a quarter past eleven. The major's cab is at the door, and your chamber candlestick's lit, and standing in the hall.'

Time to do as he was told, and go to bed. He accompanied his guest to the door, and watched as the driver settled him into the cab. Then he returned to the hall, and picked up the candlestick that would light him up to his bedchamber. As he mounted the stairs, the flickering light threw unsettling shadows on to the staircase wall.

Yes, it was a question to which he would love to know the answer.

How much did Ainsworth know?

★ ★ ★

Professor Roderick Ainsworth, having exchanged some civilities with the guard, settled himself in his compartment on the night sleeper from Edinburgh's Waverley Station to far-off Euston. It was nearly ten minutes past eleven.

His brief visit to Scotland's capital had been a brilliant success. He would certainly repeat his lecture on the following Monday in London, as planned. He had brought late editions of several Scottish newspapers, and scanned them for information about the murder in his Mithraeum, having listened to a garbled account of it from one of his Scottish friends. Yes, here it was. The sensationalists were already building it up into a vulgar mystery, but that was to be expected.

It was vexing, to say the least. The discovery of the Mithraeum had been a triumphant public success, enhancing his reputation as an archaeologist of unusual flair. The Marquess of Lorne had visited the site, thus setting the Royal seal of approval on the enterprise. And then, some weeks later, perhaps, there would have been yet another sensation in Clerkenwell to tickle the ears of the general public . . .

Would that happen now, in view of that young man's demise? That remained to be seen.

What was Wayneflete thinking about the business? Indigent old fool — no, he wasn't that. He was no fool, even though half the antiquities in his wretched house were of decidedly doubtful provenance — second-rate stuff was all that he could afford. It would be better to keep out of his way. Distant civility would be in order, but no communication of any kind. Wayneflete's star was almost set, in any case, and the general public had never heard of him. Let sleeping dogs lie . . .

But was Wayneflete sleeping? Was he a man to be cowed into inaction by a brutal slaying? No, Sir Charles Wayneflete was a dangerous man, a man to be watched.

Professor Ainsworth climbed into his bunk, and turned the little oil lamp down to a glimmer. Presently there came a triumphant emission of steam from the great engine, and the carriage began to move slowly along the platform. Ainsworth lay back on the pillow. It had been a full, rather tiring day, and he was ready to sleep. Just as he was dropping off, some lingering fragment of anxiety jerked him awake, and made him ask himself a silent question.

How much does Wayneflete know?

5

The Clerkenwell Chemist

Detective Sergeant Knollys stood for a moment on the pavement in front of 5 Hayward's Court, a gaunt, three-storeyed house in an enclave of liver-brick dwellings leading off St John Street in Clerkenwell. A brass plate beside the front door told him that this was the premises of Raymond Walsh & Son, Assayers and Samplers, established 1836.

As Knollys mounted the steps from the street, the front door was opened, and a young woman came out on to the top step to greet him.

'Sergeant Knollys?' she asked. 'We were given notice that you were coming. Please come upstairs.'

Knollys recognized the young woman immediately: he had seen her smiling out of the photograph that Gregory Walsh had kept in his wallet. 'To Greg, with love from Thelma', it had said on the reverse. He saw the flash of a diamond engagement ring as she placed her left hand on the lintel of the door.

Thelma was not smiling now, but although her eyes were red with weeping, she was clearly in full control of herself. Neatly and carefully dressed, she had drawn back her fair hair from her forehead, and tied it into a bun. As Jack Knollys stepped over the threshold, he saw her glance at the bulky valise that he was carrying. Fresh tears started to her eyes. No doubt she had realized that it contained her fiancé's clothes and effects.

He followed her up a steep and narrow staircase, its walls papered with dark brown anaglypta. She opened a door on the top landing, and as they entered a long room overlooking the court, Knollys saw an old gentleman rise from his chair to greet him. He was very tall and thin, clad in a dark-grey suit, and with a wide mourning band on his arm. When he spoke, his voice quavered a little, but that, Knollys decided, was the effect of age rather than emotion. Old or not, this gentleman conveyed a strong air of command and control.

'Detective Sergeant Knollys,' said the old man. 'I am Raymond Walsh, Gregory's father. This young lady is Miss Thelma Thompson, who is staying in the house both at my request, and out of the kindness of her generous heart. Until yesterday, she was my son's fiancée. Sit down, Mr Knollys.'

Knollys did as he was bid, and Thelma Thompson followed suit. The room was homely and comfortable, and was evidently the main living area of the house. Without more ado, the sergeant unfastened the valise and silently withdrew Gregory Walsh's clothing, which he handed, item by item, to Thelma. Trousers, jacket, cap; a discreet cloth bag containing his shirt and undergarments — all the violated relics of what had once been a living man. How he hated this particular task! Silver watch and leather guard, signet ring; an official envelope containing one sovereign, two half-crowns, four shillings, and one and sevenpence in copper. One chemical spatula.

Old Mr Walsh, who had sat silently in his chair, watching the solemn production of his dead son's effects, suddenly spoke.

'A Sergeant French came here yesterday, to break the news of Gregory's death. He couldn't tell us much, but he did say that my son had been murdered. That was true, was it?'

'It was, sir. Mr Walsh died from a single blow to the back of the head, delivered by an axe or adze — I'm sorry, Miss Thompson. Do you want to leave us alone for a while?'

'No, no! I want to stay!' cried Thelma, angrily dashing away her sudden tears. 'Let

83

me hear what happened to my fiancé.'

'Very well, miss. Death would have been instantaneous, if that's any consolation. The weapon has not yet been found.' Knollys delved once more into the valise. 'This handkerchief,' he said, 'had been used by Mr Gregory Walsh to wipe paint from his hand. I mean artists' paint, the powdered kind, that you mix with water. Could that action have any connection with his work as an assayer and sampler?'

'It could well be a part of Gregory's work,' said old Mr Walsh. 'He may have been handling a sample of paint for analysis, and stained his hands. Like many analytical chemists, his fingers got stained with chemicals and burned with acids — occupational hazards, you might say. He was a wonderfully skilful man in his profession, you know. He was only twenty-six. I handed the business over to him last year, and was looking forward to Thelma here becoming his wife. But there, it was not to be.'

His old eyes filled with tears, and he looked away, so as to hide them from his visitor.

'Mr Knollys,' said Thelma, 'why not look at the books downstairs in the laboratory? You'll be able to see whether any of the jobs going forward yesterday would have involved the handling of paint. Mr Craven, the chief assistant, will be able to tell you.'

'Thank you, miss, I'll do that, presently. And now, here are Mr Walsh's reading glasses, folded in their tin case.'

'Glasses? No, they're not Greg's,' said Thelma. 'Greg had perfect sight. He never wore glasses.'

'Never,' said Gregory Walsh's father. 'If those glasses were in Gregory's pocket, then they must have been put there.'

'Well, that's possible, sir,' said Knollys, 'though there are other explanations.'

He rummaged through the valise, and withdrew Gregory Walsh's wallet. Thelma gave vent to a stifled sob, and held out her hand, but Knollys seemed unwilling for the moment to relinquish the wallet.

'I found the cancelled halves of two tickets for the Alhambra in Mr Walsh's wallet,' he said. 'They were dated the 14 July, which was a Saturday. Returning the stubs of tickets to his wallet suggests to me that Mr Gregory Walsh was a meticulous young man — a man concerned with detail.'

'That was clever of you, Sergeant,' said the elder Mr Walsh. 'Gregory always paid great attention to detail. He noticed when things were awry, and would put them right.'

'The 14 July — that was the night Greg took me to the music hall,' said Thelma.

'Hetty Miller was on, and the Santini Brothers. When we came out into Leicester Square, the heavens opened, and we were both drenched. It was all such fun, you know. But now . . . '

The girl shook her head sadly. Knollys glanced at her, and then turned his attention once more to the murdered man's father.

'Did your son live with you, Mr Walsh?'

'He did, and if things had gone as planned, he would have married Thelma, as I told you, and they would have taken over the top floor. Who could have wished him any harm? He hadn't an enemy in the world . . . Gregory was born in this house, and will be buried from it. When shall we — when . . . ?'

'The body will be released from Horseferry Road Police Mortuary tomorrow, Mr Walsh, so you can begin making arrangements immediately. I can't tell you how sorry I am, sir, to be plaguing you with all these questions at this time. As your son lived in Clerkenwell, did he ever visit the Mithraeum in Priory Gate Street?'

'Yes, he did. He'd made several visits there, when they were still admitting the public. They stopped doing that about a fortnight ago. I don't know why. It was something to do with replacing the wooden stairs leading down into the chamber, I think.'

The old man moved in his chair, and a light of animation came to his old eyes.

'I wonder, Sergeant, whether poor Gregory went to look at the site yesterday, and was attacked by a vagrant? That would explain it all. As I said, Gregory was no stranger to the Mithraeum, and I know for a fact that he'd been allowed in there despite its being closed for the duration.'

'It could be as you say, sir,' said Knollys, though privately he thought it a very remote possibility. Murderous vagrants didn't go round with pots of honey in their pockets. 'Did your son know Professor Ainsworth, the man who discovered the Mithraeum? Did he ever mention having met the professor?'

The old man glanced at Thelma, who shook her head.

'No, Sergeant,' said Mr Walsh, 'I'm sure Gregory didn't know this professor. He'd have mentioned it if he'd known him. I must confess that I've never heard of him. I'm not much interested in ancient things. Are there any further questions that you want to ask? I'm a little tired, you know. I'd like to lie down soon.'

'Of course, sir. There is one other question I'd like to ask you, and it's this: was Mr Gregory Walsh fond of honey? Or did he ever mention honey in any particular context?'

'*Honey?*' Thelma exclaimed. 'I've no idea whether he liked it or not. What can honey have to do with my fiancé's violent death?'

'Is honey kept in the house?' Knollys persisted. 'Mr Walsh, sir — '

'No, Sergeant!' cried the old man. 'I do not eat honey. And there's none in the house. I detest the wretched stuff. Now, if you don't mind, I'll retire to my bed. Thelma will show you the way down to the laboratory, and you can talk to Craven.'

Old Mr Walsh left the room, closing the door behind him. Jack Knollys took the amulet from his pocket, and showed it to Thelma. She looked at it curiously, but it was clear to Knollys that it meant nothing to her.

'It's a pretty little thing, isn't it?' she said. 'A little lion on one side, and a seated man on the other.'

'It was found in Mr Gregory Walsh's pocket.'

'Maybe he picked it up in the street,' Thelma suggested. 'It certainly wasn't something that he had before he was killed. He'd have shown it to me, otherwise.'

As they descended the narrow staircase to the ground floor, Knollys felt compelled to ask Thelma Thompson a question.

'Will you be all right here, Miss Thompson? Haven't you got a woman friend who could keep you company?'

Thelma paused on the stairs, and smiled. She placed a hand lightly on Jack Knollys' arm.

'How kind of you, Sergeant,' she said. 'In fact, I'm quite content to stay here in the house for a few days in order to look after Greg's father. He married and became a father very late in life, which makes Greg's loss even more cruel. Greg was his only child, you see. His wife — Greg's mother — died three years ago. He and I always got along well. My parents know where I am, and they don't live far away. In a week's time, Mr Walsh's widowed sister will arrive to live with him. She's years younger than he is, so he'll be well cared for.'

Thelma paused for a moment, as though making up her mind to speak further. 'Greg's dead,' she said at last, 'and nothing can bring him back. But I do have another friend — a gentleman friend — who has already called to see me, and once things are settled here, I'll start walking out with him. Life must go on. Just go down that little flight of stairs, Mr Knollys, and through the glazed door. That'll take you into the laboratory.'

★ ★ ★

The laboratory proved to be a large, square room occupying most of the ground floor at the rear of the house. Stone-flagged and with a low, stained ceiling, it received daylight from a row of frosted glass windows giving on to a narrow passage which divided 5 Hayward's Court from its neighbour. The room held the characteristic tang of hot metal and coal-gas. An acrid vapour smarted Knollys' eyes.

Three laboratory benches, each equipped with a ceramic sink, piped water and gas, and a professional microscope, filled the centre space, and at one of these benches a man stood working. He was somewhere between fifty and sixty, and wore a long, brown laboratory coat, which concealed all but his stiff white collar and sober tie. He was holding a test tube by means of a special holder, and was gently moving it across the flame of a Bunsen burner. He looked up as Jack Knollys entered, and smiled; but it was a world-weary, cynical kind of smile, which did nothing to animate the man's pale face.

'Mr Craven? I'm Detective Sergeant Knollys of Scotland Yard. I'd like to have a word with you, if I may.'

'Bear with me a little while, Sergeant,' said Craven. 'I need to finish this test without interruption. I'll be with you in a minute.'

Still holding the test tube in its clamp, Craven poured the contents into a small glass dish, and put the test tube safely into a little wooden rack. He turned out the Bunsen burner, and wiped his hands on a cloth.

'Now, Sergeant Knollys,' he said, 'I'm all attention. I expect you're here in connection with the death of Mr Gregory. Well, I know nothing about it. On the day he was killed in Priory Gate Street, I came in here to work as usual at eight o'clock. Mr Gregory never turned up until ten, which was his agreed starting-time. So he wasn't *here*, and I wasn't *there*.'

This man, thought Knollys, didn't like the late Mr Gregory Walsh, or at least, resented him. Perhaps it would be wise to find out why.

'Mr Walsh was only twenty-six, so I've been told,' he said. 'Was he a qualified chemist? Was he skilled in the craft? These are not idle questions, Mr Craven.'

'Skilled? Oh, he was skilled enough. And he was well qualified, I'll grant him that.'

The man's voice was grudging, and held an undertone of angered disappointment, but it was clear to Knollys that Craven would never tell a lie. He might begrudge telling the truth, but he'd tell it, nonetheless.

Craven picked up the small glass dish and

peered at the liquid. Evidently, the result was satisfactory. His mind was clearly more on the day's work than the cruel fate of his employer's son.

'But I'm qualified, too, Mr Knollys, and I've worked here since I was fourteen. There's very little I don't know about this business, and until last year — '

He stopped speaking, and again took up the dish. He swirled the contents around, and gave a little grunt of satisfaction. Box heard him mutter, 'Yes, the crystals are growing nicely!'

'Until last year? What happened then, Mr Craven?'

'Old Mr Walsh — you've met him, haven't you, upstairs? — old Mr Walsh had always half promised me a partnership on account of my seniority here, and the many years that I've worked for him — fifty years, to be precise. 'Don't worry, Craven', he'd say, 'when the time's ripe, I'll make you a partner'. But then, he decided to hand over the business to young Mr Walsh, and that was the end of all talk of a share for me!'

Craven all but slammed the dish down on to the bench. For the first time since Knollys had entered the dim chamber, he looked him straight in the eyes.

'But that's all changed, now, hasn't it, Mr

92

Knollys?' he said, the bitter smile returning to his lips. 'Mr Gregory is dead, so maybe the old man will think over what he used to say about a partnership. He'll need all the dependable help that he can get, now, and there's none more dependable than me.'

Knollys felt a sudden stab of pity for the man. He had spun himself a fantasy about a partnership, which had been unkindly dangled before him for years, in order to keep him loyal to the business. To become a partner, you had to bring money into a business, and Craven was clearly not a moneyed man.

'I wish you every success, Mr Craven,' said Knollys. 'Now, let me ask you a specific question. Was Mr Gregory Walsh engaged on any experiments that could conceivably have a connection with the Mithraeum in Priory Gate Street?'

Mr Craven looked interested. He left the bench, and invited Knollys to enter a tiny office, little more than a cupboard, situated near the staircase door. He pulled down a ledger from a shelf, and turned its pages for a while.

'On these pages, Mr Knollys,' he said, 'you see all the jobs assigned to Mr Gregory Walsh this month. There's Tuesday, the fourteenth — the day he was killed. Nothing until eleven o'clock, when he was due at the East India

Dock to collect a sample of pine oil from one of the Baltic freighters. Nothing then till the afternoon, when he was due to collect some samples of paint and pigment from Thomas & Jones at Tower Wharf. That would be something to do with faults in manufacture, I should imagine. Nothing about the Mithraeum.'

Knollys had seen and heard all that was necessary. As he prepared to mount the stairs to take leave of Miss Thompson, he asked a sudden and unrehearsed question.

'Did you like Mr Gregory Walsh?'

'Like him? Well, I suppose I did. Yes, of course I did. I'll be going to his funeral, I expect. I must buy a little wreath. Old Mr Walsh would appreciate that.'

★　★　★

Jack Knollys walked thoughtfully out of Hayward's Court and into St John Street. He wondered how the guvnor was faring in Carshalton. Well, he'd find out later in the day. Sergeant Kenwright would be in the Mithraeum by now, with his sketch pads, pencils, and tracing-paper. Should he call in on him as he walked past the entrance to the site? No, best to keep his mind on the task in hand.

He turned out of Priory Gate Street and stepped on to the cobbles of Catherine Lane, glancing as he did so at the premises of the wholesale jeweller on the corner. 'Gold & Co.', it said over the door. A very apt name. A stout man with a bushy black beard was looking incuriously out of the front door. Next door to Mr Gold's workshop was the closed and inscrutable Hatchard's Furniture Repository, at the side of which was Miller's Alley, leading to Miller's Court.

His eyes still stinging from the chemical-laden atmosphere of Mr Walsh's laboratory, Knollys crossed the lane, and set out to find the premises of Reuben Greensands, the optician who had made the pair of glasses that had been found in Gregory Walsh's pocket. He found it almost immediately. It was a modest, double-fronted shop, with an open door between two display windows, one of which had been smashed, and boarded up. Wooden packing cases and heaps of shavings stood outside on the cobbles, together with a newly painted shop sign propped up against the wall, evidently waiting to be erected. 'J. Newton, Optician', it read. Above the shop the name of Reuben Greensands still stood on its painted board.

'Come in, sir! We are open — mind that ladder! I can see from here that your near sight's not all that it should be. Sit down in this chair.'

An affable, bald-headed man had come forward from some recess at the back of the shop, which was crammed with cardboard boxes and decorating materials. Before Knollys had time to speak, the man had gently guided him into a chair facing one of the walls.

'My name's John Newton, sir,' said the man, rummaging through a box of lenses, 'and I've just bought the late Mr Reuben Greensands' business from his cousin. How are you? Isn't it warm today! Now, just cover your left eye, and look through this little lens. There's a chart on the wall in front of you. Never mind the big letters. Try the fifth row.'

'Mr Newton — '

'That's right, Newton. I've another shop in Finsbury. Just read the fifth row.'

'P E C F D. My name is Detective Sergeant Knollys of Scotland Yard. I've come to ask whether you can identify a pair of spectacles that were found in the pocket of a dead man.'

Mr Newton almost crowed with delight. He put the lens down on the counter, and clasped his hands together.

'Dear me! A mystery! Do let me see these spectacles, Mr Knollys. Ah! They're in one of

Mr Greensands' own little tin cases. I'm introducing mock crocodile cases, which I think will go down well, but I'll use up Greensands' old stock first. The shop stood empty for over a fortnight, and I'm afraid people seemed to have got into it from time to time. Somebody threw a brick through that right-hand window, but that's only exuberance. Boys, I expect.'

Mr Newton had a pleasant, light tenor voice, and evidently liked to hear it in action.

'And can you identify the owner of those spectacles? Did Mr Greensands record his customers' details in a ledger?'

'He used a card index system, Mr Knollys. You can see it, over there. Now, let me see if he's scratched a reference number on the inside of the frame — where's my magnifying glass? While I'm looking at this, just read the seventh line of the chart, will you? Read it aloud, you know.'

'D E F P O T E C.'

'Well done. Yes, here's the reference number, so now I can look it up in the index. How fascinating this is! I've never helped the police in an investigation before.'

The genial Mr Newton threaded his way between the cardboard boxes and ladders until he came to a mahogany box standing on a table. He pulled open a drawer, and flicked rapidly through the stack of cards arranged in it. With a little cry of triumph, he selected a card and held it up for Knollys to see. The optician's mind, however, was occupied with more important things than mere cards.

'The beauty of it is,' he said, 'that the eye test is free. Entirely free. It's not a good thing to strain the eyes by too much peering at pages of print. I'll need to try you with four more lenses, and then I'll show you our selection of ready-made reading glasses. You were very wise to come in here this morning.'

'Mr Newton, will you please tell me the name on that card?'

'The name? Ainsworth. Professor Roderick Ainsworth. Now isn't that interesting? He's the man who excavated the Mithraeum just a stone's throw from here, in Priory Gate Street. He's in Edinburgh at the moment, addressing the Royal Caledonian Something-or-other. You know how learned the Scots are. Now cover your right eye, and look through this new lens. Can you see the third line of the chart clearly?'

'Yes, I can. So those particular glasses belong to Professor Ainsworth?'

'They do. They're for reading, you know — quite strong of their type.'

Mr Newton drew up a chair, and sat beside

Knollys. He looked both excited and intrigued.

'I wonder why Professor Ainsworth bought his glasses from Greensands?'

'It's a question that I've been asking myself, Mr Newton. I don't suppose he lives in Clerkenwell.'

'Oh, no, he doesn't. He has a beautiful house at Epsom — Ardleigh Manor, it's called.'

'You seem to know a lot about him, Mr Newton. And it looks as though archaeology pays very well.'

'I'm very interested in history, Mr Knollys, and in archaeology too, and I've read a lot about Professor Ainsworth in *The Historical Magazine*. And, of course, he's by way of being a local celebrity. It was he who discovered the Clerkenwell Treasure just across the road from here, near the entrance to Hatchard's. Have you seen it? It's in the South Kensington Museum. Ancient church vessels of gold and silver, all kinds of wonderful things. Try these steel frames on for size. It's fit I'm interested in at the moment, so there's no glass in these.'

Jack Knollys resigned himself to the fact that he was going to buy a pair of glasses. This gossiping optician was a veritable mine of information as well as being an extremely cunning salesman.

'And it was very clever how he discovered it,' Mr Newton continued. 'Quite in your own line of work, Mr Knollys. He read all kinds of old letters and chronicles in cathedral libraries and other ancient places, and from those documents he was able to deduce where the treasure had been hidden. Something like that. Wonderful, really.'

'And so he made his fortune?'

'Oh, no, Mr Knollys. I don't suppose archaeology pays all that much, or the professorship, come to that. No, Professor Ainsworth inherited a fortune from his father, who was a Tyneside shipbuilder. He's a very wealthy man, so he's been able to put all his heart and soul into his scholarly work. I went to one of his lectures, once. Fascinating.

'Now, all these pairs of spectacles in this tray are suitable for your eye condition. You can try them all on, and choose the one you like. Those steel-rimmed ones are three-and-six, and the gold ones four-and-eleven. You can pay me now, or you can make a down payment of a shilling, and pay the rest off at sixpence a week. The important thing is that you should be satisfied.'

While Newton was talking, Knollys was propounding a theory to himself. Walsh's killer must have fled quickly from the site, but had nevertheless contrived to conceal the murder weapon. What if this was a local murder, something confined to people living in Clerkenwell? True, there was the odd business of the honey, but that might have been a crude attempt to lead the police astray.

This Mr Newton had told him that the empty shop had been broken in to more than once. Had the killer been one of those intruders, using the premises as a place to conceal his deadly weapon? It would do no harm to have a look around.

'I'll take this steel pair, thank you, Mr Newton,' said Knollys, 'and I'll pay for them now. Would you mind very much if I were to look round the premises for a little while? Just out of interest, you know.'

'Of course, of course! Things are rather topsy-turvy at the moment, as you can see. Poor Mr Greensands died very suddenly, you know. Heart, it was. I don't think the doctors can do much in that line, do you? By the way, I suppose the man who had Professor Ainsworth's glasses in his pocket was young Mr Walsh, who was killed in the Mithraeum? You see, if you found those glasses in his pocket, then maybe he'd found them in the Mithraeum, and decided to return them to Professor Ainsworth.'

'Quite possibly, Mr Newton,' said Knollys. 'We'll certainly look into the matter. May I go through this door behind the counter?'

'Certainly. It leads into the back yard. There's a lot of straightening up to be done there before the week's out.'

The back yard of 14 Catherine Lane was quite small, and occupied almost entirely by a couple of tall iron middens, and a number of bulging crates of rubbish. There was a dilapidated wooden door in one of the high brick walls. It was half open, and led into an alley. It was very quiet and sunny. A few somnolent bluebottles were droning around one of the crates. Bluebottles . . . Wherever they congregated, there was bound to be organic decay.

Jack Knollys pulled aside a number of sheets of cardboard and pieces of broken wood to reveal the steel head of an adze, which was clotted with congealed blood. He permitted himself a little sigh of satisfaction: his theory had been right. This was surely a local crime, committed by a man with local knowledge. Very carefully, he drew the complete adze from the crate into which it had been thrust. This, clearly, was the instrument that had been used to strike down Gregory Walsh.

6

The Man with the Carpet Bag

'I don't know what to think, Sergeant Knollys.'

The two officers were sitting at the big table in Box's office. Each had given the other a full account of his doings on the previous day, and together they were pondering some of the ramifications. Having heard Box's account of the events at Carshalton, Knollys had conceded that the death of Gregory Walsh was something more than a local affair.

'There *must* be a link between these two murders,' Box continued. 'I'm not prepared to consider coincidence. Gregory Walsh was an analytical chemist. Abraham Barnes had connections with another chemist, a man called Bonner. Walsh had come in contact with scrapings of paint while examining that Roman shrine. Barnes was interested in the analysis of Roman cement. Why this interest in things Roman?'

Sergeant Knollys nodded his assent.

'What were they both up to, sir?' he said. 'Each man had been abused after death by

103

the introduction of a substance into his mouth — honey in one case, mercury in the other. Apart from the disgusting profanation of a dead body, what was the point of it?'

'If we contain our patience for a few days more, Sergeant, it's more than likely that the general public will start to remember things — men behaving suspiciously, furtive goings-on in the vicinity of the Mithraeum — you know the kind of thing I mean. And then, there's your discovery of the murder weapon in the back yard of the late Reuben Greensands' shop. Someone may have seen someone else 'behaving suspiciously', as they say. It might be an idea to ask a few questions in the area.

'Meanwhile, there's other work for us to do, besides the murders of Walsh and Barnes. The Balantyne brothers are coming up for trial at the Old Bailey next week, and we'll both be called as witnesses. We need to write clear statements of our own evidence, or their counsel will tie us into knots. The Balantynes have briefed Malcolm Thresher, QC, who's a real terror — '

'Sir,' said Knollys, who evidently had not been listening, 'there's a little detail concerning this Mithraeum case which I think we should both bear in mind. I'm referring to the railway line from Croydon to Carshalton. Its final stop is Epsom, and it's at Epsom that Professor Ainsworth lives. Croydon, Carshalton, Epsom — a nice convenient line.'

'Ainsworth? You think he may have travelled to Carshalton, done for Barnes, and then went on to London Bridge? Well, Jack, I suppose anything's possible, but if your friend Mr Newton the optician's telling the truth, Professor Ainsworth is in Edinburgh, giving a lecture. But you're right, Jack, we need to know far more about Ainsworth. At the moment, he's just a name and a reputation. Did he know poor Walsh? Did he know Barnes?'

'As a matter of fact, sir,' said Knollys, 'I saw in *The Morning Post* yesterday that Professor Ainsworth's giving a lecture at Exeter Hall next Monday, the twentieth. It might be an idea for us to go to that lecture, partly to listen to what the professor has to say, and partly to see what he's like as a man. Weigh him up, you know.'

'That's a very good idea, Sergeant. We'll do that. Maybe I'll introduce myself to him at the end — '

The swing doors of the office were pushed open, and a young lad of fourteen or so came into the room. He was wearing the smart uniform of a message boy, and carried a folded newspaper in one hand, and his cap in the other. The boy looked with interest around the room before his eyes rested on the giant Sergeant.

'Sir,' said the boy, 'I was sent from Fleet Street to give you this copy of *The Graphic*, which is just off the press. The policeman at the door said I could come through with it. Mr Fiske sent me.'

'He thinks you're me, Jack,' said Box, laughing. 'Go on, give him a penny for his trouble!'

Sergeant Knollys did as he was bid with a good grace, and took the folded paper from the lad.

'Mr Fiske said you're to look at page four, sir.' The boy glanced round the bare room for a second time, and pulled a face.

'It's not up to much, is it, this place?' he said. 'There's a crack in the ceiling. Why don't you move to the new building on the Embankment?'

'Because we like it here,' said Knollys, handing the paper to Box. 'So you just hop it, will you, and leave us alone.'

When the boy had gone, Box laid the paper on the table, and opened it at page four. Beneath a striking engraving of the mysterious figure painted on the reredos in the Mithraeum, a headline had been set in daringly large type, and beneath it was the deliberately sensational article that Billy Fiske had told Box he would write.

ARE PAGAN RITES STILL CELEBRATED IN MODERN LONDON?

On Tuesday last, in the Roman Mithraeum at Clerkenwell, a young man was found murdered, his body sprawled at the base of a great pagan image of the ancient god Mithras. His mouth was found to have been filled with honey, introduced there after his death. On the same day, at Carshalton in Surrey, an older man, a highly respected citizen of the town, was found murdered in the same manner. His mouth had been sacrilegiously filled with a quantity of common mercury or quicksilver.

Reader, do not be lulled into the belief that these two foul murders were not connected. Consider this. At the heart of our great metropolis there sits the ancient, hidden Roman city of Londinium. If business ever takes you south of Cripplegate, you will find yourself walking above the remains of a great Roman fort. Within a stone's-throw of London's cathedral a first-century Roman bath lies concealed. Carshalton lies near an ancient Roman staging-post, where, so I have been told, a second-century cave of Mithras once existed.

These are the dead remains of a civilization long gone. But do its ancient beliefs and practices still persist? Are these murders linked by occult practices surviving unknown and unsuspected for over a thousand years? Were these two unfortunate men adepts of some secret cult, its origins lost in antiquity? Mithraism was once a serious rival to Christianity, and may still have its secret adherents.

In the pockets of both unfortunate victims, circular tokens of lapis lazuli were found, each bearing an image of Jupiter on one side, and the depiction of a beast on the other: in Clerkenwell, a lion, in Carshalton, a raven. Is there some occult fellowship of Mithras at work in our land, and were the images of lion and raven signs of rank in a diabolical hierarchy?

You will reply that the nineteenth century is an era of progress and enlightenment, and of course you will be right. Nevertheless, we will remind you of the shocking revelations made at Naples in 1874, where the self-styled

'Mage' Alfredo Bertoni was condemned to death for offering human sacrifices to this same deity, Mithras. There were lapis lazuli tokens there, too, one bearing an engraved horned moon, and the other a sun's disc with arrows for rays. In the mouths of Bertoni's victims the authorities there found not only traces of honey and mercury, but rings, fashioned from silver wire. Surely, we must suspend our disbelief for a while, and examine the possibility of dark supernatural forces at work in our midst.

We are gratified to hear that the murders at Clerkenwell and Carshalton are being investigated by Detective Inspector Arnold Box of Scotland Yard, an officer who needs no introduction to readers of this paper. We sincerely trust that, among the many mundane details of his investigation, Mr Box will not lose sight of the grim reality that the powers of darkness, even in this, the most enlightened of ages, can be in the ascendant.

'Blimey!' cried Box, throwing the paper down on to the table. 'He doesn't half lay it on! But then, he's always known how to use words as a weapon. 'The powers of darkness'! Only think!'

'What a load of tosh, sir,' said Knollys. 'And yet — That Italian case Fiske referred to — there was the same business of honey and mercury. And silver wire rings . . . He certainly does his research, doesn't he? What can it all mean? Maybe Billy Fiske's on to something real after all.'

Arnold Box stood up, and gave a little shudder of distaste.

'I don't like all this pagan stuff, Sergeant Knollys,' he said. 'Quite frankly it disgusts me. I can't see why they don't leave all these mouldering bits of stone where they belong — under the ground, buried from our sight. It's eleven o'clock. Come on, let's go and have a glass of ale and a pie in The Grapes. There are one or two other things I want to talk about while we've got a bit of time to ourselves.'

★   ★   ★

Joe Straddling, sitting at breakfast that morning in the kitchen of his railway cottage overlooking the down line from Croydon, threw the newspaper aside, and drained his second cup of tea. He sat back in his chair, and looked at his wife. Should he tell her about the man on the train the night Abraham Barnes was killed? She always said

110

he imagined things, but he hadn't imagined that man. Maybe there was nothing to it, but he should have told Inspector Perrivale.

'Ruth,' said Joe Straddling, 'you remember that I was guard on the four o'clock milk train to Croydon on the fourteenth, the night that Mr Barnes was murdered up at the works?'

'Indeed I do, and it was the third night shift you'd been given in a row. It's not right, Joe, and the company ought to be ashamed of themselves. Twenty-five years you've been a guard on those trains — '

'What I'm trying to say, Ruth, if you'll give me a chance, is that a man boarded that train here at Carshalton just after a quarter to four. You don't often get passengers on the milk trains, on account of them being so early, which is why I noticed him. He'd got a ticket right enough — he must have bought it sometime late Monday evening — and he sat by himself in a cold compartment while we went up the line to Croydon. I've been wondering whether he had anything to do with Mr Barnes's death.'

Ruth Straddling paused in her task of clearing away the breakfast things.

'What sort of a man was he? What makes you think he had anything to do with the murder?'

111

'Well, he was a burly man, well built — not young, though. He was wearing a merchant seaman's black jacket, and a cap with a glazed peak pulled well down over his eyes. Bearded, he was. You couldn't see much of his face.'

'A workman, was he?'

'Yes, he was. He was carrying one of those big carpet bags. Maybe he had tools in it. I just wondered who he was, and what he'd been doing here in Carshalton in the middle of the night. Do you think I should tell Inspector Perrivale?'

'I think you should, Joe. It'd be just as well. He'd have had to leave the train at Croydon, wouldn't he, because that's as far as that milk train goes?'

'That's right. I watched him when he got down, lugging his carpet bag down after him on to the platform. It was still dark, of course, so all the station lamps were still lit. He crossed the bridge to Platform Seven and stood there, waiting for the London train. There were a few other men there, and he just merged in with them, if you know what I mean.'

'So he'd have gone up to London Bridge — '

'No, Ruth: Platform Seven's for the through train to Victoria. It makes you think who he was, and what he was up to. He'd have got into Victoria at seven minutes past six.'

Mrs Straddling glanced at a clock on the window sill.

'You're going to be late, Joe. Best get your coat on. Yes, I'd tell Mr Perrivale about it. Mind you, when you think about it, the conservatory door at Wellington House was open when the police came — their maid, Mary, told me that. There was no sign of a break-in. So what was Abraham Barnes doing, going in there in the middle of the night, fully dressed?'

'Well, how should *I* know?'

'He was meeting someone, you mark my words, and that 'someone' murdered him. He was supposed to be a great pillar of society, but everybody knew that Mr Barnes had some very peculiar friends. In another five minutes, Joe, you'll be late. You'd best be going. See Inspector Perrivale on your way home.'

* * *

As always in mid-morning, the back bar of The Grapes public house in Aberdeen Lane was crowded with plain-clothes policemen. They sat at tables in the discreet glazed booths, drinking beer, smoking, eating pies, and talking earnestly in low tones. None of them cared much if the others heard what they were saying, as they were all serving police officers from the Rents, or from the old headquarters of 'A' Division in Whitehall Place.

Box and Knollys nodded to one or two of the men, and sat down in an empty booth.

'What's your pleasure, Mr Box?' asked the bar waiter, a rather greasy young man who had carefully folded a grubby napkin over his arm.

'Two India pale ales, and two beef pies, with plates and knives. Put it on the slate, Louis.

'I had a note from Sergeant French in Clerkenwell this morning,' said Box, after their food and drink had been deposited on the table. 'You remember that the police surgeon never turned up? Well, apparently, he came in the police hearse, and viewed the body just after you and I had left. He agrees that the time of death was about seven in the morning. Perhaps a bit earlier, but certainly no later.'

The ale was strong and cool, and the beef pies flavoursome and garnished with jelly. Box sighed, and sat back in his chair. Around the two of them the other customers continued to mutter their professional secrets to each other. Although it was hot and stuffy in the back bar, it was a welcome change from the Rents.

'And there was a note from Dr Miller at Horseferry Road,' Box said. 'He's had the honey from young Walsh's mouth analysed. It was just ordinary honey, he said, the kind you could buy at any grocer's. So that's that.'

'What are you going to do now, sir?'

'I propose that you and I, Jack, pay a visit to this other chemist, the one who had business dealings with Abraham Barnes at Carshalton. What was his name?'

Box produced his notebook, and rapidly flicked over the pages.

'Yes, here it is. When I searched through Barnes's desk, I found four little envelopes containing small quantities of what looked like sand or mortar. There was also a note — or the copy of a note — saying that the contents of the envelopes had been analysed by someone called Bonner, whose premises were in Garrick Flags, which is just behind Charing Cross Road. Let's call upon this Mr Bonner this afternoon, and show him those envelopes. They're bound to mean something to him.'

★ ★ ★

Inspector Perrivale knocked on the door of Mr Stanley's boarding-house in Queen's Lane. His feet were hurting him, because it was years since he'd pounded so many pavements as he'd done that day. He'd visited six of the seven small hotels and boarding-houses in the Hackbridge area of Carshalton, to no avail. No one had accommodated a burly, bearded workman in a black jacket, accompanied by a large carpet bag. Mr Stanley's establishment was the last of the seven.

The door was opened by Mr Stanley himself. He was in his shirt sleeves, and had evidently been polishing cutlery, as he still held a fork in one hand and an ample cloth in the other.

'Mr Perrivale! Come in. What can I do for you? Is it about the man with the carpet bag?'

'It is, Mr Stanley,' said Perrivale, entering a narrow hallway containing an enormous hall stand and an aspidistra growing in a glazed pot on a stand. There was a strong smell of cabbage emanating from some unseen quarter of the house behind the stairs.

'He came here on Monday,' said Mr Stanley, a genial, balding man in his fifties. 'He said he wanted a room for the night, and offered to pay cash in advance. Well, that was fine, of course, so I took him upstairs and showed him one of the little attic rooms at the back. He said he didn't want a meal, and that he'd be out quite late. I gave him a latch key, and left him to his own devices.'

'How did you know that I was trying to find where this man had stayed?'

'Joe Straddling's wife told *my* wife. I don't know who told Mrs Straddling. Do you think he was the man who murdered poor Mr Barnes? Just think! We might have all been murdered in our beds!'

'What was he like, this bearded man?'

'He seemed very respectable to me. Well set up, if you know what I mean. His cap and coat were obviously brand new, and so was his carpet bag. I offered to carry it upstairs for him, but he said to let well alone. He spoke quietly, and I got the impression he'd been well educated. He was probably a skilled tradesman of some sort. He was the kind of man who didn't encourage questions, and I never asked him any.'

'When did he leave, Mr Stanley? Did you see him go?'

'No, I didn't see him go. He'd left the house long before I got up. In fact, I'm not sure that he ever returned from going out late that evening. His bed hadn't been slept in, though he'd evidently lain on the top of it for a while. He'd left the latch key on the edge of the wash-stand, together with a florin gratuity, which was very handsome of him, since I'd done nothing for him but provide him with a room and bed.'

'I supposed he signed your register? What name did he give?'

'Michael Shane, living at 4 Cobb's Buildings, Hackney. He asked me to write it for him, as his wrist was strained.'

'Well, thank you very much, Mr Stanley,' said Perrivale, 'you've been a great help.'

'Will you go after this Michael Shane?' asked Mr Stanley. 'Do you think it was he who murdered poor Mr Barnes?'

Inspector Perrivale smiled, but refused to be drawn. As he walked away from Mr Stanley's boarding-house, he thought: there'll be no such man as Michael Shane, and no such place as Cobb's Buildings, unless I'm very much mistaken. I'll telegraph the name and address to Mr Box at Scotland Yard, but it's information that will lead nowhere.

* * *

Box and Knollys saw the premises of the man called Bonner as soon as they walked into Garrick Flags from St Martin's Lane. A tall, three storeyed warehouse was topped by a long painted sign, telling them that this was the place of business of William Bonner and Company, Assayers to the Building Trade and Mineral Merchants' Samplers.

Bonner's was a much larger undertaking than Walsh's laboratory in Clerkenwell. In a cobbled yard at the side of the building they could see several wagons drawn up at a loading platform. A long, open-sided shed revealed rows of demijohns and carboys containing what Box judged to be deadly acids. A number of men were busy in the yard, and when the two policemen entered the building, they found themselves in a kind of open office, where a smartly dressed clerk rose from a desk to receive them.

Yes, Mr Bonner was available, and could see them straight away. It was a busy day, and Mr Bonner was in the main laboratory. Would they please walk this way?

When the clerk threw open a glazed door at the end of a passage, Box and Knollys could hardly contain a gasp of surprise. The laboratory was a room of vast proportions, containing an array of ten long chemical benches, at which a number of men in brown coats were working. Box was familiar with the delicate glass apparatus of chemical laboratories, but some of the devices set out in Bonner's vast room were quite unknown to him.

'Inspector Box? I thought you'd pay a call on us after what happened to Abraham Barnes. I'm William Bonner.'

Bonner, a tall, quiet man with silver hair, had emerged from somewhere at the rear of the laboratory. Like his employees, he wore a long brown laboratory coat buttoned up to the collar. He looked slightly vexed at having the routine of his laboratory disrupted, but his courteous voice held no tone of reproach. He stood for a moment observing his visitors with steady, unblinking eyes, and then essayed a slight smile.

'In a moment, Inspector,' said Bonner at last, 'one of my assistants will be testing the compressive strength of a suspect mortar, using that device over there.' He pointed to a machine that looked like a combination of book-press and anvil. 'It measures the torque at the moment of compression, and once the test starts it can be very noisy. You and I had better talk elsewhere.'

They followed Bonner out of the laboratory and into a well-furnished office on the same floor. Bonner motioned to a couple of chairs, and sat behind a cluttered desk.

'Now, what can I do for you?' he asked. 'I was astounded to read of poor Barnes's violent demise. It must surely have been the work of a demented tramp or vagrant.'

Arnold Box saw Knollys hide a smile behind his hand. It was amazing how the public tried to foist off every violent crime on a mythical army of dangerous beggars.

'First, sir, I'd like to know what connection you had with the dead man. Was he just a client, or would you have counted him among the number of your friends?'

'Abraham Barnes, Inspector, ran a very old-established cement works. He was, perhaps, a trifle old-fashioned in his industrial processes, but he was meticulous in submitting all his batches to us for sampling. Cement — I suppose you know what cement *is*, don't you?'

'Well, sir, it's — '

'Cement, Inspector, or Portland cement, which is what we're talking about in relation to Abraham Barnes's works, is a finely ground powder of cement clinker, gypsum, and certain other materials. It's the basic ingredient of concrete, mortar and stucco. Our company provides analytical and testing services to the cement industry in general. Abraham Barnes was one of my clients. I knew him well, but I'd not have called him a friend. Perhaps it would be more accurate to say that he was no stranger to me.'

From the laboratory beyond, a tremendous banging and crashing commenced. The two policemen winced. Mr Bonner smiled.

'Sir,' said Box, reaching into his inner pocket, 'I have some samples here that I'd like you to look at. I found them in the late Mr Barnes's office.'

A gleam of interest came to the steady eyes of the analytical chemist. He stretched out his hand, and Box gave him the four manila envelopes that he had found in Abraham Barnes's desk, together with the two notes that he had discovered with them.

'Oh, yes, Inspector,' said Bonner, 'these were very interesting. They were all specimens of mortar. Barnes wouldn't tell me where he got them from, but he asked me to analyse them to determine which were ancient Roman, and which were modern. He came in here with them about a month ago, as I remember, on business to do with the works, and when we'd finished that, he produced these samples, and asked me to tell him what they were.'

'Would such a task be part of your normal business?'

'Well, no, Mr Box, and I would normally have sub-contracted work of this type to people like poor young Gregory Walsh, at Clerkenwell. But Barnes was insistent that I should do the work myself, so I did. That's my writing on the envelopes. I sent them back to him a week later. I've got the full analyses here, in the office, but what's written on the envelopes is all that Barnes needed to know.'

'Could you briefly explain what your comments mean?'

'Well, the first sample was of a mortar made from freshly burnt lime, sharp sand, and water, used for slaking. It was indubitably ancient Roman mortar. The same applied to sample number three: undoubtedly Roman. Number two was modern mortar: I mean late nineteenth century. It contained neat Portland cement, something unknown to the Romans, and typical quantities of alumina. It was modern mortar. I did a full trade analysis on that one.'

'And the last sample?'

'I wasn't too sure about that one. Some of the constituents suggest that it was made about 1660. But it was most definitely not Roman mortar.'

Somewhere in the deep recesses of Arnold Box's mind a picture was forming. It was a picture that he did not much care for.

'You've been of enormous help, Mr Bonner,' he said. 'I must say, it's all very fascinating. And you charged him a guinea?'

Bonner laughed, and his sober face broke into a charming smile.

'He was always very keen on money and

receipts, was poor Barnes. Yes, I charged him a guinea, and he sent me a cheque through the post by return. He was old-fashioned in his approach to production, but he was a careful businessman.'

'That other note, sir: it seems to be from a third party. Does it mean anything to you?'

' 'Barnes, can I trouble you to get these four done? I'm nearly there, and these four, if they show what I think they'll show, will be the final proof.' Well, it obviously applies to these samples, and evidently Barnes had been asked by the writer to have them analysed.'

'That note is signed with the initials CW. Do they convey anything to you, sir?'

'Not a thing, Inspector. Evidently, CW was one of Barnes's friends, and he was engaged on some kind of research into building-materials. He could be a scientist, I suppose. Abraham Barnes was a Methodist, you know, so maybe this CW was one of his co-religionists. Perhaps it would be a good idea to check up on that aspect of his life.'

What sounded like a thunderous explosion shook the wall of the office. Mr Bonner rose to his feet.

'I must go back to the laboratory, gentlemen,' he said. 'They're testing the tensile strength of a batch of cement briquettes — you may have heard the sound just now. I'm always here at your service if you want me, and all records of my dealings with Abraham Barnes are at your disposal. I *must* go. Let me bid you good day.'

7

Some Talk of Mithras

In the large front room of her neat semi-detached villa in one of the spacious new avenues in Finchley, Louise Whittaker was busy setting out the tea-things on a round table near the fireplace. In half an hour's time, her little maid Ethel would bring in the teapot, and then she and her friend Mary Westerham, a renowned epigraphist, and a fellow lecturer at Maybury College in Gower Street, would settle down to an hour of refreshment and, possibly, enlightenment.

Mary Westerham always dressed in black, even in high summer. Her grey hair was drawn back from her forehead, and secured at the nape of her neck in a severe bun. But she was a woman of ready wit and genuine compassion, not just well respected, but well liked.

Miss Westerham's sight was not of the best, and she was sitting at Louise's paper-strewn working-table in the wide bay window, reading *The Graphic* newspaper with the aid of strong pince-nez.

'I say, Louise,' cried Mary Westerham suddenly, 'have you read this report of the so-called Mithras murders in this paper? Where on earth did their reporter find all this detail? He certainly gives the impression of knowing quite a lot about Mithraism. I wonder whether he's read Franz Cumont's monograph on the subject? Incidentally, I didn't know you read this kind of popular print. I thought you were a *Morning Post* woman.'

'Why, so I am.' Louise laughed. 'My little maid Ethel brought me that, because she knew I'd be interested in it. The lady next door gives it to her when she's finished with it, so that she can look at the pictures. Of course, anthropology's not my subject — I'm more at home with Anglo-Saxon manuscripts — but it's certainly intriguing.'

'He asks a lot of questions,' said Mary, 'to all of which the sensible answer would be 'no'. 'Are pagan rites still celebrated in modern London?' etcetera. 'Were these two unfortunate men adepts of some secret cult?' Well, I suppose that's possible . . . I wonder who wrote this? There's no name attached to it.'

'It was written by a man called Fiske,' said Louise. 'He's one of their chief reporters, and very highly regarded in newspaper circles.'

'How did you know that?'

'Somebody told me. This Mithraism, Mary — it was an ancient Roman religion, wasn't it? I should have thought that it was dead and buried long ago. Do tell me about it. I know that you once made a special study of ancient pagan cults.'

'It began in Persia,' said Mary Westerham, 'and spread throughout the early Greek empire. Then the Romans got hold of it. It was being practised in the Roman Empire by 100 BC. It was one of those shadowy mystery religions that appealed to soldiers, and slaves. To some extent, of course, so was Christianity, when you think of it.'

Louise Whittaker frowned. When this kind of thing's taken seriously in the papers, she thought, it was as though the Enlightenment had never happened. Most people outside the academic world seemed quite incapable of thinking rationally.

'I could imagine a certain kind of silly exhibitionist reinventing something like that in our own time,' said Louise, 'a made-up religion or philosophy, like Freemasonry, you know, or spiritualism.'

'Well, hardly Freemasonry, dear,' said Mary, regarding Louise severely over her pince-nez. 'Freemasons are more given to arcane rituals and solid charity than bizarre murders. Boy's stuff, of course, but hardly murderous! And apropos of that article in the paper, I note that Detective Inspector Box is on the case. Isn't he your tame sleuth at Scotland Yard?'

Louise Whittaker found herself blushing. It was her friend Arnold Box who had told her that Fiske was writing a series of articles about the Mithras affair for *The Graphic*, but some instinct had warned her not to acquaint Mary with that fact.

'He's rather more than that, Mary,' she said quietly. 'And — oh, dear! I see that I must tell you the whole truth about this afternoon's proceedings.'

'How intriguing! And what, pray, is the 'whole truth'?'

'I've invited Inspector Box to join us here for tea this afternoon. You see, I always try to help him all I can, and as you're an expert in ancient Roman cults, I'm sure that there are things that you could tell him to smooth his path during this investigation. Do you mind terribly, Mary?'

Mary Westerham laughed, and looked fondly at her younger colleague.

'Well, of course I don't mind. How splendid! In any case, I suspected something of the sort when I saw that you'd set out three cups and saucers for tea. But you should have told me, Louise, and then I could have brought some notes with me. When is he coming?'

'He'll be here any minute now, I expect.'

Louise Whittaker crossed to the window bay, and looked out into the quiet avenue. Her mind reverted to Mary Westerham's half-humorous remark about Arnold Box: 'Isn't he your tame sleuth at Scotland Yard?'

No, he was more than that. Much more. They had met a few years earlier when she had been called as an expert witness in a forgery case, and from that time Arnold Box had conducted a long, discreet and diffident courtship that had gradually won her heart. He was a renowned detective with a public reputation, but whenever he was with her, he seemed confused and tongue-tied, and she could never resist making him the butt of her deadly wit. She had never had much time for men — the self-appointed Lords of Creation — but she had plenty of time for her friend Arnold Box.

He would come out to Finchley in order to get what he called 'a female slant' on aspects of a case, and from this front window she would watch him walking rather self-consciously around the corner into the avenue. He would have caught one of the Light Green Atlas omnibuses from town as far as the Finchley terminus at Church End. Well, when he came today, he would find that she had provided him with an expert consultant on matters Mithraic. Dear, diffident man, he would appreciate that.

Here he was, now!

Louise withdrew from the window, and waited for Arnold Box's sprightly knock on the front door. There was a brief murmur of voices in the hall, and then Ethel entered the room.

'Detective Inspector Box to see you, ma'am,' she said, and stood aside for Box to come in. He looked very smart and spruce and, as always, a trifle nervous. What would he make of Mary Westerham?

'Thank you, Ethel,' said Louise, 'you can bring tea in, now. This is my friend Miss Westerham. Mary, this is Detective Inspector Box.'

She was surprised how quickly her two friends accepted each other. She had anticipated a certain awkwardness as her diffident detective friend tried to adjust to another female academic. But no: they seemed to accept each other immediately.

The door opened, and little Ethel, a pretty, cheerful girl of fifteen, came in with the silver teapot on a tray. She smiled shyly at Box, and then, recollecting the rather stern lady sitting in the window, she assumed an expression of profound seriousness, curtsied, and left the room. Soon, the three of them had settled themselves around the tea table. Louise poured tea for them into thin, patterned china cups. There were plates of ham and cucumber sandwiches, a plum cake on a stand, and some freshly baked scones.

'Mary,' said Louise, 'as you know, Mr Box is investigating two murders, both of which seem to be connected with a modern cult of Mithras. It's a strange and frightening business. Now, you're an expert in these matters. I'm sure he'd want to hear what you can tell him about this bizarre worship of an ancient god.'

Mary Westerham put down her cup, and regarded Box appraisingly for a few moments through her pince-nez.

'Mr Box,' she said, 'if I'd known that you were coming here today, I would have prepared some notes covering most of what you might want to learn about Mithras and his devotees. As it is, I'll have to rely on memory. If I seem to go off at a tangent, don't be afraid to recall me to the business in hand. And for goodness' sake, interrupt with questions when you need to. So let me talk to you first about the worshippers — the devotees of this god.

132

'As I told Louise earlier, the religion of Mithras is Persian in origin. It spread throughout the Greek empire, and was being practised in the Roman Empire by 100 BC. It was very popular, and very persistent, and was still being practised both in Europe, and here in Britain, as the Roman Empire was beginning to disintegrate.

'There were seven grades of initiation into the cult of Mithras,' Mary continued, 'and each grade was associated with a particular sign, and also with one of the ancient Roman gods. Has anyone mentioned to you the case of Alfredo Bertoni in Naples?'

'Yes, ma'am, I have heard of it. I believe he was some kind of fanatic who was exposed in 1874.'

'That's right. Well, he offered human sacrifices — and, by the way, they were *voluntary* sacrifices. Each slaughtered victim was found with the sign of his initiation about him. One man was clutching a lapis lazuli token depicting a horned moon: that was the sign of the fifth grade, known as 'The Persian'. A second man was found with silver rings fashioned from twisted wire in his mouth, a sign that he had achieved the second grade, that of 'The Bridegroom' , associated with the goddess Venus. Another victim had around his neck a token suspended on a gold chain, upon which was depicted the sun in majesty. That man had reached the sixth grade, called Heliodromus, the 'Runner of the Sun'.'

Louise Whittaker moved uneasily. She hated this kind of occult business. It was all mumbo jumbo, but none the less lethal for that.

'When I examined the body of young Mr Gregory Walsh in the Clerkenwell Mithraeum,' said Box, 'I found honey spooned into his mouth, and in his pocket a lapis lazuli token depicting a lion. Can you explain what that meant?'

'It suggests that Mr Walsh had achieved the fourth grade, that of Leo, the Lion, associated with Jupiter. Now, it's thought that each aspirant had to undergo an ordeal, either by heat, cold, or hunger. Those who achieved the grade of Lion were, in theory, to undergo the ordeal by fire, but because their grade was associated with Jupiter, the father of the gods, honey was used instead. Honey also betokened purity and cleanness of speech. I think I've got that right.'

All three were silent for a while, giving their attention to the business of enjoying their afternoon tea. Arnold Box glanced at Louise, and saw that she had fallen into a reverie. She sat with her hands in her lap, clutching her teacup, and with her mind evidently far away.

And this friend of hers, Miss Mary Westerham, was a much nicer lady than she chose to suggest with all that funeral black, and pulled-back hair. It was fascinating to listen to her.

So Gregory Walsh could have been a willing sacrifice, a man who crept out early from his own house in order to be slaughtered with an adze, as an offering to Mithras, or to Jupiter, or to any other of those obscene creations of a diseased imagination.

And then there was Abraham Barnes . . .

'And what about the second victim, Miss Westerham?' asked Box. 'A man called Abraham Barnes? He was found with mercury in his throat and stomach, and a little plaque of a bird marked 'Corax' found about his person.'

'That means that Mr Barnes was a recent member of the cult, who had achieved only the first stage of initiation, that of the Raven, which was associated with the god Mercury. That was why the poor man had had mercury poured down his throat. Not a pleasant thought, but then, this is not a pleasant business.'

No, indeed . . . Had Abraham Barnes, cement manufacturer, tiptoed downstairs on that fatal morning, to be offered as a sacrifice to Mithras?

'There's a hideous logic to it all, you see, Mr Box,' said Mary. 'These are modern people abandoning themselves to an ancient superstition, but they are doing it in an informed manner, adhering faithfully to the old rituals. Rather fearsome, I should have thought.'

The topic of Mithras seemed to have exhausted itself, and the conversation turned to more mundane matters. When tea was done, Louise Whittaker declared that she had to see how Ethel was coping in the kitchen, and left the room. Mary Westerham removed her pince-nez, leaned back in her chair, and gave a sigh of satisfaction.

'I expect you come here for the same reason as I do,' she said, glancing at Box. 'There's something cool and serene about Louise's house that makes it a kind of sanctuary from the cares of the world. Don't you find it so?'

'I do, ma'am,' said Box. 'It's all because of Louise — Miss Whittaker. She's what you might call the genius of the place.'

'The *genius loci*,' said Mary, nodding her agreement, 'that's what the old Romans used to call it. And you're right. Louise is a serene person by nature and inclination, and she can impart that serenity to her friends. She and I are colleagues at Maybury College, in Gower

Street, and she invites me out here to Finchley once a month. I live in college accommodation in a little dark street behind University College, so you can imagine how wonderful it is to come out this far, and enjoy the calm and sanity of Louise's house. Incidentally, I have a hansom cab calling by appointment in a quarter of an hour's time to take me to Gower Street. Would you care to share it with me?'

'I would, ma'am, thank you very much. I hope that you and I will meet here again sometime. Meanwhile, let me thank you for what you've told me today about this cult of Mithras and its adherents. It's given me a lot of food for thought.'

* * *

Louise watched her friends' cab turning the corner out of the avenue, and then went back into the house. She sidled her way past her bicycle, which stood in the narrow hall, leaning precariously against the banisters. It was a symbol of her independence. This was *her* house, and she was its sole mistress.

In the front room, Ethel was already clearing away the tea things.

'There are some sandwiches left over, miss,' she said, 'and the teapot's half full.'

'Well, you'd better take everything out to the kitchen, where you can consume the sandwiches and drink the tea.'

Ethel smiled, but said nothing. She knew what the answer would be to her question. The missus was very kind, as well as being very beautiful. Although it was not her place to think such things, she sometimes felt that Miss Whittaker regarded her as a younger sister. They'd had many a quiet giggle together when Mr Box first started to call, pretending that he wanted help with his cases, when all the time he just wanted to admire missus, and make friends with her! Missus would look lovely in a white brocade wedding-gown, and a bouquet of orange-blossom. Oh, well. Best wait and see what happened . . .

Ethel picked up the tea tray, and went out into the kitchen.

★   ★   ★

Inspector Box and Sergeant Knollys followed Sergeant Kenwright through the tunnel-like passage that would take them from Box's office to the drill hall. It was early on the Saturday morning following Box's visit to Louise Whittaker.

As always, Kenwright warned Box to 'mind

his head'. It was all very well, thought Box, to work all day in the company of two giants without having to be reminded of their superior stature. He obediently lowered his head, though in practice there was not the slightest need to do so. Sergeant Knollys smiled to himself.

The drill hall was a dim, forlorn place, a repository for trestle tables and folding chairs, and a few old deal tables. There had been talk since the eighties of piping gas into it from the adjacent office, but nothing ever came of it, and the walls were lined with ledges upon which stood a series of little smoky oil lamps, which glowed dimly at night. In daytime, though, a good deal of light found its way obliquely into the room through a row of small windows set high in the outer walls.

As Box emerged from the tunnel, his attention was immediately arrested by a vast painting of the reredos in the Clerkenwell Mithraeum. It had been meticulously copied on to a number of large gummed sheets of art paper, and pinned to a board leaning against the end wall. The morning sunlight fell across it, bringing out the immense skill of the copyist, and the delicacy of the colouring, done in chalks: sepia, umber, sienna, and pallid green.

'Sergeant Kenwright,' said Box, 'that's a wonderful piece of work! It gave me quite a shock, seeing it glowing there at the end of the room. How did you contrive to make it so real?'

Sergeant Kenwright blushed with pleasure. Really, he thought, everything he did in this quaint old backwater of the Metropolitan Police was appreciated and applauded. But it was all Mr Box's doing. He was only thirty-five or thirty-six, but he had the knack of finding out a man's talents, and using them creatively. He'd never met a police officer like him before, or a detective sergeant like Jack Knollys, for that matter. It was lovely at the Rents.

'Well, sir, I measured the original, and it was roughly eight feet high and seven feet wide. I've made my drawing six feet square, and reduced the image accordingly. There are ten big sheets of paper there, all gummed together, and to produce the actual picture, I made thirty smaller drawings at the site. I'm glad you like it, sir.'

It was like being in the Mithraeum again, thought Box. Kenwright's beautiful chalk drawing had the same power to create unease, to give him the impression of an atrocity suspended in time, and of a tranquil slayer-deity, forever slaughtering a bull. This was the god Mithras. Did he still have his devotees in the Age of Steam? Miss Westerham had hinted at the possibility, though she'd been too wise a lady to make any kind of positive assertion.

He drew nearer to the drawing, and saw that Kenwright had divided it with fine white chalked lines into five irregular segments. He had affixed a paper label to each segment, numbering them clearly from 1 to 5.

'What's the significance of these numbers, Sergeant Kenwright?' asked Box.

'Well, sir, the reredos seems to have been assembled from five separate pieces, which have been cemented together. You can see the irregular edges of those pieces if you get up close to the work with a lantern. I expect it must have been broken at some time, sir, and then put together again. You have to look closely to see the joins, but they're there, right enough.'

Excellent, thought Box. What a pity it was that Scotland Yard had no place like this, a forensic laboratory, a dedicated workshop . . . There was nothing like that, though, of course, there were many specialists on call to perform certain tasks for a fee.

What was that other drawing, pinned to the edge of the main display?

It was a charcoal drawing of a man in a

merchant sailor's jacket with a peaked cap pulled well over his eyes. You could see the impression of a beard, and Kenwright had managed to convey a furtiveness in the man's movements. He was carrying a carpet bag.

'Well done, again, Sergeant! I'm sure that's what our mysterious traveller must look like. I wonder who he is? He's been sighted in Carshalton, then in Croydon. What is he? Some kind of messenger for this secret cult? Come on, let's all get back to the office, and we'll brew a pot of coffee.'

There was no water in the kettle, and Sergeant Knollys went out to fill it from a tap in the ablutions. Box produced some matches, and lit a gas-ring standing in the hearth. It coughed and hiccuped for a moment, and then settled itself into a steady flame.

Box looked thoughtfully at the massive bearded clerk sergeant, who was busy retrieving a number of chipped mugs from a cupboard beside the fireplace. What was he thinking?

'Sergeant,' he said, 'what's your opinion of all this Mithras business? These sacrifices, hints in the press about secret worshippers, and so on? What's your own private opinion?'

'Well, sir, I don't like to believe anything of that sort goes on at all. Murder is murder, no matter how you disguise it. We can't ignore the evidence, of course, but it might be as well to look beyond the evidence at times in order to see the sober reality. Dress it up as fancy as you wish, sir, murder is still murder.'

'It certainly is, Sergeant, and no amount of ancient rituals will make it anything else. I've been thinking of that man in the merchant navy jacket — the man who's always seen carrying a huge carpet bag. I want you to go to Clerkenwell this afternoon, Sergeant Kenwright. Talk to the shopkeepers in Priory Gate Street and Catherine Lane. They may have started to remember things about last Tuesday — the fatal fourteenth. Ask around; who knows, you may come up with something.'

★　★　★

Mr Isaac Gold, the aptly named goldsmith and wholesale jeweller, stood at the front door of his premises in Catherine Lane, watching the giant, bearded police sergeant walking slowly over the hot cobbles. He'd be on his way back to that heathen temple in Priory Gate Street. That spade beard of his was magnificent, far superior to his own. But then, you couldn't have everything in this life.

He didn't suppose that the sergeant was as rich as he was. He'd been in the district on and off for a week, now, sometimes carrying a heavy leather satchel. He didn't look like your regular beat sergeant. Mr Manassas at number 45 reckoned he was some kind of special officer from Scotland Yard. Here he was now, crossing the road. Better put yourself in his way.

'Good morning, Sergeant,' cried Mr Gold. 'We've not met before, but I've seen you about. Gold's my name, and gold's my business. This is my workshop.'

'Pleased to meet you, Mr Gold,' said the sergeant. 'My name's Kenwright. Sergeant Kenwright. Can I help you?'

'Well, it might be that I can help *you*, come to that,' said Mr Gold. 'I didn't fancy telling the constable who does this beat — PC Gully, he's called. Do you know him? Whatever you tell him, the answer's always the same: 'Don't you worry about it, Mr Gold. We'll look into it.' But they never do. When those dratted boys got over my backyard wall — '

'And you fancy you can help me, Mr Gold?' said Sergeant Kenwright. This man, he thought, is a cheerful, gossipy kind of cove, but if he isn't stopped, he'd go on talking forever. A bit like that Mr Newton, the

144

optician, at number 14. Amiable, but a chatterbox.

'It was on the very morning that the poor young man was murdered in that heathen temple round the corner,' said Mr Gold. 'It was about half-past seven, or maybe a quarter to eight — So, we should stand here and melt in the sun? Step into the shop, Sergeant. It's cool and shady in there.'

Kenwright followed the jeweller into the premises of Gold & Company. Although it was on the shady side of the lane, the place glittered and gleamed with a thousand flashes of gold. Cases of rings and other jewellery lined the shelves behind the counter. There was no silverware, or items of glass and crystal, such as is found in most jewellers' shops. Everything, everywhere, was gleaming gold.

'Yes,' said Mr Gold, stroking his beard, 'it was about a quarter to eight on the day of the murder — Did you say you were getting married? Do you have a daughter or a niece who's getting married? Come here for the rings. Don't go anywhere else. For you there will be a discount. Everything here's twenty-two carat — '

'And what did you see, Mr Gold? Or what did you hear?'

'It was a man, Sergeant; a stranger; someone I'd never seen round here before.

He came walking quickly round the corner from Priory Gate Street — hurrying, you know, taking little nervous steps, as though he was trying not to be noticed. Hurrying, but pretending *not* to hurry, if you see what I mean. He was a big, burly man, much of your build, Sergeant. He had a beard of sorts, but not as magnificent as yours or mine, and a cap with a glazed peak pulled well down over his eyes. He was wearing one of those workmen's jackets — like a seaman's jacket — and was carrying a heavy carpet bag.'

'And what did he do, this bearded man?'

'Well, that's just it, Sergeant. I watched him hurrying furtively along the lane, and then I turned away for a moment to check that the counter door was unlocked. When I looked out of the door again, the man had disappeared. I couldn't imagine where he'd got to.'

'He couldn't have gone into the optician's shop, could he? Greensands' old shop at number 14?'

'Well, he could have, I suppose. That new man hadn't moved in at that time, and the front window was broken. But why should he want to go there? Of course, he might have crossed the road again, and disappeared down Miller's Alley at the side of the furniture emporium next door. Whatever he did, Sergeant, I thought you should know.'

8

A Born Performer

Exeter Hall, venue for rousing political meetings, religious rallies and stirring concerts, was not so much a building as an attitude of mind. In the early forties it had been the centre of the anti-slavery campaign, after which it became a focus for societies concerned with the supposedly oppressed nationalities of the Empire. To be 'Exeter Hall' was to be somewhere to the left of the Liberal Party.

Box and Knollys were nearly an hour late for Professor Ainsworth's evening lecture. They had both spent the day at the Old Bailey, where they had been required to attend as witnesses at the opening of the trial of the Balantyne brothers, forgers and murderers. In the event, they had not been called that day, but late in the afternoon they had been summoned to the office of the attorney general to countersign a number of depositions.

By the time Box and Knollys approached the impressive but sooty Corinthian façade of

Exeter Hall, it was after eight o'clock in the evening, and the sun was beginning to disappear behind the roof-tops, although, even in its decline, it was able to burnish the waters of the Thames with a coppery sheen. The bases of the columns flanking the entrance were plastered with posters announcing the lecture that was to be given that evening, under the aegis of the Artisans' Improvement League.

THE ROMAN WORLD BENEATH OUR FEET

How the ancient Temple of Mithras was discovered beneath the modern pavements of Clerkenwell.
A lecture to be delivered by
Professor Roderick Ainsworth LLD MA, etc.,
Cordwainers' Professor of Antiquities in the University of London
On Monday 20 August 1894 at 7.00 p.m.
Admission 6d

The uniformed official at the door of the lower hall was inclined to be officious. The professor had been speaking for nearly an hour. At that very moment lantern slides were being shown, and the lights had been turned down . . . Police officers? Very well, then. They could mount the stairs and sit in the gallery.

The lower hall was packed with row upon row of earnest young men and women sitting on cane-backed chairs. Box and Knollys sat down unobtrusively in the right-hand gallery, and surveyed the scene. They were prepared to be interested in what remained of the lecture, but they had really come to observe the man who was delivering it.

At the front of the hall was a high, raised platform, surrounded by elaborately ornate gilded railings. There was a long bench, covered with books and papers, above which rose a rotating blackboard. A steady stream of brilliant light shone across the hall from the rear of the balcony, where an assistant was operating a magic lantern. The gaslights had been turned down to a glimmer.

Standing in the beam of light was a tall, bearded man with abundant curling hair and bright, almost fierce eyes. Box looked at him. Here was a man who smiled easily, a man who stood poised and in full command of his attentive audience. They had tiptoed into the gallery in a brief interlude between slides. When he spoke, his voice held power and authority, but it was a friendly, endearing voice, as though this magnetic personality was

149

talking to old and valued friends.

Ainsworth had noticed their entrance, and had glanced upwards very briefly before giving his whole attention once more to the audience. By sheer force of habit, Box produced his notebook, and recorded in shorthand most of what the professor said.

'So, ladies and gentlemen, the long-awaited moment had come. We levered up the final paving stone from what had been the cellar of a demolished workman's cottage at half past eleven on the morning of the seventh of May 1893. You can imagine, friends, how thrilled and awed we were.'

He rapped sharply on the bench, and a new slide was pulled through the gate of the lantern. A dramatic black and white image appeared on the screen. It showed a burly workman in dungarees standing awkwardly beside Professor Ainsworth. The man was still leaning on the adze with which he had prised up the slab.

An adze . . . They came easily to hand in this case. A fearsome weapon indeed, and used against Gregory Walsh and Abraham Barnes to deadly effect.

'There you can see Ruddock, my foreman — now dead, alas! — resting for a moment after his exertions . . . And there's the big paving stone that he's leant against the remains of the brick foundations of the demolished cottage that stood on the site. And now — '

He tapped sharply once more on the lecture bench, and another image appeared.

'Here, you can see the pit yawning at our feet! There seemed to be no original entrance to the Mithraeum remaining. That's me, steadying myself, as I prepare to descend the long ladder that Ruddock has lowered down to the floor of the vault. Quite dramatic, isn't it?'

Tap, tap, on the bench.

'The next photograph was taken by magnesium flash, much later that day. I had descended the ladder into pitch darkness, and after I had found my bearings, the indispensable Ruddock lowered down a powerful reflector lantern on a chain. This is what I saw, by its brilliant light.'

Box drew in his breath involuntarily as, once again, he was confronted by the great image of Mithras slaying the bull. He had first seen it while he was huddled over the dead body of a young man with honey in his mouth. Later, it had appeared in the drill hall at King James's Rents, brought to life on paper by the skills of Sergeant Kenwright. And here it was again, in black and white, glowing on the great screen, projected in a stream of silvery light by the magic lantern.

'Mithras, sacrificing a bull,' said the professor, standing back from the screen to look at the image. 'A curious thing to see, ladies and gentlemen — a god sacrificing to another god, probably to the Unconquerable Sun, whose feast day was the twenty-fifth of December.' Another sharp tap on the bench.

'And now, you will see a series of five specially-produced slides illustrating some of the other finds that the lantern — and our careful searches — revealed that day in the underground temple of Mithras. This, perhaps, is the most amazing of all: a headless skeleton, that had once been stored in a leather bag. Ah! You gasp! Isn't it dramatic? It was almost certainly a sacrifice of some sort, some kind of offering. It was confirmed as dating from about AD 160 by Dr Andrew McKinley of St Andrews.

'Next — a corroded sword blade, with the name Maximus scratched on it. I wonder who he was? And now, this Roman cup, which has been proved to be of bronze. It looks dirty and undistinguished — but here, in the next slide, you can see it glowing after it was cleaned by an expert in such things at the British Museum.

'Here's a Roman coin, which we can date to AD 130. It was found at the base of the great reredos, where it seems to have been pushed half beneath the foundation. And finally, this fine belt buckle, again of bronze, which would have formed part of the uniform of a Roman foot-soldier. I like to think that some worshipper had brought it there as a simple offering, over one-and-a-half millennia ago.'

Tap, tap on the bench. Another slide was pushed through the gate.

'And here we all are, ladies and gentlemen,' said the professor, 'the intrepid band of excavators, lined up, as it were, to take a bow. There's me, with Ruddock beside me, there's Mr Thompson, the site overseer, and my colleague Dr Alan Cooper of King's College. Yes, we're taking our bow, hopeful that it will be received not with brickbats but applause.'

There was a roar of laughter from the audience, and the enthusiastic clapping echoed to the roof. Professor Ainsworth's delight was obviously unfeigned. Box watched him as he stood in front of the bench, smiling and bowing. When the applause died down, and the magic lantern had been extinguished, the professor addressed his audience once more.

'Ladies and gentlemen,' he said, 'thank you very much for those signs of your approbation. I hope that you realize how grateful I am that you are so interested in and appreciative of what we've shown you. A lecture is only successful if the audience are kindled by it to absorb its base of knowledge — and that's what I feel you good folk have done tonight.

'And now it's time for questions. We have half an hour in hand, and I hope you'll ask me as many questions as will comfortably fill that time. Now, who'll set the ball rolling?'

A fair-haired young man sitting near the front of the hall stood up.

'Sir,' he said, in a voice that could just be heard by Box and Knollys from their position in the gallery, 'I've read your account of how you discovered the Clerkenwell Treasure by following a trail through old manuscripts, and suchlike. Did you do something similar when you set out to find the Mithraeum, or did you just stumble upon it by chance?'

'Stumble, young man? That's hardly the word to describe how an archaeologist goes about things!'

Professor Ainsworth's laugh was so evidently good-humoured that several members of the audience caught his mood, and chuckled as the blushing questioner sat down.

'It's a good question,' the professor continued, 'but if I'm to answer it, I'll have to tell you a dramatic story that began in the

154

eighteenth century, and ended in my house at Epsom in October last year.' He made a show of consulting his watch. 'It'll add ten minutes to the proceedings, I'm afraid. Do you want to hear it?'

To cries of 'Yes, yes!' from the audience, Professor Ainsworth took up a position at the very edge of the platform, with his hands on the gilded rail, leaning slightly forward, as though to draw his listeners into an intimate circle.

'Three hundred years or more ago, ladies and gentlemen,' he began, 'there lived a man called Sir Robert Bruce Cotton. He was an antiquarian and bibliophile and, by the time that he died at the age of sixty, in 1631, he had amassed a splendid collection of books, manuscripts, coins and medallions. He was able to acquire many important books that had been plundered from monastery libraries during the Reformation — Has anyone here ever heard of *Beowulf*?'

A number of arms were raised, and the professor nodded in satisfaction. This man, thought Box, is a born performer. He's loving every minute of this lecture.

'Well, one of Sir Robert Bruce Cotton's treasures was the original Anglo-Saxon manuscript of *Beowulf*. Sir Robert's grandson left most of this unique library to the nation. It's in the British Museum Library now, but it was originally housed first at Essex House in the Strand, and then at Ashburnham House in Westminster. Do you want me to continue?'

'Yes, yes!' from the audience.

'On the twenty-third of October 1731, a great fire broke out in Ashburnham House, and a quarter of the collection was either destroyed or damaged. Fortunately, copies had been made of some of these manuscripts, many years before the fire, notably by a man called Elphinstone, and it was he who had copied a certain Cottonian manuscript — a single sheet of vellum known as Cotton Augustus Extra B vii — which perished in the fire. Written in Latin, it was a letter from the Abbot of Ealing, dated 1511, hinting at the existence of a Mithraeum in the vicinity of the Church of St Catherine in Clerkenwell.

'Now, I had heard rumours years ago of the existence of this copy by Elphinstone, and I used various agents to track it down. It was found in the library of an obscure country gentleman, who, when he heard of its importance, promptly insisted on sending it to Sotheby's for auction. To cut a long story short, I went to that auction, and outbid everybody else. It was the hints given in that transcript of the old abbot's letter that sent me back to Clerkenwell, spade in hand!'

Once again, the hall erupted into laughter. Ainsworth held up a restraining hand.

'And now for the final irony of this tale,' he said. 'Last October, a small fire broke out in the library of my house in Epsom. It was soon extinguished by my own staff, but a whole shelf of books and papers had been destroyed. The cause of the fire was never ascertained. Yes, friends, as I'm sure you've already guessed, Elphinstone's precious transcript perished in that fire — a curious irony indeed! How fortunate it was that I, too, had made a pen-and-ink transcript of the transcript! And now, are there any more questions? We have about ten minutes left.'

A number of hands were raised, Box's among them. He had recalled Sergeant Kenwright's impressive drawing, and that recollection determined him to ask a question. After responding to a few requests for archaeological facts, the professor pointed to Box in the gallery.

'Sir,' said Box, 'I believe that the reredos in Clerkenwell depicting Mithras has been reassembled from a number of pieces. Was it in pieces when you discovered it?'

'I wonder where you acquired that piece of information, my friend?' asked the professor, smiling. 'When I discovered the reredos, it was standing complete, just as you've seen it tonight in the lantern-slide. But it had certainly been damaged — and badly damaged — in antiquity. It may be that an earthquake had occurred, or a subterranean landslip, either of which could have shattered the monument. Or perhaps it was deliberately smashed by zealots of another faith. Certainly, the Christians of those early centuries of our era were no friends to Mithraism. Whatever the truth of the matter, the reredos had been fully restored to use in antiquity.'

Some minutes later the proceedings came to a close. There was another tremendous round of clapping, and the audience dispersed. Box and Knollys came down from the gallery, and approached the lecture bench, where Professor Ainsworth was busy packing his notes away into a briefcase.

'Ah! It's my perceptive friend from upstairs!' cried Ainsworth. 'I hope you enjoyed the lecture? It makes such a difference to have an intelligent audience, like the one we had tonight.'

'Sir,' said Box, 'I am Detective Inspector Box of Scotland Yard, the officer who is investigating the murder in the Clerkenwell Mithraeum, and a similar murder in Carshalton. I hoped that I could have a few quiet words with you — '

'Box! Of course! I thought I recognized you, Inspector. Your picture is often in the public prints. Yes, I'm more than willing to speak to you. I've been in Scotland, you know, and I had this lecture to deliver as soon as I returned to London. I've felt a bit guilty about that — about not contacting the police, I mean. Do you want me to visit you at Scotland Yard?'

'Well, sir — '

'No, better still: why don't you come down to visit me at Ardleigh Manor, my home in Epsom? You could come out for a morning, or a whole day, if you like, and we can discuss whatever topics you like at our leisure. You're very welcome to stay to luncheon. I'm sure you'd prefer that, Inspector, to interviewing me in your office. Is that your sergeant with you? Bring him too. Wait a bit, though — I know you, don't I, Sergeant? Now, where have I seen you before? Why, yes! You're Jack Knollys, who played wing three-quarter for the Croydon Ephesians against Oxford at Blackheath last year.'

'Why, sir, fancy you remembering that!'

'I'm not likely to forget that match, Sergeant. I've never seen such a versatile dropper and punter as you on any field in London. I was a useful Rugby player myself in my youth, you know. Come down, both of you, on Wednesday. Any time will do. Can you manage that? Good. Then I shall look forward to seeing you then. I'm sure there's a lot that we can tell each other.'

A few minutes later, Box and Knollys had emerged with the crowd from Exeter Hall, and were walking back along the Strand. It was dark, but the great thoroughfare was brilliantly lit by two rows of flaring gas-lamps.

'What did you think of Professor Roderick Ainsworth, Sergeant?' asked Box.

'He's rather overwhelming, sir,' said Knollys, 'and he knows how to flatter his audience — including me. I'd say he was a genuine and generous man. I'd rather not think of him as a brutal murderer.'

'Neither would I,' Box replied. 'He was quite different from what I'd expected. He's a learned man, right enough, but he wears his learning lightly. And yet . . . '

'And yet, sir,' said Knollys, 'he could have been the man in the seaman's jacket, the burly stranger who was seen by decent, reliable witnesses in Carshalton and Croydon, and apparently in Catherine Lane, Clerkenwell. Remember that railway line, sir — Epson, Carshalton, Croydon. Perhaps we should check up on the train times to Edinburgh on the day of the murder.'

'We'll certainly do that, Jack,' said Box.

'Meanwhile, we'd better suspend judgement until we've visited Ainsworth at Epsom. It's always a danger to jump to premature conclusions. Perhaps we'll have a more rounded picture of the good professor after we've spent a few hours with him at Ardleigh Manor on Wednesday.'

9

Guests at Ardleigh Manor

When Box and Knollys stepped down from the train at Epsom Station they found a coachman waiting for them on the platform. An elegant brougham stood in the station forecourt, a smart grey mare between the shafts.

They drove for nearly half a mile through the pleasant streets of the little town, eventually turning into a country lane in sight of the green expanse of Epsom Common. Soon, they passed through a pair of open gates, flanked by brick pillars, and entered a curving drive, bordered by banks of wild roses.

'There it is, Sergeant,' said Box. 'Ardleigh Manor. What a splendid place!'

He had seen a rambling sandstone mansion, cloaked by tall beeches, but with an uninterrupted view of the common. It was a Gothic fantasy of a house, evidently not more than fifty years old, but it had been so contrived to look as though it had been there, on the skirts of Epsom, since time immemorial.

The carriage turned into a formal path, with wide grass verges on either side. Box glimpsed a number of rustic brick cottages behind tall yew hedges, and the exposed rafters of a new house that was being built in the grounds of the manor. The white timbers reminded him of a freshly disinterred skeleton that he had once seen lying on a make-shift stretcher at the scene of the Hoxton murders in '86.

They came into a semi-circular court in front of the house, and a groom ran out to take the horse's head. At the same time, a sober-suited butler walked down the steps of the house to greet them. Before either man could get his bearings, the coachman delivered them to the butler, and the butler conducted them into the house.

They had scarcely set foot in the hall when Professor Roderick Ainsworth erupted like a whirlwind from a passage on the left. He seized both men by the hand, and seemed to be welcoming them as though they were long-lost relatives. The butler was given no chance to announce them, and neither man was able to utter as much as a 'good morning'.

'Ah! Mr Box! And you, Mr Knollys! Welcome to Ardleigh Manor. Take their hats and coats, will you, Mason? Put them on the

— Put them over there, on that Spanish oak chest. Did you have a good journey? They're quite good trains on this line, I find. Isn't this a splendid entrance hall? All this panelling was brought from Claygate House after the fire they had there in '58. I see you're admiring that great carved stone face of Bacchus. It startles people when they see it there, facing the front door! I found that under an old house in Bow Lane in '81. The Metropolitan Board of Works let me keep it. It's very fine of its type. What do you think, Mason?'

'It's very nice, sir,' said the butler, permitting himself a little smile. He was a man of sixty or so, with a good-humoured face and well-tended side-whiskers. 'Will these gentlemen be staying to luncheon?'

'It's very — '

'Of course they'll be staying, Mason,' said Ainsworth, cutting Box short. 'It can be served to the three of us in the conservatory, thus avoiding the absurdities of social protocol — servants' entrance, that kind of thing. Now, what was I saying?'

Professor Ainsworth was wearing a well-cut suit of green serge, which he evidently thought more fitting for the country than his usually sober attire. He was as impressive and overwhelming as he had been on Monday

164

night, when he had lectured to an enthralled audience at Exeter Hall. His eyes, dark and intelligent, seemed animated by genuine pleasure at seeing them.

The professor darted away into the passage to the left of the hall, and they followed him through a glazed door into a cavernous glass conservatory, which housed a collection of exotic plants and ferns. Between the vegetation Box could glimpse intriguing islands of furniture constituting miniature drawing-rooms and bijou libraries. The whole vast glass-roofed creation held a mystery and fascination that was all its own.

'Come and sit down here, gentlemen, where we can talk together in peace.' Ainsworth threaded his way through a bank of ferns, and they emerged into a pleasant enclave of comfort, where two upholstered settees had been placed on either side of a long glass table.

'Are you settled comfortably? Excellent. Now, what have you got to tell me? And what do you want to know? Epsom is a splendid place to live, though a base in London would be an additional convenience. This place used to be famous for its mineral spring — it's where the original Epsom salts came from. But I suppose it's the racecourse that attracts people here today — the Derby and the Oaks, you know. I must confess to a mild flutter myself on those occasions! But to business. What have you to tell me about these appalling murders, and how can I help you?'

For answer, Arnold Box removed from his pocket the glasses case that had been found on the dead body of Gregory Walsh, and handed it to Professor Ainsworth, who opened it. For the first time since they had entered Ardleigh Manor, a deathly silence reigned, and they could hear the quiet splashing of a fountain situated somewhere amidst the riot of ferns.

'Where did you find these?' asked the professor at last. 'I've missed them for over a week.'

Professor Ainsworth held the open glasses case in his right hand, looking at it with what Box thought of as an expression of concentrated bewilderment. For a moment the great extrovert was subdued and in some way nonplussed.

'We found them, sir,' Box replied, 'in the left-hand jacket pocket of the late unfortunate Mr Gregory Walsh, when my colleagues and I examined his body in the Clerkenwell Mithraeum. Sergeant Knollys traced them to you through the optician's records.'

'How strange . . . I never knew this poor young man, Inspector. How could he have acquired my glasses? They're for reading, you know, and I was very vexed when they went missing.'

'Well, sir,' said Box, 'I can only assume that you must have dropped them in some dark corner of the Mithraeum, and that Gregory Walsh found them. He put them in his pocket, meaning, I suppose, to hand them to one or other of the workmen in those huts on the site. It doesn't necessarily follow that he knew they were *your* glasses.'

Professor Ainsworth relaxed visibly. He put the spectacle case down on the glass table, and smiled. Box and Knollys could sense his usual ebullience reasserting itself.

'How simple you make it sound, Inspector! Well, I'm glad to have them back. We'll celebrate the fact with a pre-prandial drink in a minute — something cool and refreshing. But you haven't answered my question, Inspector. What's on your mind?'

'Those spectacles, sir,' said Box. 'I notice that they were supplied by an optician called Reuben Greensands, who died a few months ago. He had premises in Catherine Lane, just behind the Mithraeum. Did you always obtain your glasses from him?'

'No, no, Inspector. I go to a very good man in Bond Street. But one day last year I was working on the Clerkenwell site, and I found that I'd left my reading glasses here at home. Well, I tried to manage for an hour or so, but it was really quite impossible. Thompson, the site foreman at Clerkenwell, told me about this Greensands, round the corner in Catherine Lane. I called at his shop, and found that he had some very good ready-made reading glasses. I don't remember him very well. I thought he was a rather insipid, insignificant kind of man.'

Professor Ainsworth leaned forward, and rang a little brass bell on the table. Presently a footman appeared through the ferns, wheeling a trolley upon which stood a large silver bowl full of melting ice and a number of bottles of Bass's pale ale, which the footman served to them in tall lager glasses.

Box drank some of his beer, and then dabbed his moustache delicately with his handkerchief.

'I wonder what Gregory Walsh was doing in the Mithraeum that morning, sir?' he asked. 'He was an analytical chemist, and we found traces of pigment on his hands and clothing. Do you think he was exercising one of the mysteries of his trade?'

Professor Ainsworth laughed, and shook his head.

'I can't think what he'd find to do there, Inspector! I certainly never hired him to take samples, or scrapings, or whatever it is that analytical chemists do. I understood from the papers that he'd been a member of some kind of esoteric cult, and that he'd been offered as a sacrifice by one or other of its devotees. Do you think that's possible? Or is it just another fabrication of the Press?'

'Well, as to that, sir,' said Box, 'I was talking yesterday to a lady called Miss Westerham, and she told me all the curious details of the rituals connected with the worship of Mithras — '

'You saw Mary Westerham?' exclaimed the professor, his eyes shining. 'How clever of you to seek her out. She's very good on the history of Mithraism and similar cults, though by profession she's actually an epigraphist. What did you think of her?'

'I thought she was very clever, sir, and she didn't deny the possibility that some kind of secret cult existed. If that's the case, sir, then its murderous activities must be curtailed. Miss Westerham certainly regarded both Mr Walsh of Clerkenwell and Mr Barnes of Carshalton as men engaged in sinister rituals culminating in voluntary sacrifice. Did you know either of those men, sir?'

Professor Ainsworth had drunk his beer, and had sunk into a reverie.

'I preferred not to believe it, you know,' he

169

said, leaving Box's question unanswered. 'About the sacrifices to Mithras, I mean. It seems to negate the validity of the work I do. I want to expose the remains of past civilizations to the scrutiny of modern man: it seems perverse to me that intelligent people should profess belief in the long-buried rituals of discredited faiths. But I've spoken to Miss Westerham on a number of occasions, and she's a woman whose judgement I respect.'

As Ainsworth was speaking, Box saw the figure of a man walking hurriedly along what was evidently a path bordering the glazed wall of the conservatory in front of which the professor's couch had been placed. Ainsworth followed Box's glance, and half turned round.

'Ah!' he cried, springing up from his seat. 'Here's Mr Crale, my academic secretary! I expect he's bringing something for me to sign. I poached him, you know: spirited him away from under the nose of my dreaded rival, Sir Charles Wayneflete. As well as being a bit of an amateur, Wayneflete's also a skinflint. Mr Crale's worth far more than he was paying him.'

Box and Knollys heard a door banging somewhere beyond the conservatory, and in a few moments a tall, thin man entered the secluded island of couches. He was, Box judged, about fifty, with a balding head of brown hair, and thin, prim lips. He was dressed very elegantly in a well-cut suit of sober grey. He was holding a letter. He glanced briefly at the visitors, and then gave his whole attention to his employer.

'Sir,' he said in quiet, deferential tones, 'I am sorry to bother you, but we have received this letter from Mr Trevor, asking whether you will agree to give your talk to his boys on the twenty-first of August instead of the twentieth. In other words, the Tuesday rather than the Monday. I think it would be as well to reply at once, either way.'

Professor Ainsworth looked at the rather unprepossessing man with what seemed to be unconditional admiration.

'What do you think of him, Mr Box?' he asked. 'Isn't he a treasure? I'm having a house built for him, aren't I, Crale? A man like him shouldn't be cooped up somewhere in an attic. What do you think I should do about Trevor?'

'I would be inclined to accede to his request, sir. As well as being Headmaster of Bishop Wilson's School, he's also a man of some influence with Mr Asquith. It's always valuable to have one's name whispered into the ear of the Home Secretary.'

Mr Crale permitted himself a thin little

smile. Professor Ainsworth threw back his head and laughed.

'Didn't I tell you he was a treasure? Write the letter, will you, Crale? I'll sign it after luncheon.'

The secretary bowed, and disappeared among the foliage. Box thought: I don't much like the look of you, my lad. You're one of those sneaks who can be either a toady or a bully, as circumstances demand. Professor Ainsworth's welcome to you.

'Come along, gentlemen,' said Ainsworth, 'it's time you met my wife. She'll be thrilled to see you here at the manor. Zena!'

Ainsworth disappeared among the foliage, with the two policemen close at his heels. They emerged into a much larger island, hidden by the tall ferns and exotics artfully arranged in their brass tubs. There were more settees, arranged this time around a carved oak table, and a section of brick wall dividing two transepts of the enormous conservatory. On this wall were fixed two great oars, and above them a shield, bearing the arms of Henley Rowing Club. A pair of crossed swords complemented the oars, and hanging beneath them was a pair of boxing gloves. A small wooden shelf held a number of well-polished silver trophies. It was clear to both guests that Ainsworth had been no mean sportsman in his younger days.

'Zena!' cried Professor Ainsworth, flinging himself into one of the chairs at the table. In response to the professor's lusty call a door banged somewhere to their right, and in a few moments a lady appeared before them. She was a powerful-looking woman with frizzy red hair, and a determined countenance. She was wearing a long canvas smock, and her hands were caked with clay.

'Zena, come and meet Inspector Box of Scotland Yard, and Sergeant Knollys. Gentlemen, this is Mrs Ainsworth, a lady known more widely by her professional name of Zena Copley. She's the rising sculptress of the moment, you know — they're saying she's a second Rodin.'

'How do you do, Inspector?' Zena Copley's voice was as powerful and resonating as that of her husband. 'I don't suppose you're interested in sculpture? Or you, Sergeant Knollys — I say, aren't you the Rugby-playing Knollys? Thought you were. I suppose you're here about that young man who was killed in my husband's temple? Anyway, welcome to Ardleigh Manor.'

She turned to Professor Ainsworth, who was sitting back in his chair, openly admiring her.

'By the way, Ainsworth,' she said, 'I'm

going down to Leatherhead to see Imogene tomorrow. I'll be leaving early, so I thought I'd tell you, in case you wondered what had happened to me later in the day. I don't know when I'll be back. Did Margery tell you she's met a young man? Well, she will, I expect. She met him last week at Brighton.'

'Brighton? So that's where she went. When did she come back?'

'Don't know. She was here at breakfast this morning. That's when she told me about this young man. I must get back to my work. I'm doing a massive clay figure called 'The Sleeper'. I think it's going to be a success.'

Before anyone could reply, Mrs Ainsworth had disappeared among the ferns.

'A wonderful woman!' Ainsworth exclaimed. 'She does these massive sculptures in clay, and when they're finished, they're cast in bronze. Marvellous work! Sit down, gentlemen. Don't hover! It makes me uncomfortable.'

'Sir,' said Box, 'about the two men who were killed — I asked you whether you knew either of them, but you had no opportunity to reply — '

'I knew neither of them, Inspector. The younger man, Walsh — I'd never heard of him until I read an account of the discovery of his body in *The Scotsman*. I was in Edinburgh by then. Barnes I knew by reputation: he's a very prominent business-man in this part of the world. I saw him a number of times at public functions, but I never knew him personally.'

Box thought to himself: Shall I tell him about the mysterious samples of mortar that I found in Abraham Barnes's desk? No. Keep that to yourself, for the moment.

From somewhere in the house the noise of a piano being played very lustily came to their ears. Ainsworth woke out of a reverie, and sat up in his chair.

'That's my daughter, Margery,' he cried. 'She's just got back from Brighton, apparently. Just listen to her! That's Chopin she's playing. Very difficult, I'm told. Ties your fingers in knots. I think we'll see Margery on the concert platform one of these days. I've not much ear for music, unfortunately, but my wife tells me Margery's a second Clara Schumann.'

I hope this Clara Schumann has a lighter touch than Margery, thought Box. She'll break something if she goes on like that.

★   ★   ★

At one o'clock the footman reappeared, accompanied by a housemaid. They laid a snow-white cloth on the table, and the

175

footman deftly set it out with silver and glass. Between them they served a meal of clear soup, followed by chicken salad. The footman had brought in a silver wine bucket containing a bottle of chilled hock, which Ainsworth poured out for himself and his guests.

All the time that they were eating, Professor Ainsworth talked about archaeology. He proved to be as fascinating at the table as he had been in the lecture hall. He told Box and Knollys at length about his celebrated discovery of the Clerkenwell Treasure, and about his unearthing of many important Roman sites in London and beyond, culminating in his excavation of the Temple of Mithras.

'That, gentlemen,' he said, waving his fork at them, 'was the crowning point of my active career. Of course, I've been Professor of Antiquities at London for nearly ten years, but that post involves a great deal of theoretical work, and not a little tedious administration. But uncovering the Mithraeum — well, it's detective work in the true meaning of that word, and it was filled with an excitement that is necessarily lacking in the lecture hall.'

'I think you enjoy lecturing, though, don't you, sir?' asked Box. 'That was very evident to both of us when we listened to you at Exeter Hall the other night.'

'Lecturing? Yes, I'll confess to you, gentlemen, that I'm a showman at heart. That's why I'm prepared to travel all over the country to give those lantern lectures of mine. That's what I was doing when that poor young man met his death in the Mithraeum. In fact, I left for Scotland that very morning — Tuesday, the fourteenth, it was. I caught the nine-five from Euston. The station was very crowded, and I was relieved to find that there were only three of us in my compartment. It's a long haul to Scotland — five hours, if you're lucky. We got there some time after two. This hock's just right. Pour yourselves some more, won't you?'

When they had finished the main course, the footman reappeared, bringing them portions of summer pudding. The housemaid soon followed with coffee. It had been a perfect meal for a hot August day.

'I travelled up that day with Canon Arthur Venables of St Paul's, who was one of the scholars concerned with the Revised Version of the Bible in '85. Do you know him? Well, he's a very erudite man, and a bit of a dandy. He dresses very smartly, although, as he remarked to me rather ruefully, there wasn't much you can do to ring the changes on clerical dress.'

Ainsworth laughed. 'I was decked out in all my finery for that journey, and he admired my morning coat, and the pearl-grey stock that I was wearing. It was all I could do to take the good man's mind off tailoring and on to Biblical criticism! He got off at Carlisle, and I dropped off to sleep. I was more or less comatose until we arrived at Waverley Station in Edinburgh.'

Box thought: This whole business of Professor Ainsworth is a mare's nest. There are many other things I could be doing than enjoying this gentleman's open-handed hospitality. In a moment I'll give Jack the wink, and we'll make our excuses.

As though on cue, Jack Knollys suddenly asked a question. It was the first time that he had spoken since they had started their meal.

'You mentioned a 'dreaded rival' earlier, sir,' said Knollys. 'Sir Charles Wayneflete, I think you said his name was. Would you care to tell us something about him?'

Professor Ainsworth scowled, and threw his napkin down on the table.

'Wayneflete? Yes, I'll tell you about him, but not in here. It's getting very hot under all this glass. Come into my study and smoke a cigar. We'll talk about Wayneflete there.'

Ainsworth sprang up from his chair and strode through the ferns. The two detectives followed him out of the vast conservatory, along a carpeted corridor, and into a spacious, book-lined study, where they settled themselves in enormous leather chairs.

The professor stood by the fireplace, and pointed to a large oil painting that hung above the mantelpiece. It showed part of a busy shipyard, with the iron hull of a warship under construction. Tall steam-cranes stood at the dockside, which seemed to be alive with hundreds of shipwrights.

'Do you see that picture?' said Ainsworth. 'It shows part of the great yards of Ainsworth & Company at Newcastle. It's from that yard, and that great town, that my wealth is derived. That's where my family came from, the area known as Tyneside. Others manage that shipyard now, supervising the building of naval frigates, in which we excel. With the wealth of the yard behind me, I have been able to devote my whole professional life to archaeology.'

Professor Ainsworth sat down in his vast leather armchair. He drew on his cigar, frowning the while. Then he suddenly laughed.

'My 'dreaded rival', Sir Charles Wayneflete, is a baronet. He bears an inherited title, but the land and estates that once went with it have long vanished, and he scrapes a living from writing in the popular art magazines, supplementing that income with the proceeds of a modest annuity. In his earlier years he amassed quite a creditable collection of bits and pieces which he displays in that gloomy house of his in Lowndes Square — a house that is mortgaged to the hilt. I could buy the man up, lock, stock and barrel, with my small change, and he knows it.'

'In what way is he your rival, sir?' asked Knollys.

'Well, I call him that, but of course it's not true. Wayneflete is a dabbler, a kind of jack of all trades, with no professional training of any kind. He hates me because of my success, and because I can combine the active and passive approaches to revealing the past that get results — I can pursue a line of academic research, and then pick up a spade to prove its validity.'

'And Sir Charles Wayneflete — '

'Sir Charles Wayneflete sits in that house of his, weaving plots, and thinking up ways of undermining my reputation. His whole life centres around jealousy of others. Have you seen him? He's a thin, attenuated man with little beady eyes and a twisted, discontented mouth. He used poor Crale as little more than a slave, paying him less than I pay one of my servants. He's mean in mind, and mean in spirit.'

Professor Ainsworth suddenly blushed.

'There,' he said, 'I've perhaps said more than I should about Wayneflete. Not very charitable, and rather petty, I suppose. But you see, he has the entrée to all echelons of society, because his is an ancient family, and while he moves in those exalted circles, cadging a dinner here and a luncheon there, he creates his subtle slanders and metaphorically drops them where people who matter can find them. What was it that Pope said of Joseph Addison?

Damn with faint praise, assent with civil leer,
And, without sneering, teach the rest to sneer.

That's what Wayneflete's like.

'But, gentlemen, let me tell you something that at the moment is a close secret. Her Majesty the Queen, on the advice of Mr Gladstone, has graciously agreed to bestow upon me the dignity of a knighthood, some time in the coming autumn. As though to supplement this honour, I heard only this morning that I am to be elected a Fellow of the Society of Antiquaries. That's been in the wind for some time, but today's letter confirmed it. Wayneflete can boast of his inherited title, but mine will be bestowed upon me by our beloved Queen Victoria, in recognition of my many achievements, of which the discovery of the Mithraeum in Clerkenwell was the crowning triumph. Let Charles Wayneflete equal *that*!'

'My congratulations, sir,' said Box. 'Sir Charles Wayneflete's jealousy will know no bounds once those two honours are made public. Do you think, sir, that Wayneflete would ever contemplate doing you an injury? I don't mean assaulting you, of course — '

'I don't want to say too much about that, Mr Box, because I'm obviously prejudiced against the man. But yes, I could imagine him plotting to damage or destroy my work, if only out of spite. I've no proof, of course, but I know from Crale that he hated my discovery of the Mithraeum, and said once, in Crale's presence, that he wished the whole place would collapse and be buried for good. Jealousy, you see. I think he sensed Crale's disapproval, and dismissed him on some trumped-up excuse or other. I can tell you, I snapped the man up at once.'

Box glanced at Knollys, and the two men stood up.

'Professor,' said Box, 'I'd like to thank you for your exceptional hospitality to Sergeant Knollys and me. Really, you have treated us like honoured guests in your home. It's time for us to get back to London. Would you like me to keep you informed of any further developments in our investigation of these curious murders?'

'I would, Inspector Box. How very kind of you. If ever you want to escape from London, in order to do a bit of quiet thinking, come down here to Epsom again, and make yourselves free of the house.'

When Box and Knollys had gone, Professor Ainsworth wandered back into the conservatory. At the far end of the great glazed area there was a washroom, containing watering cans, vases, and other items connected with the maintenance of the many plants and ferns. It was a cool place, with a floor of brown and blue encaustic tiles.

Ainsworth walked over to a row of sinks fixed to the far wall beneath a long mirror. Selecting one of the sinks, he carefully balanced his still glowing cigar on the edge of a long wooden shelf running just under the mirror, and turned on the taps. With the aid of a block of fragrant lavender soap, he washed his hands in order to remove from them the lingering smells of chicken and mayonnaise. He must curb his inclination to eat chicken legs with his hands!

While he dried his hands on a rough towel, he regarded his reflection in the mirror. He still had his abundant curly hair, which was only now showing incipient hints of grey. His eyes were as bright and alert as they had ever been. He smiled, and his image in the glass smiled back at him. Whatever reasons Wayneflete had for hating him, he, Roderick Ainsworth, had reached the peak of his career. A knighthood beckoned — an honour infinitely more worthwhile than a beggar's inherited title.

Suddenly, unbidden and unwelcome memories flooded his consciousness, recollections of things too frightful to bear, and when he next glanced in the mirror, he saw looking back at him the face of a man who was racked with a spasm of bleak anguish and despair.

10

Wet Night for a Murder

Arnold Box stood on the cramped foredeck of the police launch and blinked the rain out of his eyes. There was an awning above his head, but it was no protection against the seemingly endless downpour. It had been close and humid all day, and minutes after he had received a summons by telegraph at the Rents, just before nine o'clock, the summer tempest had begun.

> *Box, King James's Rents*, the telegraph message had read. *Come at once to Gas Street, Rotherhithe. Man murdered, with honey, etc., present. Street disturbance followed, but contained. Murder suspect killed by crowd. T. Lambton, Sergeant.*

What a night to be out in a flimsy launch on the busy Thames! He would have used the train, but, as fate would have it, one of the locomotives out of Liverpool Street had broken down in the Thames Tunnel. Some yards off their port side the penny steam ferry

185

from Wapping to Rotherhithe was toiling through the mist. Should he have swallowed his pride and travelled on that? No. The police launch would take him direct to Beaver's Dock Ladders, where this Sergeant Lambton would be waiting for him.

Was it only yesterday that he and Jack Knollys had been guests in a country house? That had been a curious day, a day in some ways detached from the everyday realities of police work, but it had determined him to start looking elsewhere for the Mithras murderer. Roderick Ainsworth was not the stuff of which vicious killers were made.

He'd known earlier in the evening that the Wapping Tunnel was blocked, and had telegraphed back to tell this Sergeant Lambton that he would arrive by way of Beaver's Dock Ladders. Perhaps this new ritual killing would give him a fresh lead.

Despite the driving rain and mist, the river was alive with vessels, lamps glinting high on their masts. As they came nearer to the vast expanse of the Surrey Commercial Docks they found themselves weaving their way through a score of trading vessels lying at anchor.

Presently, Box discerned the high and intimidating river wall at Beaver's Dock rising above the churning waters of the Thames.

There were figures standing on the dock wall, and he could see the fitful glow of a rain-battered gas standard, which had defied the wrath of the summer storm, and remained alight.

The launch shut off steam, and the pilot manoeuvred it alongside the massive slime-covered stone wall, where it bobbed up and down uneasily on the choppy waters. Box looked up through the rain at the four iron ladders rising vertically above him to the men waiting on the quay above. Standing on the gunwale, he stretched gingerly from the launch, secured his footing on the iron rungs of one of the ladders, and began to climb. Don't look down, people said; but it was impossible to look upwards in this blinding rain. Clinging grimly to the cold iron rails, he made his way slowly up the twenty feet to the rim of the quay.

Within a foot of the ladder's top he ventured to squint up through the rain, and saw a bearded face half-hidden by an oilskin hood looking down at him. A pair of stout arms reached down to haul him up on to the flags of Beaver's Wharf.

'I thought you'd better come straight away, Inspector,' said the man with the beard, 'seeing as how you're the expert in these heathen murders. I'm Sergeant Lambton, of

'P' Division, sir, out of Peckham High Street. I'll take you to Gas Street straight away, if that's in order.' As he spoke, other policemen, clad in dripping cloaks, appeared out of the rain, and moved into the circle of light cast by the single valiant gas standard.

Sergeant Lambton set his face away from the river, and Box followed him, clutching his rain-sodden overcoat around him. What a night! What a benighted place! The eight to eight night shift at the Rents was usually a quiet affair, with plenty of time to catch up with paperwork. Evidently, this particular Thursday night shift was to be an exception.

Gas Street lay among a huddle of crowded lanes and alleys in one of the most neglected and desperate areas of Rotherhithe. Thick, acrid smoke rolled down from hundreds of chimneys to lie as choking mist in the streets. What street lights there were had long ago been smashed, and Gas Street was lit that night by portable gas flares, brought in by the police to illuminate the scene of a minor riot that had culminated in murder.

The carriageway was strewn with broken bricks and uprooted cobbles, and a crowd of women, moaning, and clutching thin shawls to their bodies, stood on the pavements, seemingly impervious to the rain. Halfway along one side of the road a house stood burning, the flames from its rafters so fierce as to set the relentless rain at defiance. A fire engine stood in the middle of the street and, as they looked, men in brass helmets emerged from an alley, carrying an inert form on a stretcher.

The women in shawls began screaming, holding their arms up to the heavens. Sergeant Lambton looked at them without emotion.

'So there's the physical proof that poor Tommy Bassano is dead,' he muttered, 'and they know that one or other of their brutes of husbands will hang for it, unless I'm very much mistaken. This is the aftermath of the disturbance I told you about in my message, Inspector. 'Riot' would be too strong a word to describe it, but it was bad enough to lead to a second murder here tonight — for murder it is, in my book. I'll tell you all about that later, Inspector, if I may. That's just *our* murder, as you might say; *your* murder took place further down the street.'

They moved away from the burning house and the keening women, and came to a mean little pawn-shop on the corner of the street. The inscription JOHN CORNISH, PLEDGES, was painted on a board above the single shuttered window. Sergeant Lambton hammered on the door, which was immediately opened by a thin, frantic man with wide haunted eyes staring from a narrow, unshaven face. The man seized Lambton by the sleeve.

'He's not dead, too, is he? Poor Tommy Bassano? He isn't — he didn't — '

'Get back into the kitchen, will you,' said Sergeant Lambton roughly, 'and sit there quietly with PC Glover until I'm ready to talk to you again. As for Tommy, he's dead right enough. But that wasn't your fault, so stop that caterwauling and do as I tell you.'

They had entered a dim, cluttered shop, lit by a couple of candles standing in the necks of beer bottles and placed on the counter. The walls were shelved from floor to ceiling, and the shelves were crammed with ticketed pledges waiting to be redeemed. Piles of garments, labelled and done up into bundles, were heaped up on the floor. A few sets of fire-irons and a couple of steel fenders were propped up against the wall behind the door.

The frantic man retreated through a door at the far end of the room, shading his face with a hand as he passed the inert figure of an elderly man lying half hidden behind the counter. Box could detect the sickening smell of the abattoir, and saw that the dead man was lying in a pool of his own congealing blood.

'He was killed no later than eight o'clock,

Inspector,' said Lambton. 'That's what the local doctor said. He's been and gone this half-hour. This is the body of John Cornish, licensed pawn-broker, aged seventy. He's run this shop for nigh on twenty years. That frantic scarecrow of a man that you've just seen was his assistant. Victor Freestone, his name is, and it was he who found him dead, and ran down to us at the police station. When I saw the honey around Cornish's mouth, and the little piece of slate with a raven scratched on it, I thought I'd better send for you.'

'You don't much care for the people round here, do you, Sergeant?' asked Box.

The burly, bearded police officer looked at him with something like reproach.

'It's no bed of roses working round here, Mr Box,' he said, 'and a man can get cynical in his way of speaking about folks. We've got a lot of mindless brutes and merciless thugs on our patch, sir, but there are many very good, decent people living here as well. They're the ones that don't cause trouble.'

Arnold Box nodded his understanding, and then knelt down beside the dead man. A sudden wave of nausea made him shudder. How long were these foul murders going to continue? Was there a plan to immolate all the members of this unknown coven? Who

191

were they? Who was their leader? Could this aged man, with the stubble beard and a disfiguring growth on his right cheek, be a devotee of Mithras? It sounded too silly for words, but murder wasn't silly at all.

He raised the dead man's head from the pool of congealing blood, and examined the site of a fatal blow which had caved in the right side of his skull. Whatever had been used to inflict the wound, it had not been an adze. The indentation was too wide, and too shallow to have been caused by a sharpened blade. Something heavy and round had made that fatal, crushing wound.

Yes, there it was: the pool of honey beside the dead man's head, formed there as it had oozed out of his mouth. Box smeared some of it on his finger, and tasted it. He recalled the sticky patch of honey, no bigger than a penny, which he had found beside the body of Gregory Walsh in the Mithraeum. Here, beside the corpse of the pawnbroker, the honey formed a little pool. It was as though —

He was suddenly alert to the danger of drawing facile conclusions from the physical traces of a crime. The case of John Cornish, pawnbroker, had unique qualities of its own. He sat back on his heels, and looked at the sergeant, who was standing quite still near the counter, watching him.

'Have you got the little piece of slate with the raven carved on it, Sergeant?' he asked. 'I'd like to see it, now, if I may.'

The sergeant unbuttoned one of his jacket pockets and produced a piece of slate, no more than an inch square. Its edges had been smoothed with a file, and on one side of it had been scratched the figure of a bird, with the word 'corax' written beneath it. Box's mind reverted to the scenes of the two previous ritual murders. On those two occasions costly lapis lazuli had been used to fashion the tokens, and he had assumed, probably rightly, that they had been antique. The images, too, the lion and the raven, had been artistically depicted, with the care that one would expect where some kind of devotion, however misplaced, had guided the hand of the devotee.

But this, he could see, was part of an ordinary roofing slate, bought for sixpence a dozen at any builder's merchants. The drawing was little more than crude scratching. An idea began to form in his mind.

'Did you check the till, Sergeant?' he asked. 'Just for form's sake, I mean?'

'The till, sir? Why, no, I — '

'Do it now, will you?'

Sergeant Lambton pulled upon the drawer

in the desk which served as a till.

'Empty, sir! There's nothing in it but three halfpennies. So it was murder in the pursuit of theft . . . Or maybe poor Cornish emptied it himself, sir, and put the takings away for the night in his strong-box — '

'His strong-box? Do you know for certain that he had one?'

'He showed it to me once, sir, after we'd had a spate of burglaries round here. Poor old chap, he wasn't exactly rich, but I do remember a roll of sovereigns wrapped in greaseproof paper. I told him to bank it, but, of course, people like him don't trust banks.'

'And where is this strong-box?'

Sergeant Lambton lowered his voice, and glanced at the closed door of the back room, where the wretched assistant Victor Freestone could be heard lamenting the death of his master.

'It's under this loose board in the corner, sir. You see, it just lifts out, like so — and here's the box. Hello! The lock's been forced — it's empty!'

'Yes, it's empty, Sergeant,' said Box, sitting down on one of two rickety chairs that stood in the room. Lambton watched him slip the piece of slate into one of the pockets of his overcoat. 'It's empty, as I thought it would be, and in a minute I'll explain to you what that means, and what you and I will do. But first, you'd better tell me about this disturbance in the street earlier tonight.'

'Well, sir, Victor Freestone — him that's moaning and snuffling in the back room there — came into the police station at a quarter to nine, as I told you. He'd found poor Cornish dead, and had noticed the pool of honey near his mouth. Everybody knows what that signifies now, sir. The papers have been full of these Mithras murders for the last ten days.'

'I know, Sergeant, and it's a pity, because the Press accounts are becoming more and more sensational. I'm beginning to believe them myself. So what happened next?'

'Before he came to us, sir, Freestone had run into the public bar at the Vasa Arms in Sweden Street and told his mates what had happened. They were all blind drunk by that time, and they looked to the leader of the pack to tell them what to do. Patrick Brannigan — that's the leader of the pack — told them that poor Tommy Bassano was behind it — '

'Just a moment, Sergeant, you're losing me. Who is this Tommy Bassano?'

'He was a simpleton, sir, who made a living from selling bunches of herbs and so-called cures for common ailments from door to door. The women liked him well enough, because he was quite good-looking in a pinched, half-starved kind of way, but all the men round here hated him, on account of him being simple, like, and a foreigner into the bargain. He was supposed to be some kind of an Italian.'

'And this Patrick Brannigan — '

'Brannigan declared that poor Tommy was a wizard, and that it was he who must have murdered John Cornish. There was something more to that — some grudge that Brannigan held against poor Tommy. We'll get that out of him, later.

'So Brannigan and his mates poured out of the Vasa like a swarm of hornets, and laid siege to Tommy Bassano in his lodging further up the road. To cut a long story short, Mr Box, they broke the windows with uprooted cobbles and stones, and then someone threw a lighted torch into the house. You saw the result of that yourself. The woman who rents out the rooms managed to escape through the back. It could have developed into a full-scale riot, Inspector, but we had enough police to disperse the mob. We've arrested the ringleaders, and they've been lodged in the cells at Peckham until tomorrow morning.'

'Where's your inspector, Sergeant Lambton?' he asked.

'He's gone to Peckham High Street, sir, to consult Superintendent Butt about the riot.'

Box rose from his chair, and began a swift search of the shelves. Lambton watched him as he rummaged behind the rows of pledges, and then turned his attention to the piles of baled clothing lying on the floor. What was he looking for?

Box gave a little cry of satisfaction, and motioned to the sergeant to join him in the space behind the front door. He pointed to one of the two brass fenders leaning upright against the wall.

'You see that, Sergeant?' he said. 'There's a heavy ornamental ball at one end of this fender, but the other one's been screwed off. Do you see? The thread in the socket is still clean and bright, so it hasn't been removed very long. A round, heavy brass ball — does that suggest anything to you? Bring that empty strong-box over to the table, will you — quiet, man, or they'll hear you in the back room.'

'What are you going to do, sir?' asked Sergeant Lambton. 'Why are you unscrewing the remaining ball from that fender?'

'Listen, Sergeant,' said Box in a low voice. 'There's no need for me to go into details, but I had a long talk about this old religion of Mithras with an expert on the subject, a lady called Miss Mary Westerham. She told me that spilt honey always went together with the symbol of a lion, and that the sign of a raven was associated with mercury.'

'But that's wrong, sir, because — '

'It's wrong, Sergeant, because poor Mr Cornish's killer got his facts wrong. In this case, the case of John Cornish, there's honey, all right, because it's easier to procure than mercury. I expect you'll find an opened jar of honey in the kitchen back there. But the sign's wrong — a raven instead of a lion. Whoever carved that crude little bit of slate carved the wrong image. He'd read about the murders at Clerkenwell and Carshalton in the newspapers, you see, and used what he'd read there to concoct this fake sacrifice to Mithras —

'Do I have to say any more, Sergeant? You know what we've got to do. After that, you can send a constable to fetch the van for poor Cornish's body. Come on, let's get it over and done with. When I give the nod, fling open that kitchen door.'

Box stooped down and, holding the heavy brass knob by its screw, trawled it through the pool of congealed blood. He placed it in the rifled strong-box, and signalled to the sergeant, who suddenly threw open the door to the back room. The haunted Victor

Freestone, who was sitting motionless beside a uniformed constable, looked up in terror as the inspector slammed the open strong-box down on to the table.

'What did you do with the money?' cried Box. 'Do you think you can fool a Scotland-Yarder?'

The quaking Freestone uttered a howl like that of a scalded cat, and rose from his chair. He pointed at the bloodstained brass fender-ornament.

'How did you find it?' he shrieked. 'I threw it into the storm drain across the road! No one could have found it in this rain . . . '

He began to mutter a kind of confession, mingled with an attempt at self-justification. Old Cornish had been a skinflint, an exploiter, he had cheated him out of his due share of the profits. The thin whine continued until it petered out in a strangled sob. Sergeant Lambton produced a set of handcuffs.

★　★　★

At the end of an hour's activity, the body of the murdered pawn-broker had been removed in a police hand-ambulance, and Victor Freestone had been conveyed by van to the holding cells at Putney. Sergeant

Lambton had prevailed on Box to come back for a while to the local police station in Canal Street. They were sitting together in front of a blazing fire in a cramped but cheerful office looking out on to the wet cobbles. A constable had brought them two enamel mugs of steaming coffee.

'It was obvious to me, Sergeant,' said Box, 'that John Cornish's murder had been tricked out to look like one of these Mithras slayings. The details had been culled from papers like *The Graphic*, but Freestone had got the symbols mixed. It was a crude affair, and my little ruse with the brass knob worked like a dream. And you're my witness that I never enticed him into a confession by drawing his attention to that fender-ornament. It wasn't a case of entrapment.'

'It was very clever of you, sir, if you don't mind me saying so,' said Lambton. 'Very clever. Don't you think so, Father Brooks?'

Box had noticed a stout, elderly clergyman enveloped in a serge cloak, who was sitting at a desk in the corner of the office, and had wondered who he was. He had been reading an evening newspaper with the aid of a pair of steel spectacles, which he used folded, rather like a magnifying glass. He had looked up when the two police officers had entered from the street, and had then turned to his newspaper once again. A broad-brimmed hat reposing on the desk in front of him suggested to Box that he was a Roman Catholic priest.

'Very clever, Tim,' said Father Brooks, treating Box to an elfish smile. 'But then, Inspector Box is a very clever man.'

Sergeant Lambton rose from his chair, and went towards a door leading to the back premises of the police station.

'If you'll excuse me, gentlemen,' he said, 'I'll go and see if all's well out the back.'

He quickly left the room, closing the door behind him.

'It's probably an act of Providence,' said Father Brooks, 'that you and I have met here tonight, Mr Box. I've followed your investigations of these Mithras murders in the daily Press, and I've been longing to talk to you about the matter. Have you ever seen the Clerkenwell Treasure?'

'Well, Father, I've heard a lot about it recently, but I've not actually seen it — '

'May I counsel you to go and see it, Mr Box? It's in the South Kensington Museum. They do a very informative leaflet, too, which you might care to buy. It's only a penny. And when you've seen it — but not before — come out to visit me at Saint Joseph's Retreat, in Highgate. Do you know it?'

'I know of it, Father, because it's only a couple of years since the great chapel was completed, round about the time that Sir Sydney Waterlow presented that fine park of his to the public. May I take it that you're an antiquarian, Father?'

'You may take it, Inspector, that I'm an observer of human nature,' the priest replied. There was a slight acerbity in his voice. 'When you come to see me — as I hope you will — I'll tell you something about the foibles and follies of mankind. I'm speaking, you understand, about this business of the heathen god Mithras, and his devotees. 'They have mouths and speak not: they have eyes and see not'. You've heard those words, I expect, or something like them. Well, they're true.'

Box looked at the priest, and saw the intense seriousness of his expression. This was a man content for the moment to speak in enigmas. He's telling me something, thought Box, and warning me about something. Maybe their meeting had indeed been providential.

'I promise you, sir,' he said, 'that I will visit the Clerkenwell Treasure this very week.'

'Excellent, Mr Box. And yes, I will admit now that I am something of an antiquarian.

Many people would regard me as an expert on the Clerkenwell Treasure, and they would be right. Go and see it, and then come out to visit me at Highgate. I think you'll find the journey well worth the trouble.'

11

A Bad Time at the Rents

It was well after midnight when Arnold Box got back to King James's Rents. When his business in Rotherhithe was done, one of Sergeant Lambton's constables walked with him through the rain to Union Street, where there was a cab rank. He'd secured a lumbering old four-wheeler, which had taken him into the Borough, and then across Southwark Bridge. When the cab had deposited him at the threshold of Cannon Street, he had hailed a hansom cab, which had taken him through the now diminishing rain to Whitehall.

It was very quiet and rather eerie late at night in King James's Rents. When Box entered his office, he found that the gas-mantle had been turned low, and the embers of the day's fire still glowed in the grate. He sat down in his usual chair at the long table. The ancient pile of buildings continued its creaking and settling of timbers, and from somewhere near the dark rear part of the office, a rat pattered and squeaked its way to some secret destination.

What a squalid, petty murder! Fancy being dragged out that far on a stormy night to expose the likes of Victor Freestone! If Lambton's inspector hadn't gone running off to Putney after the riot, he could have wrapped the whole thing up himself in half an hour. Well, he'd better write the case up for Old Growler to see in the morning.

He took a fresh sheet of paper from a drawer, and drew the inkwell towards him. *Thursday, 23 August 1894*, he wrote. It was actually Friday, now, but the murder of that poor wretched pawnbroker had taken place on Thursday evening. He wrote for ten minutes or so, rapidly covering the page with his neat copperplate handwriting. Then he threw the pen down, and sat back in his chair.

He was getting nowhere with this Mithras investigation. He'd been on the case since the fourteenth, and still he'd made no arrests. He'd not even brought anyone in for questioning. What about that chemist's assistant, who hoped to gain promotion from the death of Gregory Walsh? What about the bland, uncommunicative works manager who was now free to marry into the family of the murdered Abraham Barnes?

He got up from his chair, and groped his way down the dim tunnel that led to the drill hall. Two small oil lamps had been left lit, so that Sergeant Kenwright's large drawing of the reredos at Clerkenwell stood in a pool of flickering light. The face of Mithras seemed to be wreathed in a mocking smile. He could just make out the edges of the piece of stone containing the face, one of the several pieces that had been broken in antiquity, and reassembled. It looked to Box like a rough outline of the Isle of Wight. Hateful, alien thing!

Box returned to his office, and sat down again at the table. No, there were no fresh leads. He'd still no idea who these fanatics were — if, indeed, they existed at all. And now, petty killers like Freestone were staging their own 'Mithras murders' . . . Where was he going? Who would be murdered next, with honey in his mouth and a carved image in his pocket? He needed a new impetus. Something, anything —

The swing doors of the office were pushed open, and an elderly man in shirtsleeves and a long waistcoat came in to the room. He was carrying a wooden tray, which contained a small brown teapot, a homely collection of saucerless cups, and a couple of tin spoons. There was also a bowl of brown sugar, and an enamel jug of milk.

'Hello, Charlie,' said Box. 'Have you

brought me some tea? I don't suppose there's any toast, is there?'

'It's just outside the door, sir. You pour yourself a brew, and I'll bring it in.'

Box watched as Charlie limped out of the dim room. Charlie had been night-helper at the Rents for well over thirty years. He'd been invalided out of the Royal Engineers after suffering an accident to his spine, and had been given light work in the Metropolitan Police. He'd come to the Rents in 1862, and had worked there ever since.

'You don't look your usual cheerful self tonight, Mr Box,' said Charlie, when he had returned with the toast. 'I hear you've been out for most of the first watch.'

'I have, Charlie. I've been across the river, solving a silly little murder which didn't need a detective to do it. This toast's lovely. And so is this tea. Thanks very much. You're a shining ornament, Charlie.'

The old man chuckled, and walked round the table. He pulled down one of the chains on the mantle. The burners spluttered and hissed, and the shadows receded a little into the corners of Box's office. Discreet use of the poker coaxed a little spurt of flame from the remains of the fire.

'Mr Mackharness came in here just after ten, Mr Box,' said Charlie. 'Just called in on his way back from his club, he said. He wanted to know where you were. When he heard that you'd been called out to a case, he said he'd see you first thing in the morning. 'Tell Mr Box not to go off duty until he's seen me', he said.'

'I wonder what he wants?' asked Box, half to himself.

'He didn't say, sir. He said he wouldn't keep you more than a few minutes.'

'He always says that, Charlie. Mr Mackharness's 'few minutes' can last half an hour.' He yawned, and covered his mouth with his hand. 'I don't think I'll finish this report tonight,' he said. 'I'm too tired to be bothered.'

'Why don't you go up to the bunks for a couple of hours, Mr Box?' said Charlie. 'No one's going to bother you again tonight, and there's a sergeant borrowed from 'A' Division manning the front office for the night.'

'I'll do that, Charlie,' said Box, rising from his chair, and stretching. 'Maybe things will be more cheerful in the morning. Good night.'

'Good night, Mr Box.'

Box left the old man in the office, and made his way slowly up the stairs from the vestibule, where a dim gaslight glowed. He glimpsed the duty sergeant in the office

— the man borrowed for the night from 'A' — but didn't recognize him. He passed the door of the superintendent's office on the first floor and ascended to the floor above. There was no gas laid on above the first storey, and the little passage at the top of the second flight was lit by a shaded oil lamp standing in a tray of sand on a ledge.

He entered a small room overlooking the cobbled square in front of King James's Rents. It contained two double bunks, furnished with pillows and blankets. There was no light provided, and Box left the door half open, so that the oil lamp in the passage would help to illuminate the little room. He removed his jacket and shoes, and stretched out on one of the lower bunks, pulling the blanket up over himself.

Even up here, you could hear the creaking and settling of the fabric, and the scuttling of rats in the passage, inured, apparently, to the trays of poison left out for them. That Father Brooks . . . There was a man who spoke in riddles. He'd go out to Highgate and see him. He might have something useful to tell him. This bunk was very comfortable, and he was very tired. Charlie was right. No one would disturb him again tonight . . .

There came the sound of footsteps in the passage, a sudden leap of shadows across the wall, and Sergeant Knollys entered the room. He sat down on the adjacent lower bunk, and looked at Box for a moment. Then he spoke.

'Sir,' said Knollys, 'we're making no headway with this Mithras business. What have we achieved, so far? No one's been brought to book. Poor young Walsh is still unavenged, and your investigation of Barnes's murder led to nothing. And what about tonight's escapade? Maybe it'll be the first of many.'

Knollys shifted on the bunk. Box could not see his features, as he was silhouetted against the lamplight in the passage. But he could sense a growing aggression in the big sergeant's demeanour.

'What do you propose to do next, sir?' Knollys continued. 'All we've done so far is take a genteel luncheon with our only suspect, and then walked away from him! What use is that? Why don't you admit defeat, and hand the case over to someone else? You're not fit to be on this case. You're not fit to be an inspector — '

Box jerked awake with fright. His stomach churned, and he could hear the blood drumming in his ears. The room was empty. Jack Knollys would never have spoken to him like that. The dream-figure had been a vehicle for his own misgivings and sense of failure.

Something would have to be done, and soon. The 'ghost' had been right: he wasn't fit for the case.

He lay back disconsolately on the bunk, and immediately fell into a deep, untroubled sleep, from which he was awakened at seven o'clock by a rough shaking of his shoulder by the incoming duty sergeant.

Downstairs, Charlie accosted him at the door of his office.

'There's a bacon sandwich and a mug of tea for you on your table, sir,' he said. 'I've put a bit of soap and a razor out in the ablutions, and a can of hot water. Mr Mackharness came in at six, as usual. I'll be off now, sir.'

It was too early for Jack Knollys to have come in from Syria Wharf. Perhaps it was just as well. He could still recall the dream-figure who had told him that he wasn't fit to be an inspector. He ate his sandwich, drank his tea, and went out to the ablutions, a chilly stone passageway, half open to the sky, in what Mr Mackharness called 'the exercise yard'.

The shaving things had been arranged neatly beside one of the brownstone sinks, and behind them was propped a piece of cardboard, upon which Charlie had written in chalk: 'For Use of Insp. Box.' As Box shaved, he thought to himself, I've gone badly wrong over this case. I'm getting nowhere . . . He wondered why Old Growler wanted to see him so early in the day. Well, in a minute or so, he'd find out.

* * *

'Sit down in that chair, will you, Box, and listen carefully to what I'm going to say.'

Superintendent Mackharness sat behind his ornate desk, upon which he had placed a collection of folders and papers, all neatly arranged for instant reference. He waited for Box to sit down, looked fixedly at his inspector for what seemed to Box like minutes, and then began to speak.

'Over the last few days, Box,' he said, 'I have been reading through your reports on these murders in Clerkenwell and Carshalton, together with your account of what seems to have been a social visit to Professor Roderick Ainsworth out at Epsom.'

Box moved uneasily. In his mind he could hear the words of the phantom Knollys: '*All we've done so far is take a genteel luncheon with our only suspect, and then walked away from him! What use is that? Why don't you admit defeat, and hand the case over to someone else?*'

'Throughout your reports,' Mackharness

continued, 'there are many references to the cult of Mithras, the significance of honey and mercury to the various kinds of sacrifice connected with Mithraism, and a very cogent account of your interview with — what was her name? — Miss Mary Westerham, an expert in these matters. Am I right in assuming that you regard all these details as germane to the cases in hand?'

'You are, sir. I'm convinced that there is a hidden society at work, some kind of fanatical brotherhood that won't scruple to sacrifice its members to the god of their choosing. I'm afraid that I've made no progress in uncovering that brotherhood. For a time, I suspected Professor Ainsworth himself of being involved in the business, but I can see now that I was entirely mistaken. But it was his uncovering of that ancient shrine, sir, that animated the members of this secret cult to resume the abominations that I believe must have been practised there in antiquity — '

'*Tripe!*'

Superintendent Mackharness's face had grown redder and redder as Box talked. His sudden verbal explosion was accompanied by the crashing of one of his massive fists on the table. Box jumped in alarm, and stared at his master as though he had gone mad.

'Tripe, I say! Tripe and drivel! I'm sorry to

use such language, Box — I'm usually calling *you* to book for employing the expressions of the fishwife or Billingsgate porter — but I'm horrified to hear you spouting all that rot to me as though it were true. It's not. I'll tell you what it is: it's obfuscation. Legerdemain. Do I have to tell you what has really happened in this case?'

'Sir — '

'Don't interrupt. Just listen. We have here, Box, two murders. Never mind all the fancy dressing. Gregory Walsh was murdered in the Mithraeum by a single blow from an adze. I have the autopsy report here, on my desk. Abraham Barnes, the cement manufacturer out at Carshalton, was similarly murdered by a single blow from an adze. There's the autopsy report on *that*.' He flourished a paper briefly at Box, and then threw it down on the desk.

'*Murders*, Box! Not ritual sacrifices, offerings to pagan gods — where did you get those addled notions from? I blame the Press. That fellow Fiske started it all with his tosh in *The Graphic*. Fiske is a dangerous man, because he can serve up ignorance in a dressing of erudition. All reporters do that — even the gentlemen of *The Times* when it suits their convenience. Well, you've got to cleanse your mind of all that rot, Box, and concentrate on what it is that you're supposed to be investigating. Murders! Your task is to find the killer, and bring him to book. Why do people commit murders, Box? Come on, tell me that.'

'Sir, they commit murder for financial gain, or out of hatred, or to achieve security by silencing those who could uncover a misdeed — '

'That's right. So what you must do now, Box, is find out *why* Gregory Walsh was killed. You don't know the whole story there. And find out *why* Abraham Barnes was killed. Forget these wretched legends. This case centres on archaeology, and it's time for you to do much more digging and delving of your own than you've done so far. Go out, Box, and uncover the past. Look for practical motives, and see where your fresh investigations take you.'

Box rose from his chair. The guvnor was right. He'd make a start that very day —

'In God's name, man,' cried Mackharness, 'where are you going? I haven't finished talking to you yet. Sit down. Now, let me talk for a little about one very interesting lead that you were developing before all this . . . this *tripe* overwhelmed you. The man in the seaman's jacket. You found him at Carshalton, and then at Croydon, and had begun to track him back across the river when you seemed to abandon that particular chase, even after Sergeant Kenwright had uncovered evidence of his presence in Clerkenwell. Why did you not follow up that line of investigation?'

'Sir, I'd more or less made up my mind that the man in the seaman's jacket was none other than Professor Ainsworth. But that could not have been so. The professor caught the nine-five train to Edinburgh from Euston on the morning of the fourteenth — '

'How do you know that?'

'He — he told me.'

'Box!' Mr Mackharness shook his head and sighed. 'So he told you, did he? Did you check up at Euston?'

'No, sir. But he told me that he'd talked to a Canon Venables of St Paul's on the train, and this canon had commented on Ainsworth's smart turn-out — morning coat, pearl-grey stock, and so on. Dressed like that, sir, he couldn't have been the man in the seaman's jacket.'

'And have you checked that little story with Canon Venables? No, I thought not. Didn't it occur to you that Ainsworth was detailing his alibi to you? All that talk of morning coats, and so on — it sounds as though Ainsworth may have forced the topic on to this Venables so that he could repeat it to the police later. You're not going stale on me, are you, Box? Do you want to be taken off this case — ?'

'No, sir! But you're making me feel ashamed. I'm very sorry.'

'Yes, well, never mind all that. I want you to probe more deeply into this business of the man in the seaman's jacket. Follow those trains that he took, and see where they went. Go to the stations, and ask questions. Take Sergeant Knollys with you.

'Another little point: Sergeant Knollys recovered the adze, but what happened to the big carpet bag? Find out. Or if you can't find out, draw some sensible deductions. Question this Canon Venables of St Paul's. Ask him about Ainsworth, how he seemed on the journey. Did Venables really alight at Carlisle? Do I have to go on, Box?'

'No, sir.'

'Very well. Now, before I move on to other matters, you'd better tell me what happened to you last night. I gather from the duty sergeant that you were called out to Rotherhithe.'

When Box had finished his account of the murder of John Cornish, Mackharness treated him to an unpleasantly triumphant smile.

'There you are, you see? Obfuscation.

Already, a common criminal crudely fabricates one of these so-called Mithras murders. Well, I'm suggesting to you, Box, that *someone else* had already fabricated two such atrocities. All the honey and mercury, all those little plaques with lions and so forth engraved on them, were put there to mislead an intelligent man like yourself into believing a lot of tosh, and mistaking it for truth.'

Superintendent Mackharness began to rummage round on his desk, until he had gathered a number of specific documents, and placed them neatly on his leather-bound blotter.

'I want to turn now, Box,' Mackharness continued, 'to the immediate vicinity of the site of Gregory Walsh's murder. You furnished me with a very full and detailed account of that rough square bounded on two sides by Priory Gate Street and Catherine Lane. I was particularly interested in the building called Hatchard's Furniture Repository, which you described as being in good repair, but seldom open to the public. Why do you think I should be interested in that particular building?'

'Because — because it stands on the site of the place where the Clerkenwell Treasure was discovered. It also extends backward from Catherine Lane to very near the excavated

Mithraeum. In a street of thriving businesses, sir, it's a bit of an anomaly, if that's the right word.'

'It is, Box. Well done! It struck me immediately that Hatchard's Furniture Repository deserved special attention.'

The superintendent picked up an envelope, and extracted a letter.

'I wrote to the Registrar of Companies, Box, asking them about Hatchard's Furniture Repository, and received this reply. The premises are owned by a holding company, called The North-Eastern Storage Association, with an address in Sunderland. That in turn is a subsidiary of Thomas Ainsworth & Son, shipbuilders, of Newcastle. What do you think of that?'

'Sir, I'm stunned. That piece of information opens up all kinds of possibilities.'

'It does, Box, and to my way of thinking they're very sinister possibilities. So among other things, bring your attention back to Clerkenwell for a while, and to the milieu of poor Gregory Walsh's murder. Investigate that building — you'll have no trouble with warrants, if you need them. And examine all that business of the cement samples again. Find out who commissioned them. That piece of knowledge in itself could well provide the solution to the whole business.'

'Sir, do you think I should visit this Father Brooks out at Highgate? He talked in riddles when I met him in Rotherhithe. Perhaps he's just a well-meaning eccentric.'

'Perhaps he is, and then again, Box, perhaps he isn't. Go and see him; but before you do, go to the South Kensington Museum, and have a look at the Clerkenwell Treasure. This Father Brooks seemed to think that you should do so before you pay him a visit. Humour him, Box. It might lead somewhere.

'Oh, yes. I knew there was something else. I think you and Sergeant Knollys should visit Sir Charles Wayneflete, who's supposed to be Ainsworth's rival in the field of archaeology. You've heard Professor Ainsworth's biased account of the man; go and find out for yourself what this Wayneflete's like, and what happened to that man of his — Crale, I think his name was.

'And now, Box, there's something else I've found out for you — someone, in fact, that I feel you should visit. I was told about this person by my friend Lord Maurice Vale Rose, whose people live near her people in Essex. Lord Maurice has very kindly agreed to furnish you with a letter of introduction to this lady, whose name is Mrs Warwick Newman. She lives in an ancient former rectory in the village of Melton Castra, in the deep countryside a few miles north-west of Chelmsford. Go down and see her, and see what she can tell you.'

'But who is she, sir? This Mrs Warwick Newman?' asked Box in some bewilderment.

'What? Oh, yes. She's Professor Roderick Ainsworth's second cousin. According to what Lord Maurice Vale Rose told me, the two of them became estranged many years ago, but she's thought in the neighbourhood to know some very interesting things about Roderick Ainsworth's activities in his youth. Delve, Box. Be your own archaeologist, and turn up old scandals and secrets to the light of day.

'It's just on eight o'clock, so I've not kept you beyond your time. I want you to take the rest of the day off, and to consider everything that I've said to you very carefully. Take all these documents with you, and let Sergeant Knollys know what you intend to do — draw up a plan of action with him, if you like. I think that's all, Box. Good morning.'

'Sir,' said Box, 'thank you very much for putting me back on the rails. I hate to think what you might have been thinking about — '

'What? Nonsense. I have a very high opinion of your abilities, as you know. I just don't like you being misled by superstitious tripe. Your almost instantaneous solution of that murder in Rotherhithe last night was typical of your special kind of expertise. So go to it, Box, and let me see some positive results next week. Send me a daily report each night before you leave.'

★   ★   ★

In a secluded gallery leading off one of the cramped courts of the South Kensington Museum, Arnold Box sat on a bench facing a glazed cabinet that contained twelve chalices of gleaming gold, each one set with precious stones. They were standing on a strip of red velvet, which enhanced their overpowering splendour. Gold, they said, never tarnished, and these vessels looked as though they had been created only that week. But they were, in fact, centuries old.

This, then, was the Clerkenwell Treasure. Box had bought the penny pamphlet on entering the gallery. It recounted the story of how the treasure was discovered, following an ingenious and diligent search by Professor Roderick Ainsworth, who had tracked the items down after a long perusal of ancient manuscripts and letters, in English, Latin and French, assembled from widely dispersed archives in county houses and obscure libraries. It was in itself a fascinating tale, but it was time for Box to read about the sacred vessels themselves. He turned his attention once more to the penny pamphlet.

THE CLERKENWELL TREASURE

The twelve solid gold chalices constituting what we now call the Clerkenwell Treasure were known collectively as The Patrimony of the Twelve Apostles. Each chalice was assigned to a particular apostle, and the Masses at which they were used were known by the names 'Mass of St Peter,' 'Mass of St Paul', etc.

The Patrimony was one of the prized possessions of the Priory of St John at Clerkenwell. At the time of the Reformation the collection seemed to have disappeared, and it was rumoured that it had been prudently removed some years before 1532, to the Order's house in Malta. Thomas Cromwell shared this opinion, and ascribed no sinister purpose to it. It was not until 1887 that the brilliant research of Professor Ainsworth led to the discovery of a cache hidden beneath the foundations of a now long-vanished church in Catherine Lane, Clerkenwell.

The following brief notes describe the individual chalices and their provenance.

1. Small gold chalice, with heavy base, ornamented with twenty fine rubies. Florentine, dated to about AD 300 Inscription: *Calicem salutaris accipiam et nomen Domini invocabo* (Psalm 105, Sarum Breviary). *St Paul.*
2. Chalice with plain cup, but with the stem adorned with finely incised quatrefoil tracery from top to bottom. Six fine opals set into the base. London hallmark, AD 1484. Donation of Richard III. *St Peter.*
3. Chalice with unusual wide bowl, the base etched with the symbol IHS, and set with six diamonds. Hallmark erased. Provenance uncertain, probably from the Netherlands, early sixteenth century. *St Thomas.*
4. Very early chalice of late Romanesque design, the base set with emeralds. Much worn and indecipherable inscription under the base in medieval French. Dated in Arabic numerals 1368. *St Andrew.*

There were eight more ancient gold chalices in the display, all ornamented, and studded with precious stones, and each with its own fascinating history. It was upon the discovery of this great treasure that Professor Ainsworth's public reputation had been founded.

Box recalled Superintendent Mackharness's words, uttered only that morning. He'd more or less ordered him to make this visit to the South Kensington Museum, and had then advised him to follow up the visit with a call on Father Brooks at St Joseph's Retreat. 'Humour him, Box,' he'd said. 'It might lead somewhere.' Well, he'd already arranged to visit the enigmatic clergyman on the following afternoon, which was a Saturday. There was evidently something that Father Brooks knew about the Clerkenwell Treasure that was not common knowledge. It would be foolish, to say the least, not to hear what the Highgate priest had to say.

12

Provenance Uncertain

'It has always been the practice of the Passionist Fathers, Inspector Box,' said Father Brooks, 'to build their monasteries outside the towns. I venture to suggest that we chose no finer site when we selected this particular corner of Highgate for our English house.'

Box was inclined to agree. The handsome Italianate chapel occupied a commanding position overlooking Waterlow Park on its west side, and the elegant villas of the leafy North London suburb to the east. The air was fresh and invigorating, and the weather bright and sunny. The gloom and tempest of the previous day, with its crosses and nightmares, had been swept away.

'I'm glad you've come, Mr Box,' Father Brooks continued. 'This retreat of ours is comfortably distant from the curious eyes and ears of Whitehall, and I'll be able to speak to you frankly and freely. I want to talk to you first about the Clerkenwell Treasure. From some words about that, I hope that we'll progress naturally to the subject of Professor Roderick Ainsworth.'

The two men were sitting in a cramped study on the second floor of the monastery, which clung like a limpet to the side of the great chapel. It was a building that looked as though it had been transported by miracle straight from Tuscany. The room was filled with books, big art folders full of engravings, and a disconcerting number of religious paintings and statues. An intimidating portrait of Cardinal Manning hung over the mantelpiece. In the midst of all this sat Father Brooks, his stout form covered by a suit of clerical black, his steel spectacles resting on his nose.

'You have seen the Clerkenwell Treasure?'

'I have, sir. I went to see it yesterday. I did as you advised, and bought the penny pamphlet. I was quite overawed by all that gleaming gold, sir, and more so by the sheer age of those cups. They were all centuries old, yet looking like new!'

'Well,' said Father Brooks, 'now that you've seen the treasure, you must let me tell you some little-known facts about it — you'll see where all this is leading presently. In 1535, Henry VIII was declared supreme head of the church in England, and in the following year Thomas Cromwell became vicar-general.

From that year, 1536, the dissolution of the monasteries commenced, and it was not long before Clerkenwell Priory was plundered and destroyed. The last effective prior, Sir William Weston, was bought off with an annuity of a thousand pounds.'

Father Brooks rummaged through the papers on his desk and produced a faded little book bound in cheap cardboard. He peered at one or two of its pages before continuing his narrative.

'As you can imagine, Mr Box, Thomas Cromwell was most eager to get his hands on the Patrimony of the Twelve Apostles. With the precious stones gouged out, and the gold melted down, it would have provided a welcome addition to the King's ever-yawning coffers. Are you, perhaps, an admirer of King Henry, Mr Box?'

'Not particularly, sir, I can take him or leave him, as they say.'

'Very well. So Cromwell cast around to find the Patrimony. One of his searchers questioned an Augustinian brother of the Clerkenwell foundation, a certain John Pringle, a man who seemed very eager to co-operate with the new state of things. Pringle was able to persuade Cromwell's agent that the Patrimony had been removed to the Order of St John's house in Malta, in

1532. Pringle must have been a good equivocator, because Cromwell believed him, and rewarded him with fifteen shillings. I have part of a letter that Cromwell wrote to the Duke of Somerset pasted into this little book. This is what he told him.

''I can assure Your Grace that the whole parcel of gold cups fancifully called the Apostles' Patrimony was conveyed away some years since to Malta; which conveyance was done with no malign motive, but at the request of the Prior of Malta there; which thing is a matter of regret, but now of no moment, as very much remains at Clerkenwell that can be converted to the King's use.''

'But what this Pringle told Cromwell couldn't have been true, could it, Father Brooks?' said Box.

'No, it wasn't true. The truth of the matter was that, in 1532, the prior, who could see very clearly the way events were shaping in England, entrusted that very same Augustinian brother, John Pringle, with the task of spiriting the Patrimony away, and concealing it. This he did, contriving a small stone cyst beneath the north wall of the church of St Catherine of Sienna in Clerkenwell, a church which was served by Augustinian priests connected to the Priory. And there the treasure remained until it was discovered by

Professor Roderick Ainsworth in 1887.'

Father Brooks stopped speaking, and looked at Box in a way that suggested he was waiting for some kind of comment.

'A fascinating story, sir,' said Box. 'I suspect that the doings of that man Pringle are part of a secret history, known only to a few — to people like yourself, for instance. But are you suggesting that Professor Ainsworth never did discover the treasure? I can't quite see where your story's taking me — '

'Bear with me, if you will, Mr Box,' said Father Brooks. 'All will be revealed presently. *Of course* Professor Ainsworth discovered the Clerkenwell Treasure! He conducted a brilliant investigation, admired by anyone with scholarly pretensions. Ainsworth was able to wrest the secret of John Pringle from the Catholic clergy at St Etheldreda's, Ely Place, the current guardians of the deposit of secret documents pertaining to Clerkenwell Priory. Brilliant work! But there was a very peculiar flaw in Ainsworth's discovery.'

'And what was that, sir?'

'In reply, let me ask you a question, Mr Box. How many chalices comprised the treasure as you saw it yesterday in the South Kensington Museum?'

'Why, sir, there were twelve — that was the

whole point of the treasure, wasn't it? The Patrimony of the Twelve Apostles. I've brought the penny leaflet with me. It lists them all — '

'Yes, it does, Mr Box, but I can tell you, with absolute certainty, that when John Pringle hid the treasure in his little stone chamber beneath St Catherine's Church in 1532, it contained only *eleven* chalices. The one designated St Thomas had been given to the Cathedral of St Rombold at Malines, in what is now Belgium, in 1494, in exchange for a grant of land to build a new hospital near Antwerp. I am one of the few people to have been shown the St Thomas chalice in the cathedral treasury there. The exchange, like all these things, was done with subtle propriety, so that it does not enter the common chronicle of history. There are few people today who are aware of the fate of that ancient gold cup.'

Arnold Box had retrieved his penny pamphlet from his pocket. He held it up for Father Brooks to see.

'Then what are we to make of this chalice, Father, which is on show in the museum? '3. Chalice with unusual wide bowl, the base etched with the symbol IHS, and set with six diamonds. Hallmark erased. Provenance uncertain, probably from the Netherlands, early sixteenth century. *St Thomas*.' It's as clear as day!'

'Some days, Mr Box,' Father Brooks replied with a wry smile, 'can be decidedly murky. Let me draw your attention to the 'unusual wide bowl'. In the Catholic Church, where the wine at Communion is drunk only by the celebrating priest, the chalice bowls are small. But in the Anglican and Lutheran churches, where the wine is delivered also to the laity, the bowls tend to be wider, because they are designed to hold a greater quantity of wine.'

'So what you are saying — ?'

'I'm saying, Inspector, that the chalice labelled St Thomas in the Clerkenwell Treasure is a very fine example of a Lutheran Communion chalice. You notice that the hallmark has been erased? That, surely, should have aroused scholarly suspicion when the treasure was finally unearthed. I've been allowed to handle that so-called St Thomas chalice, Mr Box, and I have established to my own satisfaction that it is of Lutheran provenance; I would date it about 1540. The workmanship is certainly Flemish. Granted that you believe me, can you see where all this history is leading?'

'You're beginning to lose me, I'm afraid, Father,' said Box. 'You say that only eleven chalices were buried under St Catherine's Church, which means, I suppose, that Professor Roderick Ainsworth must have added a twelfth — presumably this Lutheran cup. Are you saying that it is a fake?'

'No, no, Mr Box, you're not seeing what I mean. It's a genuine sixteenth-century chalice, but it's been *doctored*, if you'll excuse the expression. Professor Ainsworth would have paid a goodly sum for that cup — perhaps several hundred pounds.'

'But why should he do such a thing?' asked Box. 'What was the point of it?'

'The man's a perfectionist, so when the Clerkenwell Treasure proved to be imperfect — eleven chalices instead of twelve — he set out to remedy the matter. A twelfth cup was needed, and it had to be a genuine sixteenth-century one. So he found one, somewhere, filed off the hallmark, and added it to the treasure. Behold! The great archaeologist has unearthed the full Patrimony of the Apostles! History had let him down, but he was not a man to be browbeaten by history.'

As the elderly priest spoke, Arnold Box realized that he was waking up to reality. Father Brooks was talking about interfering with evidence for private gain, something that belonged not to the realms of the supernatural but to the mundane world of the wrongdoer. He saw that Father Brooks was watching him, gauging whether or not the underlying meaning of his words was taking hold in the inspector's mind.

'You can see where all this is leading, now, can't you, Mr Box? If Professor Ainsworth didn't scruple to fabricate part of the Clerkenwell Treasure, thus compromising its integrity, *what else may he have fabricated?* And who may have found that out? All those artefacts which he unearthed in the Mithraeum — how many of those are genuine? Or are there more artefacts that could be labelled 'provenance uncertain'? Perhaps an investigation is necessary. 'Seek and ye shall find'.'

'And what is *your* motive for telling me these things, Father?' asked Box. 'What is *your* connection with Professor Roderick Ainsworth?'

A slight flush of anger reddened the priest's face, but it had gone in an instant.

'My motive, Inspector, is a disapproval of murder. Amid all these shams of quicksilver and honey, all these little tokens culled from the forgotten back drawers of museums and left lying around for you and your colleagues to find, lurks the spirit of murder. Two men have been slaughtered — why? Not as sacrifices, but because they posed a danger to someone. Both men evidently knew something very damning about someone — damning enough for that man to murder in order to silence them.'

'Are you saying that Professor Ainsworth — ?'

'I'm saying nothing about any named person, Mr Box. I'm simply pointing out to you that there are some men in high places who will murder to preserve a reputation that they have knowingly tarnished. I hope that I've proved to you today that Ainsworth is a man who has compromised his reputation, and that if the truth of the Clerkenwell Treasure became public knowledge, his position in the academic world, and in society at large, would suffer irreparable damage. I accuse no one, but I set out for you certain possibilities. Do you believe what I have told you today?'

'I do, Father. As you said on a previous occasion, it was Providence that brought you and me together in Canal Street Police Station.'

'It was. I was there to visit a dying prisoner in the Bridewell, a man whom I'd known in happier times when I was working in Southwark. Sergeant Lambton is one of our flock, and knows me well.'

'Why have you not revealed what you know about the Clerkenwell Treasure before now?'

'It's not for the likes of me to cause

scandal, Mr Box. In any case, I'm a secretive man by nature. Discreet, you know. But murder — well, when murder rears its ugly head, a man can't afford the luxury of total discretion. So I determined to tell you what I know. My superior here gave me full permission to do so.'

Arnold Box rose from his chair. It was time to leave this quiet sanctuary in Highgate, and get back to the Rents. Father Brooks and he shook hands.

'Goodbye, sir,' said Box. 'You've opened up a whole new world of possibilities by what you've told me today. As far as the Clerkenwell Treasure is concerned, I'll try and be as discreet as you have been. Perhaps, after this business has been brought to its rightful conclusion, I'll come out here again, and tell you the whole truth.'

★ ★ ★

Inspector Box, standing in the dusty upper front room of an old bookshop in St Paul's Churchyard, watched Canon Arthur Venables as he lifted down a slim leather-bound book from one of the packed shelves, and blew the dust off it. A handsome man in his sixties, he was very smartly dressed in a suit of clerical black, relieved by a carnation bud in his buttonhole. He treated Box to one of those smiles designed to give a man time to think before he ventures an answer to a particular kind of question.

'Did I travel on the Edinburgh train, you ask. Travel there on the fourteenth? Why, yes, I did, now that you remind me. And I caught the nine-five from Euston, as you suggested. What is this all about, Inspector? I did pay for my ticket, you know!'

It would be both crass and unprofessional, thought Box, to ask the canon outright whether he had travelled in the company of Professor Roderick Ainsworth. This occasion called for a little harmless subterfuge.

'I'm sure you'll realize, sir,' said Box, lowering his voice, 'that some investigations require a great deal of discretion. There was a man travelling up to Edinburgh that day who is one of England's most notorious swindlers. He attaches himself to clergymen, and solicits them for large subscriptions to non-existent charities — '

'Well, I can assure you, Inspector, that no such person attempted to relieve *me* of my ill-gotten gains. There were four of us in the compartment, as I recall. One of the others was unknown to me, another was a City broker whom I'd seen before, and the third was an acquaintance of mine, Professor

Roderick Ainsworth, whose name will not be unknown to you.'

Box received another of Canon Venables' rather unnerving smiles. He began to feel uncomfortable. Canon Venables continued his observations.

'I read in the papers that you're busy investigating that murder in the Clerkenwell Mithraeum — Professor Ainsworth's Mithraeum, if I may put it like that. What a coincidence. But I didn't see your notorious swindler.'

'And did you speak to Professor Ainsworth on the journey, sir?'

'Yes, indeed. We talked about archaeology, and I told him a few things he didn't know about the recent excavations at Jericho. Then we discussed tailors, after I'd admired the cut of his morning coat and his silk stock. Very dapper he looked; 'dapper', of course, is not a word I'd apply to myself. But it suited him.'

An elderly stooping man in an alpaca jacket came in off the staircase. Venables waved the slim book vaguely in his direction.

'How much is this edition of Paley's *Evidences*, Carter?'

'To you, Canon, half a crown.'

'And how much to anyone else?'

'Much the same, sir.' The man smiled. 'Shall I wrap it up for you?'

'Do so. I'll pay you when I come downstairs. Now, Inspector Box, is there anything else that you'd like to ask me? I'm due at a meeting in the Deanery at eleven.'

'Just one more question, sir. Did you travel all the way to Edinburgh with Professor Ainsworth?'

'Dear me, no. I got off at Carlisle. What happened to Ainsworth after that, I've no idea. Is that all, Mr Box?'

'Yes, thank you, sir. You've been very helpful.'

Canon Venables laughed, and made towards the staircase.

'Well, Inspector,' he said, 'I hope you catch your swindler. And in future, if you wish to check up on Professor Ainsworth's movements, it would be easier to ask the man himself!'

★   ★   ★

'This Canon Venables, Sergeant,' said Box, drawing appreciatively on his tankard of Burton's Ale, 'fancies himself as a wit. He saw right through my attempts to shield Ainsworth from suspicion by inventing a fugitive swindler.'

'Perhaps he wasn't able to cope with your well-known subtlety, sir,' Knollys suggested.

239

'You cheeky man!' Box laughed. 'I'll have you know, Sergeant Knollys, that I'm a byword for finesse at the Rents! Still, he did confirm that Professor Ainsworth caught the nine-five on the fourteenth, and that he and the professor discussed various points of fashion, among other things. What Ainsworth told us at Ardleigh Manor wasn't an alibi, Sergeant, it was the simple truth.'

It was eleven o'clock on the morning of the 27 August. After talking to Canon Venables in the bookshop, to which the canon's housekeeper had directed him, Box had walked down to Ludgate Circus where he had arranged to meet Jack Knollys in the King Lud, his favourite public house. Glancing up through a window near where he sat, he could see the gleaming railway bridge, with its ornamental shields, spanning the roadway outside.

As the two men discussed tactics, frequent trains thundered across the bridge, and the air drifting in through the open windows became heavy with black smoke. Arnold Box loved this particular spot. With its noise and bustle, and its constant air of activity, it seemed to him the hub of the Empire.

'Where do we go from here, sir?' asked Knollys.

'We go to Euston Station, Sergeant, and

talk to some of the porters who were on duty that day — the day of the two murders. But before we do that, I want to hear you construct a narrative in which Professor Roderick Ainsworth and the Man in the Seaman's Jacket are one and the same person. That's what Superintendent Mackharness more or less hinted the other day when he was turning me on the rack.'

Jack Knollys finished his pint tankard of ale, and sat back in his chair. The two men were sitting in a quiet corner of the front bar, where they could not be overheard by other customers. He felt a sudden surge of excitement. This habit of suddenly handing over the conduct of a case to him as part of his professional development was one of the guvnor's great strengths.

'Sir, as I recall, Inspector Perrivale ascertained that a man calling himself Michael Shane secured a room for the night of Monday, 13 August at the boarding-house of a Mr Stanley, at Carshalton. He paid in advance, and said that he would be out late. He was dressed like a workman, and his cap, coat and carpet bag all seemed brand new. I'm suggesting that 'Michael Shane' was none other than Professor Roderick Ainsworth, disguised. He — he was about to embark on a very energetic course of action, namely, sir, two murders, to be committed many miles apart and on different sides of the river. One of his weapons was to be a workman's adze. The other weapon was to be the railway system — '

'Pause there, if you will, Sergeant,' said Box, holding up a hand. 'Let me be the devil's advocate for the moment. You say that our man was to embark on a very energetic course of action. That's true enough. But could a middle-aged academic man like Ainsworth pursue such a course?'

'I think so, sir. Remember, that he was a Rugby player in his youth, and that there were all kinds of trophies hanging on the walls of that great conservatory of his. He's a strong man, sir, well able to undertake this course of murder. Also, he had the sense to come early in the evening to Carshalton and take a room in Mr Stanley's house. It would give him time to collect himself, and rest for a while before going out in the middle of the night to put paid to poor Abraham Barnes.'

'Very well. But how was he able to leave his own house without being seen? He must have left Ardleigh Manor at Epsom about half-past eight or so, and caught a train to Carshalton. Would he have left his home in disguise? Wasn't the risk of being seen and remembered too great? Come on, Sergeant, tell me what he did!'

'Sir, he donned his disguise while he was at Ardleigh Manor, and then he — yes, I know! — he walked through the country lanes to the next station along the line and caught a train for Carshalton there.'

'Why wasn't he missed at home?' Box persisted. 'Why did nobody see him?'

'Because — because nobody at Ardleigh Manor ever knows where *anyone* is!'

'Well done, Jack! You've remembered that conversation between Ainsworth and his wife Zena, a conversation that showed how independent of each other the members of the Ainsworth family are. She was going to — Leatherhead, wasn't it? — and thought she'd better let him know in case he wondered what had happened to her. Their daughter Margery had evidently been to Brighton. Her mother didn't know when she'd left to go there, and her father didn't know that she'd returned. So Ainsworth could have slipped out of his house at any time, and no one there would have been curious enough to wonder where he was. Go on, Sergeant.'

'Ainsworth, calling himself Michael Shane, waited until early morning, and then left the boarding-house. It was the typical act of a gentleman to leave a gratuity together with the latch-key on the wash-stand. He makes his way under cover of darkness to Abraham Barnes's house, and enters the grounds. He must have arranged some kind of appointment with Barnes — that needs to be established, later — and when the poor man comes down to the conservatory, Ainsworth is waiting there with his adze — '

'Where did he get it from? Would he have risked keeping such a weapon at home? Or did he take the risk, and hide it in his carpet bag?'

'Sir, he — perhaps he'd come out to Carshalton earlier, maybe days earlier, and hidden the adze somewhere in the grounds of Barnes's house — what was it called? — Wellington House. That's what I would have done. When Barnes comes into the conservatory, Ainsworth kills him with the adze. It was about three in the morning. He crams the adze into the carpet bag, and sets out on the second part of his deadly venture.'

'You've done very well, Sergeant,' said Box. 'You're painting a very credible picture of what could have happened between Epsom and Carshalton. I'll give you a rest, now, and take up the story as far as Croydon. We've agreed that Abraham Barnes was murdered at about three o'clock in the morning. At just after a quarter to four that same morning, a railway guard called Joseph Straddling saw our man — it must have been our man — board the four o'clock milk train to Croydon at Carshalton Station.

'The timing's right, Sergeant. A vigorous man could walk briskly from Barnes's house to the station in well under half an hour. I can imagine how he felt. Trembling inwardly with fear, but impelled by his iron determination not to lose his public position — he'll commit murder rather than face social ruin.'

'He wouldn't be the first to have murdered for that motive, sir.'

'No, Sergeant, he wouldn't. And now, having silenced Barnes, he must do the same for poor young Walsh in Clerkenwell. Incidentally, we still don't know *why*. But motive must take second place for the moment. It's *means* that we're examining. Again, he must have arranged some kind of meeting with Walsh. Maybe he passed himself off as someone else; or maybe - wait! Maybe he used that new man of his, Crale, as a go-between. Yes, that could well be so . . .

'Anyway, Joseph Straddling saw our man, still carrying his carpet bag, cross to Platform seven, where he would catch a train that would take him through to Victoria. Straddling was able to tell Inspector Perrivale that the man would have caught a train that would

245

have got him into Victoria at seven minutes past six.'

'Sir,' said Sergeant Knollys, 'that would give him about an hour to get from Victoria to Priory Gate Street in Clerkenwell for seven o'clock. He'd need all that time, because it's a long way from Victoria to Clerkenwell, and there wouldn't be many omnibuses running at that early hour.'

'Maybe not, Sergeant, but he could take a cab from Victoria Station, and alight from it somewhere near the Mithraeum. If he'd any sense, that's what he'd have done. And so, he'd either get there before Walsh, and lie in waiting for him, or get there after Walsh, creep up on him, and kill him. Your Mr Gold evidently saw him soon after the murder, hurrying up Catherine Lane, in order to hide the fatal adze in the middens behind Greensands' shop. I think you said that there was an alley at the side of the premises, giving access to the back yard.

'Now, Sergeant, what did he do next? What would you have done had you been in his shoes? Pausing only to add that all this is mere supposition. It would be impossible to prove Ainsworth's complicity in any of this business.'

'Sir,' said Knollys, ignoring Box's proviso, 'I'd have made my way to Euston, probably on foot, or perhaps in a cab, in order to catch the nine-five train to Edinburgh. I see no problem about that for a man who's obviously very fit and determined. However — '

'Yes, Jack, *however*. However did he transform himself from dour workman to scintillating gentleman? What happened to the seaman's jacket, the peaked cap and the carpet bag? The answer, I think, lies at Euston Station, and that's where we'd better betake ourselves, in order to hear a few answers.'

'Now, sir?'

'No, Sergeant, not now. Have you forgotten that it's the last day of the trial of the Balantyne brothers? We need to be in at the kill, as they say, when old Mr Justice Hillberry dons the black cap. No, we'll go first thing tomorrow, and watch the nine-five for Edinburgh start on its long and weary way up north. Having that particular train at the platform may jog a few memories.'

13

The Melton Giant

The nine-five train for Edinburgh stood at the platform, waiting for the signal to depart. Although stationary, it looked to Box like an impatient horse at the start of a race, chafing at the bit. Little wisps of steam rose from below the edge of the platform. A wheel-tapper passed along with his long, slim hammer, intent on confirming the integrity of the wheels.

'It was exactly as you see it now, Mr Box, just a fortnight ago today. Tuesday, fourteenth August. What is it now? Eleven minutes to nine. That train will depart for Edinburgh in just sixteen minutes.'

The speaker was a very smart, handsome ticket collector in his thirties. He sported a luxuriant moustache, and wore a well-pressed frock coat and dark trousers. His glazed peak cap was pulled smartly forward over his brows. His lapel and cap badges had obviously been newly polished, as had his boots.

'It's very good of you to help us, Mr

Cotton,' said Box. 'It's an exercise in elimination that Sergeant Knollys and myself are carrying out, which is why we're asking you if you can remember any regular passengers who boarded the Edinburgh train on the fourteenth.'

'Well, now, let me see,' said Cotton. He and the two policemen were standing beside a line of ornamental railings separating the platform from the concourse beyond. 'There *were* some regulars who came through my ticket barrier that day. There was Canon Venables of St Paul's — yes, that's right. He's got family in Edinburgh, I believe, and goes up there once or twice a month. And then there was Mr Louis Rosen, the stockbroker, well-known in railway circles for his generous tips. He was there. It was quite a busy morning, Inspector. There must have been forty or fifty passengers boarding the train.'

'I don't suppose you saw a man called Professor Ainsworth — '

'Oh, yes, of course! I'd forgotten him for the moment. I didn't actually know who he was at the time, you see, but someone told me, later. He came rushing up at the last moment — there were only two minutes to spare. He was very hot and bothered, and couldn't find his ticket at first. Bearded gent, he was. Yes, Ainsworth — that was his name.'

'And was he carrying a big carpet bag with him?'

'A carpet bag? No, his only piece of luggage was a smart overnight valise. He would have sent his heavy luggage ahead the day before, as like as not. He didn't need a porter. Very nicely dressed, he was, though a bit untidy, I thought. He probably came here in a shared hansom, which is never very good for your clothes.'

So far, thought Box, we're merely confirming what we know already. Professor Ainsworth caught the nine-five train to Edinburgh. It was an interesting fact that he had been 'hot and bothered', as Mr Cotton put it. There'd be a reason for that.

'Mr Cotton,' said Box, 'I don't suppose you can recall any unusual incident that morning? Any odd little thing that didn't seem to make sense?'

Cotton shook his head, suddenly recollected something, and smiled. He pointed down the platform to where a stout, genial-looking porter was standing beside one of two long wheeled trolleys drawn up in front of the open door of the galley at the end of the first-class restaurant car.

'Do you see that man, Mr Box? We've been ribbing him for the last couple of weeks over his 'ghost story', as we call it. He says that he saw — well, why don't you go and ask him? It happened on that day, the fourteenth, about twenty minutes before the nine-five moved out. It was unusual, now I come to think of it.'

As he spoke, there came a slamming of doors, and stern cries of 'Stand back from the train!' Whistles shrieked, flags were waved, and the long train began its stately progress out of Euston Station.

'Yes, go and have a word with him, Mr Box. He'll stay where he is for a while, because that's the nature of his job. He'll wait there for the nine-thirty for Liverpool to come in from the sidings. So there's plenty of time to speak to him. Joseph Potts, his name is. Joe Potts. I'll have to go now, Inspector. Duty calls!'

★   ★   ★

'It was like this, Inspector,' said Joseph Potts. 'On that particular day, I was here where you see me now, standing between these two big trolleys, making entries in the book that you can see standing on this sort of wheeled lectern. My job is to victual the restaurant cars on the long-distance trains. All the provisions have to be just right, and properly stowed away in the galleys; and then there's

251

all the table linen, the silver cutlery — everything has to be accounted for, and ticked off in that book.

'Now, from where I stand behind this lectern, I can see right through the barrier railings and across the concourse to the gentlemen's wash-room. It's directly to the right of the station entrance from this side. That wide doorway serves as both entrance and exit. Can you see it?'

'Yes,' said Box, smiling. 'It's got an enormous black and white sign above it on the wall: 'Gentlemen's Wash-Room', it says.'

'That's right,' said Mr Potts. 'Well, Inspector, on the morning in question — the fourteenth of the month — I saw a man go into that wash-room who never came out, and another man come out who never went in!'

Mr Potts looked at the two officers defiantly for a moment, as though challenging them not to believe him, and then gave vent to a good-humoured chuckle.

'I've been the butt of the other porters' jokes for the last fortnight,' he said. 'They reckon I must have been drunk, and seeing things, like. Or maybe I was going mad. 'We'll have to call you Potty Potts', they said. One of the ticket inspectors wondered whether I hadn't seen a ghost — the inspectors are a better class altogether than the porters, of course.'

'But the important point is, Mr Potts,' said Box earnestly, laying a hand on the man's sleeve, 'the important point is, that you believed that you'd seen something strange and inexplicable. Well, I rather think you did. So please tell Sergeant Knollys and me what it was exactly that you saw.'

'Well, gents, it so happened that on that particular Tuesday morning there'd been an overflow from one of the tanks feeding the stalls in the wash-room, and the floor was flooded. The foreman cleaner closed the door of the wash-room for fifteen minutes while he mopped up the mess and the station plumber adjusted the tank. So the door was closed for a while. This was at about twenty to nine — '

'And you were standing here, in this same spot where you are now?'

'Exactly the same spot, sir. I'd finished servicing the restaurant car, and was waiting for the train to depart. There was no point in going away, because another train with restaurant facilities was due in from the sidings ten minutes after the Edinburgh train had gone out.'

'So you had a bit of time on your hands. What happened next?'

'I saw the first of my two men hurry in

from the street, and make as though to enter the wash-room. When he saw that it was closed, he actually started back as though he'd been shot! Hello, I thought, what's up with him?'

'What kind of a man was he?' asked Box.

'He was an artisan of some kind, Mr Box. He wore a seaman's black jacket and a peaked cap, and carried a big carpet bag. A bearded chap, he was.'

Box took from an inside pocket of his coat the drawing that Sergeant Kenwright had made of the man who had called himself Michael Shane, and who had stayed at Mr Stanley's boarding-house in Carshalton. He showed the picture to Potts, who started in surprise.

'Why, that's him! Fancy you knowing that! Who is he? Some famous criminal, I'll be bound. Well, he hovered around impatiently until the door was opened again, and then he rushed in. Poor man! I thought he must have been desperate to obey a call of nature. In he went, Inspector — and never came out! I was there all the time, looking across the concourse, and the man in the naval jacket never came out of that wash-room. No wonder that Mr Cotton suggested that I might have seen a ghost.'

'It wasn't a ghost, Mr Potts. Not by a long

chalk. Now tell me about the other man — the man who came out of the wash-room who had never gone into it.'

'It was just after nine, as I recall,' said Potts, 'when a gentleman came hurrying out of the place as though the devil was after him. He was almost running, and I imagined that he was fearful of missing one or other of the trains. I could have sworn that the gentleman had never entered the wash-room in the first place. In fact, I *know* he hadn't. I'd have seen him, sure enough, if he had.'

'You didn't see him come through that barrier over there to catch the nine-five train to Edinburgh?'

'No, Inspector. There was quite a crush of passengers at that time, and in any case my attention was taken up with preparing for the next train.'

'Can you describe the man?'

'Yes, sir, He was a distinguished kind of man, bearded. I think he wore an eye-glass, though I'm not sure. He wore a frock coat and shiny top hat, and carried a light valise. So there's all I can tell you about my two men: the one who never went in, and the one who never came out.'

'Well, Mr Potts,' said Box, 'I can't tell you what all this is about, I'm afraid, but I can tell you that you've been of enormous help to the police. When your colleagues start ribbing you again about your two men, tell them that you were personally thanked for your assistance by Detective Inspector Box of Scotland Yard.'

* * *

'I think that ties it up, sir,' said Sergeant Knollys as the two men made their way across the crowded concourse to the men's wash-room. 'It was Professor Ainsworth, right enough. He arrived in his character of the workman with the carpet bag, went into a cubicle, and changed into his own gentleman's clothes. The delay at the door made him slightly late, but he caught the train none the less.'

'It would seem so, Sergeant,' said Box. 'But of course, all our supposition doesn't amount to legal proof. What did he do with the carpet bag? Incidentally, everyone's noted that it was a very large bag. It would need to be, if it were to carry not only the professor's outer clothes, but a top hat and valise into the bargain.'

'He would leave the carpet bag in the cubicle, sir,' said Knollys, 'knowing that it would be found, and lodged in the lost property office. It was a neat, clever plan.'

'It was, Sergeant, and, of course, it succeeded. No one would have found out about it if it hadn't been for Mr Mackharness shaking me out of my dreams of ancient magic and putting me on the right road again. Come on, let's have a word with the man in charge of the wash-room.'

The foreman cleaner occupied a narrow glazed booth at one side of the vast tiled wash-room. He was sitting on a chair, surrounded by mops and mop buckets, and what looked like drums of carbolic disinfectant. Yes, he remembered that day. No, he couldn't remember any particular man, workman or gentleman. All sorts came in there, and he was too busy mopping and cleaning up after them all to notice any individual customer.

Yes, he did remember finding a big carpet bag in the last cubicle on the far wall. He took it to the lost property office. People were always leaving things, umbrellas and walking-sticks, mainly. They propped them up against the walls while they were making use of the facilities, and then walked out without them. Some folk would leave their heads behind if they were loose.

They had no trouble in finding the carpet bag when they called at the lost property office. The counter clerk returned with it from his long lines of racks in minutes, and after they had shown him their warrants, he allowed them to open it. It contained a workman's trousers, jacket and boots, together with a peaked cap. This, without doubt, was all that was left of the fictitious Michael Shane, of the non-existent Cobb's Buildings, Hackney.

'There's dried blood on the bottom of the bag, Sergeant,' said Box. 'That's from when he put the bloodstained adze back, after killing Gregory Walsh in the Mithraeum. Afterwards, he hid his deadly weapon in the midden behind Greensands' shop.'

Sergeant Knollys turned his back on the carpet bag and leaned against the counter, looking across the station concourse. Hundreds of people were busily concerned with their own business, and none of them glanced in the direction of the two detectives. How many of those people, he wondered, harboured vile secrets?

'Sir,' said Knollys, 'all this means that the business of the honey, and the business of the mercury, were simply blinds. The honey and the mercury were no different from the crude imitations manufactured by your paltry murderer over the river in Rotherhithe. What kind of a man will violate the bodies of the people he had just slaughtered?'

'What kind of a man? A man who's had his moral senses blunted by fear — fear of discovery, I mean. And fear of exposure can make a decent man hate the one who's doing the exposing. Hatred, resentment — with sentiments of that kind to the fore, Sergeant, the frightened man ceases to see his prey as victims at all. He's simply annihilating living dangers. So he'll not scruple at pouring mercury down a dead man's throat, or spooning honey into his mouth. I've seen that kind of thing before.'

'It's horrible, sir.'

'Yes, it is, and that's why we've got to get on with the business of bringing this man to justice. I'm going to come out in the open, now, Sergeant, and name that man, without beating about the bush. No more ifs and buts. The ruthless and cruel killer of Gregory Walsh and Abraham Barnes is Professor Roderick Ainsworth! To my way of thinking, there can be no doubt whatever about that. But we're a long way from proving it, Jack, and there's a lot to be done yet.'

'Have you a plan in mind, sir?' asked Knollys.

'Yes, I have. First, I want you to reopen your investigation of Gregory Walsh's death. I'm still not clear *why* he was silenced. What did he know? Go and find that young woman of his — Thelma, wasn't it? — and talk to her and her new gentleman friend. Find out if Walsh had a particular friend, someone who he might have confided in. He didn't seem to have told Thelma very much, and after all, he didn't appear to be very welcome in the family laboratory, did he? That man Craven was jealous of him.'

'That's very true, sir,' said Knollys. 'I'll go to Hayward's Court first thing tomorrow. What are you going to do?'

'I'm going down by train to a place called Melton Castra, in Essex,' said Box. 'There's a lady living there who evidently knows a lot of interesting things about Professor Roderick Ainsworth. She's his second cousin, apparently, and an acquaintance of Mr Mackharness's old friend Lord Maurice Vale Rose. Lord Maurice has given me a letter of introduction to this lady — well, he actually gave it to Old Growler to give to me, if you see what I mean.'

'I wonder how it is that Mr Mackharness is so friendly with a lord?'

'Well, Sergeant, whatever else Old Growler is, he's definitely a gentleman. He's out of the top drawer, all right, is our guvnor. Lord Maurice is the younger brother of the Marquess of Killeen, and the two of them were together in the Crimea. That's the bond

260

that links them. They were both 'stormed at with shot and shell', and were glad to survive.'

'Well, I never knew that, sir. Thanks for telling me. Shall I give them a receipt for this carpet bag, and lug it back to the Rents?'

'Yes, Sergeant, do that. And then tomorrow, you and I will embark on what I hope will be the final leg of our journey to bring the killer of Gregory Walsh and Abraham Barnes to justice.'

★ ★ ★

Melton Castra proved to be a very ancient, straggling village of some size, with many picturesque houses adorned with the particular kind of pargeted plaster work found throughout Essex. Arnold Box booked a room for the night at a hostelry called The Sun Inn, and set out to interview Mrs Warwick Newman, the lady known to Lord Maurice Vale Rose, Superintendent Mackharness's old friend.

He walked to the end of the village street, and saw an old church set in a swathe of mature woodland, above which rose what looked like the extensive excavations of some prehistoric British archaeological site. A signpost placed at the entrance to a rustic path told him that it led to Melton Church. After a few minutes' walk he emerged from the trees into a clearing, where he saw a stone church with a squat tower and massive carved porch. It stood in an overgrown churchyard, bright with summer flowers, its many gravestones almost hidden by long, untrimmed grass. Both church and church-yard looked as though they had fallen asleep long ago, and would never waken.

Facing the church was an old Tudor house, its timbers twisted, and its roof covered with lichen. This, then, would be the Old Rectory, home of Professor Roderick Ainsworth's second cousin. Arnold Box walked through a riotous garden until he reached the house, and knocked on the black oak door.

★ ★ ★

'Lord Maurice tells me here in his letter,' said Mrs Warwick Newman, 'that you want to hear about Roddy Ainsworth's youthful days. He doesn't say why, and I'm not sure that I want to *know* why. Roddy and I are second cousins, but I'm much older than he is — I think there's fourteen years between us. You'll understand, I think, that I have not seen him for many years. We were not close, you know, though I liked him well enough. It would have been impossible not to like Roderick Ainsworth when he was a boy.'

Box listened to Mrs Warwick Newman's well-enunciated and silvery voice as he tried to form an estimate of her character. The parlour in which she had received him was well furnished, and everything was highly polished. A soothing old grandfather clock ticked away against one wall. Books and magazines were everywhere, but carefully arranged so as not to create any kind of disharmony. This lady believed in organization and neatness. No doubt her mind functioned in a way that was reflected in the arrangements of her home.

Mrs Warwick Newman was a woman well over seventy, with grey hair and rather faded blue eyes, that regarded Box appraisingly through gold-rimmed glasses. She was very well dressed in the fashions of the seventies, and Box realized that in addition to the elderly maid who had opened the door to him, she probably kept a personal maid to help her maintain her love of fastidiousness.

'Now, Mr Box,' she said, 'where shall I begin? Roderick, as you know, belongs to the Ainsworth family of shipbuilders up in Newcastle. They were related both to my late husband's family and to mine, and from the time that Roddy was fourteen, he came down here every year to stay with us for a few weeks in July and August. I was nearing thirty when he first came, and I immediately assumed the role of an admonitory elder sister.'

'Did you have to do a lot of admonishing, ma'am?' asked Box. His hostess laughed.

'Well, he was a lively boy, you see, the type of boy who falls out of trees, or breaks glasshouse windows — he was a very *physical* boy, if you can understand what I mean. He was very good-looking, and unfailingly cheerful and, despite his family's wealth, he mixed easily with the local boys. They went fishing together, and encouraged each other in all kinds of boyish mischief . . . '

Mrs Warwick Newman paused for a while, and Box watched her as she began to look more closely into the past.

'He had to have his own way, you know,' she said at last. 'My parents were alive then, of course — it was long before I married — and they tended to indulge him. I think they had been disappointed in having only one child, and that a girl into the bargain — me, you know! But I tried to teach him that the world had not been made entirely for him to bustle in. 'Yes, Bella', he'd say, and look suitably crestfallen, but he was never sincere in his repentance.'

'And did he always get his own way with

the village lads?' asked Box.

His hostess threw him a shrewd glance of understanding.

'He did not,' she replied. 'Boys of any class won't put up with anything like that. There were fights from time to time — quite ugly, bloody affairs, as only boys can manage. When these fights occurred, it would take a couple of grown men to pull Roddy away from his opponent. Thank goodness that he was only here for part of each summer! All that belligerence, I'm glad to say, stopped once he'd passed his sixteenth birthday, and he began to realize that there were other things in the world than fighting, playing village cricket, and so on.'

'What other things did he discover, ma'am? This is all very interesting.'

'He discovered the old earthworks above the village, Mr Box, and from that moment, I think he dedicated his whole life to archaeology. He was still only a youth, but he discovered a horde of Neolithic flint weapons up there on the ridge. It caused quite a stir, and brought Roddy to the attention of Mr Marcus Kent, the antiquarian, who lived some three miles from here. He took a great interest in Roddy, helped him to classify his finds, and lent him a quantity of books on prehistory, all of which he devoured. His personal collection of artefacts grew to quite impressive proportions, and his father realized that the boy had a promising future as an academic archaeologist.'

'I imagine that was unusual for an industrialist, ma'am,' Box ventured.

'I suppose it was, Inspector, but Roderick's father was a man of broad vision — perhaps that's why his shipyards prospered as well as they did. When Roddy was eighteen, his father made him experience the business at first-hand, and he spent three years in all departments of the yard. Roddy was more than willing to do this, as he knew that a successful business would furnish all his needs for the future.

'When the three years were up, Roddy entered upon what I call his academic phase. He entered London University as an undergraduate, and progressed from there. His rise was rapid, and his excavations, both in Britain and abroad, were of a high order. The rest of Roderick Ainsworth's career, Inspector, is public knowledge.'

Mrs Warwick Newman stopped speaking, and sat back in her chair. The old grandfather clock ticked away. Through the open window, Box could hear the sultry murmur of bees in the garden. She's waiting for me to challenge her story, he thought. Unless I do, she won't tell me the whole of it.

'I think there's more to Mr Ainsworth's early life than you've told me, ma'am,' he said, and fancied that the elderly lady gave an almost imperceptible sigh of relief.

'You're right, Mr Box,' she said. 'There is something that I haven't told you, and it's this: Roderick Ainsworth couldn't keep his hands off other people's goods. The difference between 'thine' and 'mine' was very blurred where he was concerned. He'd help himself to small sums of money lying around the house, or filch food from the larder, always from the back of a dim shelf, so the loss wasn't immediately noticed. Light-fingered, was my young cousin.'

'And it led to trouble?' Box hinted.

'It did. How clever of you to realize that. Certain items began to disappear from Mr Marcus Kent's house — medieval coins, old Celtic brooches — and it soon became obvious that they must have been purloined by Roddy. He hotly denied the suggestion, but it was all bluster. Mr Kent broke off all relations with the family, and soon afterwards Roddy's father called him back to Newcastle. He was nineteen by that time. He has never visited us here at Melton Castra since.'

Mrs Warwick Newman rose from her chair, and motioned to Box to follow her.

'Enough of Roderick for the moment, Inspector,' she said. 'Let me show you over our ancient church of St John the Baptist. Its foundations date back to the sixth century, and there's a lot of surviving Norman work. It's well worth a visit.'

They left the old rectory, and crossed the lane to the church. It was a hot, intensely quiet day, and Box could hear the crickets singing among the long grass growing up between the graves. They passed under the great carved porch and descended three steps into the cool, gloomy nave. Box followed his hostess as she walked slowly up towards the sanctuary, stopping occasionally to point out some carving or unusual feature that had survived from pre-Reformation times.

When she came to the chancel steps, Mrs Warwick Newman stopped, and pointed to a tall empty niche let into the north wall of the choir. Above it was an inscription in convoluted blackletter, painted on to the stone wall in a fanciful scroll. Box was no expert in such matters, but he could tell that the inscription was not of ancient date.

'Can you read what that says, Mr Box?' asked Mrs Warwick Newman. 'It's not in Latin, for a change. It was put up there on the wall in 1752.'

Box peered up at the scroll, and slowly read the inscription.

''I am that Great Giant, Old Bobbadil, who guardeth the folk of Melton'. And who was this Old Bobbadil, ma'am?'

'He was a piece of sculpture found buried beneath the chapel floor at Sir Lewis Dangerfield's house near Saffron Walden. He declared that it was Old Bobbadil, a giant-figure that features in many local legends and epic poetry in this corner of Essex. Dangerfield was patron of the living here at St John the Baptist's, and had the thing brought here and fixed into that niche. Before the Reformation, it had contained a shrine to the Baptist.'

'But Old Bobbadil's gone now, ma'am.'

'Yes, Mr Box, he's gone. He stood there, in that niche, guarding the folk of Melton Castra, for one hundred and thirty-seven years. And then, in 1889, he was stolen. Some villains came in the night, forced entry to the church, and carried Old Bobbadil off. No one ever found out who did the deed, and the rector, who's what I call a black gown and Bible man, was relieved to see the thing gone from his church. He came here in 1880, found candles and surplices in use, and initiated a second Reformation. He was no friend of Old Giant Bobbadil.'

Mrs Warwick Newman treated Box to an amused smile, and led the way out of the gloom of the church and back to the bright comfort of the Old Rectory.

'I have an old photograph of Bobbadil somewhere,' she said, when they had settled once again in their chairs. 'As far as I know, it's the only image of the thing extant. It was taken in 1858 by the rector in those days, Canon Julian Rodgers. I'll fetch it for you.'

Why has she drawn my attention to this old country legend? thought Box, when his hostess had quitted the room. She's gone as far as she dare in talking about young Roderick's indiscretions, but she's given me a lot to think about. Old coins, brooches . . . Did Ainsworth's light fingers run to acquiring post-Reformation chalices, ancient Roman artefacts, Mithraic seals?

'Here you are, Mr Box,' said his hostess, suddenly returning. 'It's rather faded, but you can see Old Bobbadil quite clearly, standing proudly in his niche.'

She placed the old photograph in Box's hands, and he studied the likeness of the legendary giant that had been wished upon the village by an eighteenth-century enthusiast for such things.

Box found himself looking at an emotionless, almost tranquil face, surrounded by a halo of curls, and topped with a leathern cap. Painted on to a slab of stone roughly resembling the Isle of Wight, it was, beyond all doubt, the same image, and painted on to the same piece of stone, that he had first seen in the Mithraeum at Clerkenwell.

14

Sir Charles Wayneflete's Story

In one of the airy classrooms at Glover's Lane Board School, a tall, redbrick building rising from a paved playground skirted with black railings, Sergeant Knollys found Ronald Evans, a friend and confidant of Gregory Walsh, the murdered analytical chemist. He had spoken earlier that morning to the dead man's former fiancée, Thelma Thompson, who had told him the name of the man who she thought was probably Gregory Walsh's closest friend.

'Greg wasn't a very sociable man, Mr Knollys,' she had said, 'and he met with little friendship from that dreadful fellow Craven in the laboratory. But there *was* another young man whom he saw quite often. They'd go for long walks together, and visit all kinds of museums and art galleries. Ronald Evans, his name was. He's an assistant usher at Glover's Lane Board School in Shoreditch.'

Evans proved to be a good-humoured, stolid young man of thirty or so, smartly dressed in a grey suit, and sporting one of the new round-ended stiff collars. He sat at a table raised upon a dais, where he was apparently making notes from a number of books laid open in front of him.

'Gregory?' he said, putting down his pencil, and sitting back in his chair. 'I still can't believe that he's dead, Sergeant Knollys. Who would want to kill a harmless fellow like Greg? He was just an ordinary man, you know, no different from me. Nobody important.'

Jack Knollys looked round the bright, spotless schoolroom. Gas lights with white enamel shades hung from the ceiling above the rows of desks and benches. The walls were adorned with charts and maps, including a massive representation of the British Empire. There was an illustrated table of the Kings and Queens of England, a glazed case containing a brilliant array of preserved butterflies, and shelves of well-used books. Beside Evans on the desk towered a pile of slates, each in its wooden frame.

Nobody important? To Knollys' way of thinking, men like Walsh, and this self-effacing board-schoolteacher, represented the future of the country. It was August, but in a week's time the summer recess would be over, and a crowd of boys, eager for knowledge, would flood back into this government school, where men like Evans would help to equip them for the better world that was coming in the next century.

'I've called on you here, Mr Evans,' said Sergeant Knollys, 'to ask you if Mr Walsh ever mentioned having been commissioned to perform some kind of task in the Mithraeum at Clerkenwell. Miss Thelma Thompson says that you were probably Mr Walsh's closest friend. Did he ever discuss what I'd call professional matters with you?'

'Yes, Mr Knollys, he did, from time to time. As for the Mithraeum — now I come to think of it, I remember his being engaged by a man to do some work there. What was it? Yes, he was to secure samples of paint from the great figure of Mithras, and analyse them. What he was supposed to find — or not find — I can't say, and he never told me.'

'And he was to take those samples on the morning of Tuesday, fourteenth August — '

'What? No, not at all, Sergeant. That's what puzzled me about his death. What was he doing in the Mithraeum on the fourteenth? No, he'd been engaged to procure the samples on the twenty-sixth of July. I assumed that he'd done the work, given this man the results, and been paid for it.'

'The twenty-sixth of *July*? Are you quite sure of that, Mr Evans?'

'Most assuredly, Mr Knollys,' said Evans, smiling. 'You see, I was actually present when he was given the commission! Let me tell you how it was.

'You know that Gregory lived with his father in Hayward's Court, over in Clerkenwell? Well, as you turn out of the court and in to St John Street, you'll find a quiet little public house called The Lord Nelson. One evening in July — I can't recall the exact day, but it would have been about the twentieth — Greg and I were sitting at a little table enjoying a glass of beer. I'd brought a newspaper with me, and I was holding it up, open, to read an article inside. You'll see why I mention that in a moment.

'Suddenly, I heard someone speaking to Gregory, and realized that a man had joined us at the table. 'Mr Walsh?' I heard this man say. 'You were recommended to me as a skilful chemical analyst. I'd be most grateful if you would undertake a small commission for me. It's a matter of taking samples of paint from the great reredos in the Mithraeum at Clerkenwell, and analysing them to determine the age of the paint that had been used to colour the image. Could you undertake the work for me?'

'At that moment, Sergeant Knollys,' said Evans, 'I put the paper down, and the man suddenly realized that I was a friend of Gregory's. He seemed very embarrassed, and rather vexed. I think he felt that he was betraying a business confidence by speaking so openly in front of a third party. He nodded civilly to me, but made no attempt to include me in the conversation.'

'This man — '

'He was a tall, spare man of about fifty, with thinning brown hair. Rather prim in his manner, and very well spoken, but not a gentleman.' Evans laughed with evident good-humour, and added, 'People in his walk of life, which is the same as mine, Mr Knollys, should never pretend to be what they're not!'

'And what did Mr Gregory Walsh say to this man?'

'He said that he'd be glad to accept the commission, and the man told him to meet him at the Mithraeum at seven o'clock on the morning of Thursday, twenty-sixth July. He apologized for the unusual way of doing business — he meant approaching Greg in a pub, you know — and half-produced a five-pound note from a pocket, which raised my eyebrows a little, but Gregory said that all commissions were welcome, and that an advance was entirely unnecessary.'

Jack Knollys finished writing his transcript

of Evans's account in his notebook, and looked once more at this unassuming schoolmaster. Why had he not told all this to the police? Almost immediately his own faculty of common sense told him the answer. The transaction in The Lord Nelson had seemed to Evans nothing more than a piece of professional business, which had been concluded long before poor Walsh had been murdered. In addition to that, the police had been chasing after practitioners of a non-existent cult of Mithras, and the papers had been full of that sensational development.

'You have an excellent memory for conversations, Mr Evans,' said Knollys. 'I don't suppose this man told Mr Walsh his name? I'm almost certain that I know who the man was, but the name would clinch the matter.'

'The man seemed unwilling to give his name, Sergeant, but, of course, Gregory insisted. He'd no intention of doing work for a man who was afraid to give his name. So Gregory asked him, and the man told him that his name was Crale.'

Jack Knollys took his leave of the Shore-ditch schoolmaster, and walked thoughtfully away from Glover's Lane. When Mr Box returned from Essex that afternoon, they would have much to tell each other. But wherever the guvnor's tale took them, it was time for them both to pay an official call on prim Mr Crale's previous employer, Sir Charles Wayneflete.

★ ★ ★

Box and Knollys called upon Sir Charles Wayneflete at his house in Lowndes Square on the following morning. Neglected and forlorn, its peeling white stucco and crumbling stonework contrasted tellingly with the smart town houses on either side. In response to their ringing of the bell, a grim woman answered the door, and stood back to let them enter.

'Sir Charles is expecting you, Mr Box,' she said, and there was something in her tone that told the inspector that she had expected him to ring the tradesman's bell at the kitchen door down the area steps. 'I am Mrs Craddock, the housekeeper here. Please follow me.'

The woman preceded them to Sir Charles Wayneflete's study on the ground floor, announced them both, and withdrew.

Box's first impression was that he had entered a small provincial museum. The room was crammed with antique tables and bookcases, upon which had been arranged collections of coins in velvet-lined cases, busts of the Caesars, pieces of Renaissance sculpture, and dark old paintings in dull gold frames. A curious set of chess men, carved from some kind of green stone, stood on a small table.

As the inspector's eyes became more accustomed to the dim light of the room, he saw more and more souvenirs of a long life of exploration emerging from the shadows. Everything, he noted, had been carefully dusted, and although the carpet was threadbare and the upholstery of the modern chairs thin and frayed, the room was spotless. The grim custodian of all these antiquities who had admitted them to the house was evidently devoted to her master.

Two men were sitting in chairs on either side of the fireplace. One of them was smartly dressed in a morning suit with frock coat. The other was wearing an old tweed suit that had seen better days, and Box noted that he was wearing detachable paper cuffs to his shirt.

'Inspector Box,' said the smart man, 'I am Sir Charles Wayneflete. I received your note this morning. Sit down. And you, Sergeant Knollys. This gentleman is my friend Major Baverstock. You may speak quite freely in front of him. Now, state your business, if you please.'

The voice was that of a man who had once

assumed that all his commands would be obeyed; but now there was something provisional in his tones that suggested a failing authority. His frail, narrow face, with its fringe of old-fashioned whiskers, betrayed a man in poor health who at that very moment was experiencing acute fear. Was Sir Charles Wayneflete afraid of the police? It might be a good idea, thought Box, to startle this gentleman into talking by dispensing with any preliminaries.

'Sir Charles,' he said, 'I am the officer investigating the murders of Gregory Walsh and Abraham Barnes, the former in the Mithraeum at Clerkenwell, and the latter at his residence in Carshalton. In connection with these murders, I want you to tell me all that you know about Professor Roderick Ainsworth, and his impostures.'

That's done the trick, thought Box, as he saw the baronet flinch and turn very pale. If Jack and I just wait, he'll start to speak without prompting. He's looking at his old friend Major Baverstock, now, and the major's just given him the nod.

'This is all in the strictest confidence, mind!' said Wayneflete.

'Of course, sir,' said Box. 'Please continue.'

'I'd had my suspicions about Ainsworth's Mithraeum from the beginning,' said Sir

Charles, 'long before he lured that damned scoundrel Crale away from me. You know who Crale is, I expect?'

'Yes, sir,' said Box. 'I know all about Mr Crale and his doings.'

'I wish I'd consulted you earlier,' Sir Charles continued. 'Josh, there — Major Baverstock — wanted me to go to Scotland Yard with my suspicions, but I didn't. I was afraid, you see. Afraid of him. I'm helpless here, partly crippled by a stroke, and if he found out that I'd been giving voice to my suspicions, he'd come here and do for me — '

A note of panic came into the old baronet's voice, and he began to tremble.

'Steady on, Charles,' said Major Baverstock. 'Get a grip, there's a good fellow!'

You're old, my friend, thought Box, glancing at the major, but you're still a military man. Those are keen, resolute eyes peering out from beneath those bushy brows.

'I'd known for years that much of Ainsworth's work lacked integrity,' Sir Charles continued, 'and there had been rumours in certain circles that all was not quite right with the inventoried items of the Clerkenwell Treasure, which he discovered in '87. Nothing was said openly, you understand.'

'You say there had been rumours, Sir Charles,' said Box. 'What kind of rumours were they, and who spread them?'

Sir Charles Wayneflete frowned, and bit his lip. He looked both vexed and petulant. He glanced at Major Baverstock, as though seeking his opinion as to what he should reply to Box's question.

'For goodness' sake, Charles,' said the major, '*tell him*! He's already promised you that everything you say is in the strictest confidence.'

'Oh, very well,' said the old baronet. 'You don't know what it's like, Box, crawling round the house, never getting out, having to rely on one domineering old woman for everything — I'm helpless! And I'm frightened, I tell you — frightened of what Ainsworth may take it into his head to do. Crale will have told him everything about me, and revealed to him all that I already know — '

'Then why don't you tell me what you know, sir? I can use that knowledge for your protection. Now, what were these rumours about the Clerkenwell Treasure, and who spread them?'

'I don't know whether you know or not, Box,' said Wayneflete, 'but I am a Roman Catholic — all the Waynefletes are — and there are certain priests and others who know a great deal about that treasure. The Rector of St Etheldreda's knows all about it, and so does the superior of the Redemptorist Fathers out at Highgate. It was from one of their priests that I learnt about certain irregularities — '

'Would that priest have been the Reverend Father Brooks, of Highgate?'

'So you know him? Then I expect you know what I mean by irregularities?'

'I do, sir. And if you will confide to me your thoughts about the Mithraeum, I believe I can tell you something that is almost certainly unknown to you. What made you think that the Clerkenwell Mithraeum was not all that it seemed?'

Sir Charles Wayneflete settled himself back in his chair, and motioned towards the little table drawn up to the fireplace. His old friend the major rose, and mixed him a whisky and soda, which he placed into his hand. Sir Charles sipped the drink slowly, at the same time fixing his eyes on Box. Eventually, he spoke.

'There was never the slightest suggestion in the academic journals of a Roman temple in Clerkenwell, Box, but there *was* talk of a Roman grain store that had been preserved somewhere in the neighbourhood. It had been mentioned in an eleventh-century manuscript kept at a place called Morpeth, and there were fragmentary references to it in a collection of thirteenth-century merchants' correspondence preserved in Dr Lewis's Library at Lambeth.

'I wondered whether Ainsworth had not stumbled upon that grain store at the time that he discovered the Clerkenwell Treasure, and saw possibilities in its future exploitation. It would have been like him, you see. He is an expert archaeologist, but he has the soul of a charlatan.'

'And how would he have exploited that place, sir?' asked Box. 'What do you think he did? All this is in complete confidence. This conversation will not be written up in my notebook, or that of Sergeant Knollys.'

'I'm glad to hear it,' said the old baronet drily. 'I think Ainsworth must have contrived to assemble a collection of quite genuine pieces of Roman sculpture and incorporated them into something resembling a pagan altar. I remember how he claimed to have found various artefacts — coins, and so on — and that he was careful to have them validated by unimpeachable experts. I don't doubt their validity, but where did they come from? I couldn't fathom how he got all that stuff down there into the old Roman vault, but once it was open briefly to the public, I saw one way of finding out if the whole thing was a fraud or not.'

'The mortar between the pieces.'

'Ah! You know about that? Well, of course you do. Yes, the mortar. I hit upon the idea of secretly procuring samples of the mortar between the fragments, and then hiring an expert in such matters to analyse them. The results, I am convinced, would have been conclusive. The next thing I did — '

'Would you pause there, if you please, Sir Charles,' said Box, holding up a hand. 'Let me see if I can piece together from my own thoughts and certain knowledge what you did. First, you told your secretary Crale to go to the Mithraeum at some early time in the morning, and take scrapings from between the separate pieces from which the reredos was created. This would have been in early July.'

'Quite right, Inspector! How clever of you!'

'Crale did as he was bid, and returned with four samples — '

'*Three* samples. It was I who added a fourth one, scraped from an old wall in my rear garden here in Lowndes Square. That was a sort of private test, you see. I wondered what an analytical chemist would have made of it. Anyway, Crale brought back those samples, and I added my fourth sample to the collection. Then I wrote to a professional man who had been of great service to me over twenty years ago in determining the age of some stone footings which I had unearthed at a dig in Essex. Damn it, man, you'll know who I'm talking about. It was Mr Abraham Barnes, who was recently slaughtered in his own house at Carshalton. His murder was disguised as a ritual sacrifice, wasn't it? What rot! I can imagine who did it, right enough — '

'Charles!'

'Oh, don't worry, Josh, I'll not risk slander over such a serious matter. Anyway, Inspector, I sent off those samples to Mr Barnes, knowing that he had a great interest in cement and its history. I didn't tell him why I wanted the work done, you understand. I told him that it was part of an intellectual exercise.'

Sir Charles Wayneflete sighed, and shook his head rather mournfully.

'And then, Box,' he said, 'I heard nothing from Barnes, and when I read of his death in the papers, I took fright. Cause and effect, you know. I assume that he didn't live long enough to undertake my commission, and that his executors would dispose of the samples as something poor Barnes had just hoarded out of curiosity. I don't suppose I'll ever know what became of those scrapings.

Damn me, what a mess it all is! I should have left well alone — What's this you're showing me? Good God!'

While the old baronet was talking, Box had produced the old photograph that Mrs Warwick Newman had given him during his visit to Melton Castra.

'So I was right!' cried Wayneflete. 'The fellow assembled various obscure pieces of genuine Roman work, cemented them together, and set them up in that old Roman grain store. I wonder where he got that head of Mithras? And the other pieces, come to that. And how did he put them all together without anyone seeing him?'

'I don't know, sir,' said Box, 'though I mean to find out. And now, here's something else that will please you. These four packets contain the samples that you sent to Mr Barnes. He in turn sent them to a man called Bonner, who analysed them, and returned them on 23 July. For some reason, Mr Barnes delayed sending the results to you, and he died before he could do so. But as you can see, Mr Bonner, the chemist, inscribed each envelope with a brief description.'

'So he has!' cried the old baronet. 'Really, Inspector, you've excelled yourself in this business. Let's see what they say. 'Definitely Ancient Roman. Lime, Sand, Water.' That was the first sample, which Crale told me he'd scraped from between two slabs of stone near the base of the reredos. 'Modern, i.e. this century' — Crale told me that that was taken from around the section containing the head of Mithras that you've just shown me.

''Definitely Ancient Roman': Crale scraped that from between two of the dressed stones constituting the right-hand wall of the vault. That confirms my belief that the vault itself is indubitably Roman. And finally, 'Not Roman, Probably 17th century.' That was the sample which I scraped from my garden wall here, in Lowndes Square. I know for a fact that it was built just after 1605. So there you have it, Mr Box. Professor Roderick Ainsworth's Mithraeum is a monstrous fraud!

'It's very interesting, you know,' he continued. 'Although Ainsworth's reredos was made up of separate fragments, some of the fragments themselves must have been damaged and repaired in antiquity. I refer to the two slabs of stone near the base of the monument. The mortar joining them together was indubitably Roman. A fascinating puzzle, Inspector!'

Major Baverstock, who had made no attempt to join in the conversation, suddenly asked a question.

'What will you do now, Mr Box? This

business is bound to cause a great scandal.'

'Well, sir,' said Box, 'this kind of academic fraud is not strictly a crime, unless the perpetrator profits from it financially. Academic reputations are not my concern. What *does* concern me is murder, and the motives for murder. So I have a few more questions to ask, and then Sergeant Knollys here will have something to say.'

Box turned once more to Sir Charles Wayneflete.

'Will you tell me, sir, when Mr Crale left your employ? Did you dismiss him?'

Box saw how Sir Charles Wayneflete glanced uneasily at his old friend Major Baverstock. Perhaps the two men had disagreed over the fate of Sir Charles's secretary.

'I received a letter,' said Sir Charles, 'saying that Crale had been pawning things of mine at a shop in the City Road, and that he'd done the same kind of thing when working for a previous employer. The letter mentioned some of the items — an old silver cruet, a couple of Meissen figurines. It was signed 'A Well-wisher'.'

'An anonymous letter . . . What did you do about it, sir?' asked Box.

'Mrs Craddock looked for those things, and found that they were, indeed, missing. I confronted Crale with the letter, but he denied all knowledge of the thefts. He was very calm and dignified about it, I must say, and he tendered his resignation with immediate effect. That was on the 28 July. He left the house the same day, and wrote a brief note on the following Monday to tell me that he'd accepted employment in the household of Professor Ainsworth.'

Poor old gentleman, thought Box, He's not wise to the sinister tricks that men like Crale can play. What he'd just heard was a prime example of the Footman Tanner imposture. This was a wheeze for leaving one employer in order to carry all his secrets to another, who'd pay well for them. You got yourself dismissed for a crime that you'd never committed, in order to take up a post with a man who wasn't too meticulous about the truth.

'If you get your housekeeper to search more thoroughly, sir,' he said, 'I think you'll find that those little treasures of yours are still in the house. Crale would have hidden them, and arranged for that letter to be sent, so that he'd have a decent excuse to leave your service. It's an old wheeze, sir, as we say in the trade.'

'Well, I'm damned! Did you hear that, Josh? So that villain Crale will have told

Ainsworth all about my attempts to prove his precious Mithraeum to be a fraud. He'd have known all about poor Barnes — '

'Yes, sir, he'd have known all about Mr Barnes, and all about Mr Gregory Walsh, too. I can see that you're about to draw some very unpleasant conclusions, but I'd beg you not to give voice to them. Leave those conclusions to the police. I want you to listen now to what Sergeant Knollys has to say.'

Box glanced at his sergeant, who drew a notebook from his pocket, and opened it. As Knollys spoke to the old baronet, he refreshed his memory from time to time by glancing at a closely written page of notes.

'Sir Charles,' Knollys began, 'this man Crale, while he was still in your employ, commissioned Mr Gregory Walsh to secure samples of paint or pigment from the reredos in the Clerkenwell Mithraeum. Did he do so at your instigation?'

'Yes, that's right, Sergeant. I was vexed at having to wait so long for Abraham Barnes to return the analysed samples of mortar, and decided to look into the matter of the pigments used on that monument. I told Crale to find someone suitable to undertake the work, and to engage him as though the commission were his instead of mine. He found this young man Walsh, and arranged for him to go to the Mithraeum on Thursday, 26 July, at a time when I knew that Ainsworth would be engaged elsewhere.'

'And did you ever receive the results of that commission, sir?' asked Knollys.

'No, Sergeant, I did not. In the event, I received *nothing*, either from this man Walsh or Abraham Barnes. And then, on the fourteenth August, both men were murdered . . . I drew some very sinister conclusions, looked to my own safety, and decided to forget the whole business. But your visit today had shown that I was right in believing Ainsworth to be a charlatan.'

There was little more to be said, and some minutes later Box and Knollys took leave of Sir Charles Wayneflete. Major Baverstock accompanied them into the hall, and himself opened the front door. Box detained him for a moment, by placing a hand on his arm.

'Major,' he said, 'I think that Sir Charles Wayneflete is in very real danger, and I intend to place a police guard on this house night and day until this murderous business is finished. Would you undertake to tell him that?'

'I will, Inspector, and I'll say at once how relieved I am. He might be titled, but he's quite powerless and without influential friends. Consider this Ainsworth business for a moment: who would believe anything that Charles said against the popular idol? They'd say it was sour grapes, jealousy — or, worse still, senility. That's why he's kept silence for so long. He's supposed to be an amateur, but for all that he's a very exact scholar, who's admired in the more informed university circles.'

The untidy, rather neglected old soldier glanced around the gaunt, faded hall of the house with honest distaste.

'You know, Mr Box,' he said, lowering his voice, 'Mrs Craddock and I are hatching a plot to get poor Charles out of this place. I've a little put by, and if he would sell the lease of this house, and some of those awful antiquities of his, we could buy one of those snug little cottages they're building out at Chiswick. They call them cottages, you know, but they're really gentlemen's bijou residences. The three of us could live there in comfort.'

'I wish you well in that project, Major Baverstock,' said Box. 'Sir Charles might not have powerful friends, but he's certainly got a very loyal one — I mean you, sir! And now he's got another friend, one that I think has more power than Professor Ainsworth could successfully resist.'

'And what powerful friend is that, Mr Box?'

'Scotland Yard,' Box replied.

He and Knollys shook hands with the major, and stepped out into Lowndes Square.

'Sergeant,' said Box, as the two men walked out of the square in the direction of Hyde Park, 'when that man Crale arranged for Walsh to go to the Mithraeum on the 26 July, he'd already been lured away from his employer by Ainsworth. He pulled the Footman Tanner wheeze on the 28th, and by the following Monday he was working for Ainsworth. I bet you anything that Crale cancelled that appointment for the 26th, and told poor Walsh to turn up on the 14 August instead — '

'The very day,' said Knollys, 'that the good professor was due to entrain for Edinburgh. So we could say that Ainsworth conspired with Crale to lure Gregory Walsh to his death. Perhaps Crale was used in some way in the Carshalton murder, too.'

'Perhaps he was, Jack, and I've already concocted a little plot to make Mr Crale eat out of our hands when the time comes. I want to pay another visit, first, to the late Mr Barnes's house and works at Carshalton. There are a few questions I want to ask the impudent widow, who's probably now in complete charge of the place.'

'And after that, sir?'

'After that, Sergeant, I'll give our Mr Crale my full attention. And then you and I will pay a call on the Subterranean Pipe Office of the London County Council, which, as you know, is in Spring Gardens, just five minutes' walk from King James's Rents. There's something they've got there that I very much want to see.'

15

The Ubiquitous Mr Crale

Arnold Box stood in front of the solid, four-square granite house in Carshalton where the murdered cement manufacturer Abraham Barnes had lived and died. The name 'Wellington House' on the gateposts had been freshly gilded, and new, crisp lace curtains adorned every window. Evidently the predatory widow, Laura Barnes, had started to make her presence felt.

What, Box wondered, had happened to the thin, pale and tearful daughter, Hetty Barnes? The widow had told him that Hetty would have to manage on a competence elsewhere: it had been clear even then that Laura would not suffer her stepdaughter to remain at Wellington House.

He rang the bell, and in a moment the front door was opened by a smart, pretty girl of twenty or so, wearing the black dress and ribboned cap of a house parlour-maid. She curtsied, took Box's card, and asked him to sit down in the hall. Missus, she told him, would be out in a moment.

There was a strong smell of paint everywhere, and the gloom that had pervaded the house on his last visit seemed to have been very effectively dissipated. He wondered whether the widow had married the shifty Mr Harper yet, and whether all this decoration was a celebration of their tasteless and rather sinister alliance.

The door of the drawing-room opened, and an elegant woman emerged to greet him. She wore a fashionable morning dress of brown silk adorned with cream lace. 'Inspector Box!' she exclaimed, giving him her hand. 'This is an unexpected pleasure! Come into the drawing-room.'

Box followed the lady of the house into the room where he had first encountered the family of Abraham Barnes. His mind was reeling! He had only just recognized the lady as the tearful, faded daughter, Hetty. What miracle had transformed her into this commanding and handsome lady? And where was the hard-bitten widow, Laura Barnes?

'I can see that you're rather nonplussed, Mr Box,' said Hetty, smiling, and motioning him to sit down. Like the hallway, the drawing-room was in the process of being redecorated. Rolls of red flock wallpaper stood upright like ship's funnels against one wall. 'Let me very briefly explain what occurred here after your last visit.

'My father's will was produced and read on the 17 August, just two days after you came here. He left his widow Laura an annuity of a hundred and fifty pounds. Everything else, including this house, the cement works, and all his accrued savings, he left to *me*.'

'I'm delighted to hear it, Miss Barnes,' said Box, and the sincerity of his words was so obvious that Hetty knew they were rather more than a conventional reply. His kindness would encourage her to speak more frankly to him of family matters.

'I was astounded,' Hetty continued, 'and somehow, realizing that poor Father had loved me best all along, brought me out of my shell. I don't just *seem* a different woman — I *am* a different woman! I've decided to develop the works along the lines suggested by Mr Harper, and I think that, in a year's time, the Royal Albert Cement Works will be transformed.'

'And have you engaged a new manager to assist you, Miss Barnes?' asked Box. 'I should think you'd need an experienced person to help you manage a concern of this nature.'

The elegant lady suddenly treated Box to a smile of triumph, a smile that was at one and the same time joyful and cruel. She pulled the bell hanging beside the fireplace, and almost immediately the pretty young maid appeared. She glanced rather apprehensively at Box, and then addressed her mistress.

'You rang, ma'am?'

'Mary,' said the lady of the house, 'tell the master to come here at once.'

The maid curtsied, and went out. Within the minute the door opened, and the handsome young works manager, Mr Harper, came in to the room.

'Did you ring for me, my dear?' he asked. Seeing Box, he actually blushed in confusion, rapidly turning his discomfiture into a kind of servile bow.

'It was just to let you know, James, that Inspector Box has called to see me privately. I thought it right that you should know. Have the furnace-liners arrived yet? They were due here at ten.'

'They're here now, my dear. I'd better go and attend to them. Goodbye, Mr Box, Pleased to meet you again.'

As the young man left the room, Hetty held up her left hand for Box to see the thick gold band gleaming on her marriage-finger.

'Yes, Mr Box,' she said, 'I am Mrs James Harper, now! We were married by special licence ten days ago. James and I will agree well together, and between us we'll make our name resound in the building industry.' She glanced briefly at her father's portrait where it hung over the fireplace, surrounded with black mourning-crape.

'Dear Father! He left everything *entailed* to me, you know. If James wants to make his fortune, he'll have to make it from the future profits of the company. He knows that, too.'

Mrs Harper treated Box to a shrewd but not unpleasant smile. She was evidently enjoying her new status as the undoubted mistress of Wellington House and its occupants.

'I always liked him, you know,' she continued, 'even though I pretended not to. That's because Laura — well, never mind about her. James has got a good business head on his shoulders, as well as being a very presentable man.'

'And what happened to Mrs Laura Barnes, ma'am, if I may be so bold as to ask?'

'Laura? Well, she's fled across the river to live with her spinster sister in Somers Town. I hope she'll be very happy there. But I don't suppose you've come down here to ask after Laura, have you? It'll be about poor Father's murder. How can I help you?'

'I want to ask you a question, ma'am, about some samples of mortar that your late father had sent to a man called Bonner to analyse. Mr Bonner returned these samples by post on the 23 July. Your father was supposed to forward them to a gentleman living in London, but never did so. I gather that Mr Barnes was an efficient business man. Can you account for his failure to forward those samples?'

'Father was very busy all July, and he probably thought that these samples could wait until he was less pressed for time. What were they — some private matter? Yes, I thought so. Father would have let them wait until he had time to see to them. Matters concerning the business always had priority.'

'Was Mr Barnes away from Carshalton at any time in July?'

'Yes, he was. He went up to Birmingham to see our accountants on the 31 July — which was a Tuesday — and returned here on the third. After that, Inspector, I suppose he kept putting off this business of the samples until — well, until it was too late.'

Mrs Harper glanced briefly at her father's portrait, and bit her lip. She seemed to be struggling with some emotion which Box thought might have been vexation. She's making up her mind to tell me something, thought Box, and if I just stay quiet and say nothing, she'll tell me what it is. Something to do with her late father, I'll be bound.

'I'll leave you now, Inspector,' said Mrs

Harper, rising from her chair. 'I'm going to send my maid, Mary, to talk to you. You guessed, I think, that she was my only confidant when this house fell under the bane of that woman? Well, she remains so still, and very recently she told me something about my father which I think you should hear. It explains why he came down, fully clothed, into the conservatory on that fatal night — the night when he met his terrible death.'

★　★　★

At Box's bidding, the maid Mary had positioned herself gingerly on the edge of an upright chair. Like any well-trained servant, she felt uncomfortable at sitting down in the reception rooms of her mistress's house. She was nervous, Box noted, and a little frightened.

'Sir,' Mary began, 'I'm going to tell you what happened on the night of the fourteenth, when Mr Barnes was killed, but before that, I'm going to tell you about him and Mrs Barnes, and what took place on 8 August — '

'When you say Mrs Barnes — '

'Sir, if you interrupt me, I'll get all flummoxed. Just let me tell you things in my own way, asking pardon, sir, for being so

302

forward. The first Mrs Barnes was a nice lady, but the second one, Mrs Laura, was very flighty. I don't think there was much to it, myself, but she had an eye for attractive men like Mr Harper. And there were others she'd make up to, if I cared to name names, which I don't. There was no real harm in it, but Mr Barnes, he was ever so jealous! He used to lay traps for her, and later you'd hear him saying things like, 'Who was that young man you were speaking to in the shrubbery? Why do you go into Carshalton every day? Who are you seeing?' Things like that.

'And then one day — it was the 8 August, a Wednesday — a man called at the house while she was out, and asked to see Mr Barnes. He wouldn't give his name. I showed him into the morning-room, and Mr Barnes came through from the works to see him. There's a little pantry leading off the morning-room, and I went in there to dust some crockery. I wasn't really listening, but I heard this man say that he was a private detective, and that he had evidence to show that Mrs Barnes was seeing a man secretly in Carshalton. He used a funny word — candlestine, some word like that.'

'Clandestine. It just means secret.'

'That's right: that's the word he used. I shouldn't have stayed, but I was ever so interested! The master was very upset. 'I knew it!' he cried, and things like that. The detective then told him that he could prove what he'd said, by taking him to a place here in Hackbridge, where he'd find the couple, meaning this man and Mrs Laura Barnes, together in — in something or other. It was French, I think.'

'*In flagrante delicto.*'

'That's right. Master and Mistress had separate bedrooms, you see, so I suppose it was possible. And then the detective said that he would meet Mr Barnes in the conservatory at three o'clock in the morning of the 15 August, and lead him to the house where Mrs Barnes and this man would be. I wondered, myself, who'd engaged this detective, because poor Mr Barnes obviously hadn't. Anyway, the master never asked him. Had it been me — '

The maid stopped speaking, and looked a little confused.

'Had it been you, Mary, what would you have done?'

'Well, sir, I'd have waited until the morning of the fifteenth, and then I'd have peeped into the mistress's room to see whether she was there or not. But he didn't, when that day dawned.'

'What happened after Mr Barnes and the

detective had finished speaking?'

'They left the morning-room, sir, and I slipped back to the kitchen. In a moment the hall bell rang, and I went to show the detective man out.'

'Can you describe this detective to me, Mary?' asked Box. 'You've told me some very valuable things so far. What did this man look like?'

'Well, he was about fifty, I'd say, with brown hair going bald. Nicely spoken, he was, with a quiet voice. He was wearing a dark overcoat and a black bowler hat. He was tall, and rather thin. He looked more like a manservant than a detective, but that might have been a disguise, mightn't it?'

'Perhaps,' Box replied. Secretly he thought to himself: no, he wasn't a detective, and he wasn't a manservant. He was a certain Mr Crale, secretary and sneak. He asked Mary to continue with her story.

'I thought about that man, and what he'd said about Missus, for a long time, and then I made up my mind to watch what happened in the early hours of the fifteenth. I didn't mean any harm, and I never thought there was going to be a murder — '

'Of course you didn't, Mary,' Box reassured the now tearful maid. 'Now, don't start to cry. Just tell me what you saw.'

'At about half past two — this was in the dark hours of the morning, on the fifteenth — I crept downstairs and went into the little flower-room off the conservatory. I hid myself in an alcove beside the big cupboard there, and left the door slightly open. Nothing happened for what seemed ages, and while I waited, the pitch dark seemed to grow lighter, and I could see the potted plants, and some pieces of furniture. They say, don't they, that your eyes can get used to the dark?

'Suddenly, I heard the French window creak open, and a man stepped quietly into the conservatory. It was him — the detective man. I watched him as he stood there, and I could hear his breathing. He sounded as though he'd been running. But — '

Mary suddenly turned pale, and began to tremble. Box placed a reassuring hand on hers. What ailed the girl? What had she seen?

'Sir,' said Mary, making an effort to regain her composure, 'I suddenly felt that there was *someone else* in the conservatory! There was a kind of stirring in the darkness at the far end, as though someone was concealed there. It was horrible! I think the detective man felt it, too, because he made a funny little frightened sound, and half made to bolt for it. But he held his ground, and a few moments later the master came in from the house. He

306

was fully dressed, but he hadn't put on an overcoat.

''Is that you?' he whispered, and his voice sounded cruel and gloating. Somehow, it didn't seem like the master at all, but it was him, sure enough. 'Yes, it's me', the detective said. 'Follow me quietly, Mr Barnes'. The detective turned and almost ran out of the window into the dark garden, and then — and then a black shadow suddenly reared up out of the darkness, Mr Barnes cried out, and there was a terrible thud, followed by the sound of something heavy falling to the floor. I saw and heard nothing else, sir, because I fainted away with fright.'

The girl now began to sob quietly, hiding her face in her hands. Here was the witness I should have interviewed at the outset of this case, thought Box. She was here when I first visited the house, but I never thought to speak to her. She witnessed her master's murder, but fear made her keep her own counsel. What had made her tell him the truth now?

'I was terrified, sir,' Mary continued, 'and told nobody about what I'd seen, not even Miss Hetty, as she was then. I tried to forget it, and pretend that it had been all a dream. But when Miss Hetty became mistress of the house, and married Mr Harper from the works yard, I told her the whole story. She and I had been good friends, in spite of our different stations, and the time had come for her to know the whole truth. When she received your letter, saying that you were coming to see her again, she said that I had to tell you everything.'

So, thought Box, Ainsworth hid in the darkened room, and used Crale as his bait to lure his victim within striking-distance of his murderous adze. Had he used Crale in the same way at the Mithraeum? Crale could have made an appointment to meet young Gregory Walsh there, and Ainsworth could had been waiting, concealed in the vault, until Crale had left. Was Crale, then, privy to the two murders? It didn't necessarily follow. Crale was a mean-spirited, treacherous sneak, not the kind of man who would have the stomach for murder. What was the girl saying?

'I won't go to gaol, will I, sir? I was ever so frightened, and I'd no business to be out of my room in the attic when Master went downstairs to meet that detective man.'

'You should have told Inspector Perrivale at once, Mary,' said Box, 'and then you should have told *me*. It was very wrong of you to withhold evidence, and if you do anything like that again, you'll be in real trouble. But for this time we'll forget all about it. You see,

I know who the detective man is, and I also know who the shadow-man is. You told your story very well, Mary, which makes me suspect that you went to a good school. Am I right?'

'Yes, sir. I was educated at Epsom Church of England School for Girls. They wanted me to go on to train as a board-school teacher, but Mother couldn't afford to let me go. So I went into service. And you won't send me to gaol?'

'I will not, Mary. You'd take up a place there that someone more 'deserving' could occupy! It's time I caught a train to Epsom. There's more work waiting for me there.'

*　*　*

Box found Mr Crale sitting on one of several basket chairs set out in the garden of a rustic brick cottage, part of Professor Ainsworth's estate of Ardleigh Manor. He was wearing his well-fitting suit of sober grey, and on the grass beside him he had deposited a black bowler hat and a pair of dark gloves. He was smoking a cigarette, and looking across the garden hedge to the neighbouring garden, where his new house was rising. He caught sight of Box, half rose from his chair, and then apparently thought better of it.

'Why, Detective Inspector Box!' he said. 'How nice to see you again, sir. I'm afraid Professor Ainsworth is in London today. He's attending a meeting of the Senate at London University. Won't you sit down?'

'Thank you very much, Mr Crale,' said Box. 'So the professor's in Town today, is he? Well, it can't be helped.'

He knew perfectly well that Ainsworth would not be at home that morning. But then, it wasn't the professor he'd come to see.

'Having half an hour to spare, Mr Box,' said Crale, 'I thought I'd come out here and view the progress of my new house. It was originally intended for the head groom, but the poor fellow died in a fall last May, and when I came into the professor's employment, he very kindly offered the house to me. So very kind, you know, but then Professor Ainsworth is a very kind man.'

'I'm sure you're right,' said Box, settling himself beside the secretary in one of the basket chairs. 'Well, if the professor's not here today, I'll while away the time by telling you a story. Once upon a time, there was a man who worked for an elderly, crippled baronet, who was something of an invalid. The man proved very useful to his employer, and the old baronet made the mistake of thinking him trustworthy.

'One day, the old baronet told this man to engage an analytical chemist to examine the pigments used on a depiction of an old Roman god, which had been discovered by his rival, a famous archaeologist, in what was supposed to be an ancient Mithraeum. He suspected, you see, Mr Crale, that the depiction, and the monument containing it, were both fakes.'

'This man — who are you talking about, Mr Box? I fail to understand the purpose of this 'story', as you call it.'

Box watched the secretary as he licked his dry lips before venturing these few words. He's like that man in *The Ancient Mariner*, he thought. He'd like to cut and run, but he cannot choose but hear.

'Bear with me, Mr Crale,' said Box, 'and you'll see where all this is leading. The man — he was the old baronet's secretary — did as he was told, and contrived to meet a young man called Gregory Walsh in The Lord Nelson public house on the corner of St John Street in Clerkenwell. Acting as though for himself, the man arranged for Walsh to secure the paint samples on Thursday, 26 July.'

'Mr Box,' said Crale, 'there's no need to present all this as a story. 'The man', as you call him, was myself. I make no secret of the fact. Sir Charles Wayneflete told me to make those arrangements, keeping his name out of the matter if possible, and I did so.'

'Very commendable of you, Mr Crale,' said Box, 'no doubt they'll engrave those well-known words, 'Well done, thou good and faithful servant', on your gravestone — if you ever have one. It's possible, you know, that you'll end up under a prison flagstone, packed in quicklime. But you were not good and faithful, were you? You arranged to have yourself accused of a non-existent theft, so that you could resign with honour, and allow yourself to be lured away from Sir Charles and into the employ of his arch-enemy, Professor Roderick Ainsworth — '

'This is too much!' cried Crale, springing to his feet. 'I have no need to stay here listening to your insulting innuendoes. I shall make a complaint to Professor Ainsworth when he returns from London. Meanwhile, I'll leave you here to indulge your fantasies by yourself.'

'Sit down, Crale,' said Box quietly, 'bluster won't work here, my lad. Once in the professor's employ, you revealed all Sir Charles Wayneflete's secrets and suspicions to him. It was then that Ainsworth, realizing that exposure would mean the loss of his impending knighthood, and fellowship of the Society of Antiquaries, determined to silence the two men who could prove his frauds — Gregory Walsh, and a man living further up the line from here, at Carshalton, a man called Abraham Barnes. He decided to *murder* them, Mr Crale, and in you, his new secretary, he found a willing accomplice.'

'It's not true!' Crale's voice rose to a scream, and his face became drained of all colour. 'I knew nothing about murder!'

'Really? Do you think I'm naïve enough to think that Ainsworth gave you a brand new house out of the goodness of his heart? He knew that you'd do anything he asked for money, and decided to make you a down-payment of a desirable residence. Although you began to work openly for Ainsworth in August, you'd approached him earlier, and soon after you'd engaged Gregory Walsh to go to the Mithraeum on the 26 July, you saw the poor young man again in The Lord Nelson, and cancelled that appointment, knowing that your new master would be pleased that you'd forestalled Wayneflete in the exposure of his frauds. I'm right, aren't I?'

'Yes, but — '

'You and Ainsworth put your heads together, and chose the fourteenth August, which was a Tuesday, as the day on which, together, you would kill two birds with one stone. It was a well-laid plan. First, you went down to Carshalton, and posed as a detective, in order to deceive Mr Barnes, who had incriminating evidence against Ainsworth in his possession, into thinking that his new wife was being unfaithful. You said that you would furnish him with living proof if he would present himself in the conservatory of his house at three o'clock on the morning of the fifteenth August — '

'Yes, yes, it's all true!' cried the terrified secretary. 'But I tell you I knew nothing about murder. Ainsworth told me nothing. He just gave me orders, and I carried them out.'

'I see,' said Box, 'so you've now decided that Ainsworth is to take all the blame! I suspect that you were always a sneak and a toady, so it's no surprise that you're going to become a Judas as well. Did you know, that when you met poor Abraham Barnes in the conservatory of his house on that fatal night, there was a witness, watching you? That witness *saw* you do the deed — '

'It's a lie! Ainsworth told me to say a few words to Barnes, and then leave the house immediately and return to Epsom. It wasn't me that felled him with the adze!'

'Who was it, then, if it wasn't you? You must have known that Ainsworth had concealed himself somewhere in that conservatory.

My witness saw you quite clearly, and heard you exclaim as you realized that there was someone else there. The witness saw a shadow rise up and strike poor Abraham Barnes down. Whose was that shadow? Was it yours, or Ainsworth's?'

'It's not true,' moaned the terrified secretary. 'I knew nothing about murder.'

'I think otherwise, Crale, and so will any jury, when they've heard all the evidence. The two of you travelled by train to London immediately after Barnes's murder, and lay in wait for Gregory Walsh in the Mithraeum at Clerkenwell. It doesn't much matter which one of you committed that second murder, either. One of you was accessory to the other. You'll both hang.'

The ashen-faced man seized Box by the sleeve.

'What can I say to convince you that you're wrong?' he whispered. 'I admit that I carried out all Ainsworth's orders, and that I wasn't too particular about their consequences. I admit that I was in the conservatory of the house in Carshalton that night, because that was part of the pose of a detective that I had been told to adopt. But I swear to you that I thought the conservatory was empty. I fancied I heard a noise, but was convinced that I was mistaken. I came to that house alone. How was I to know that Professor Ainsworth was concealed there, bent on murder? I tell you, I knew nothing about murder! A servant does as he is told; he doesn't ask his master for reasons.'

'And what about your presence in the Mithraeum?' asked Box.

'I tell you, I was never there on that fatal morning! I can prove it. I was back here in Ashleigh Manor, and Mason, the butler, can vouch for the fact that I was here. He saw me at six o'clock, and I was here, in sight, all that morning.'

The man suddenly began to wring his hands in anguish. He looked the picture of despair. What a wretched, cringing fellow he is! thought Box. I never believed for one moment that he'd have the courage to commit murder, but I wanted to see him squirm. When Ainsworth tries to enlist his aid again, he'll find himself up against a brick wall.

'Very well, Crale,' said Box, standing up. 'I'm prepared to believe you. But you must take it from me that Professor Ainsworth is a double murderer, and that when he's brought to trial, it will be very difficult for you to claim that you weren't his accomplice. You'll be called as a witness, you see. I'll do what I can, but until then, do nothing more than

316

your duties as a secretary here. If you as much as listen to any further confidences from Professor Ainsworth, you'll make yourself an accessory after the fact of murder.'

16

Depths of Deceit

The Subterranean Pipe Office of the London County Council occupied premises in Spring Gardens, within a stone's-throw of Whitehall Place. In a long room on the first floor, Inspector Box and Sergeant Knollys stood at a draughtsman's table, examining a plan that the deputy engineer, a smart young man who had introduced himself as Percy Phelps, had just laid out for their inspection.

'It's very good of you, Mr Phelps,' said Box, 'to come in on a Saturday morning like this. It's much appreciated.'

'Not at all, Inspector,' said Phelps, 'I'm always happy to explain the fascinating business of public drainage. It's one of the great unsung triumphs of the late nineteenth century! We inherited boxes of these plans from the old Metropolitan Board of Works, and only a fraction of them have been freshly mapped. This one, as you can see, is one of our own devising, made earlier this year. It shows the area of Clerkenwell lying between Priory Gate Street — here, on the right of the plan — and Catherine Lane, at the bottom.

'Priory Gardens, which were laid out in 1890, are at the top. Below the gardens is the large area of slum clearance, which was done by the council between 1893 and 1894. The site contains the entrance to the Mithraeum, and abuts on to the derelict Miller's Court. At the bottom of the plan, in Catherine Lane, you can see the premises of Mr Gold, the wholesale jeweller, and the building known as Hatchard's Furniture Repository.'

'What is this little red square marked 'Flagstone', Mr Phelps?' asked Box. 'It has been drawn in the middle of the rectangle representing the premises of Hatchard's.'

'That flagstone can be found in many plans of this area,' Phelps replied. 'It was the entrance to the vaults of the old Church of St Catherine that used to stand on this site. It was situated on the south side of the nave floor. The church was burned down in the Great Fire of 1666, and never rebuilt. The present basement floor of Hatchard's is actually the cleared pavement of the old church's nave. Planners need to know about entrances to subterranean cavities, especially when contemplating the construction of new sewers.'

'And these thin lines in red, blue and green, criss-crossing the plan — '

'They are the various service pipes, Mr Box. The blue lines are water mains, and the red lines are live sewers. The green lines show sewers and water mains that have been closed off and sealed. As you can see, the whole upper area of the plan contains very little in the way of water and drainage. The whole area is due for redevelopment, you see. All the water pipes and sewers serving the buildings in Catherine Lane have been redirected to meet the new mains and deep sewer laid two years ago to the east of the site, beneath Phoenix Place.'

Phelps stopped speaking, and in the ensuing silence — for Mr Phelps was rather fond of his own voice — Box studied the plan. The whole area from behind the premises in Catherine Lane to Priory Gardens was a mass of green lines, each line bearing a reference number. It was, in effect, an arid desert, with minimal water and sewage.

'What can you tell me about the Mith-raeum site itself, Mr Phelps?' asked Box. 'I mean from your own professional point of view. I know all I need to know about the archaeological aspect.'

'Well, Inspector, that particular site is not only derelict but dangerous, and in the next six months it will be filled in, landscaped, and planted as an extension of Priory Gardens. Professor Ainsworth knew that the site could remain open for no longer than six months at the most. I believe he has planned to remove the antiquities from the old Roman vault, and present them to the British Museum.'

'He knew all along that the Mithraeum would have to be destroyed?' Box exclaimed. 'Are you sure of that?'

'Yes, indeed, Inspector. You sound as though you don't believe me. I told the professor myself. He came here, you see, to ask about the nature of the site, and whether it would be suitable for preservation. Very responsible of him, I thought. I told him that the exhibition of the antiquities could only be temporary.'

'And was he put out when you told him that?' asked Box.

'No, not really. He took the matter philosophically, and we parted in great amity.'

'Why do you say that the site is dangerous, Mr Phelps?'

For answer, Phelps produced another, much older, plan, which he laid on top of the first. It was dated 1854, and showed the clear outline of a medieval church lying beneath what was now Hatchard's Furniture Repository. A series of dotted lines delineated the long nave of the church, and its semi-circular apse. Once again, a little red square marked 'Flagstone' had been drawn at a particular spot in the floor of the nave.

'I'm showing you this plan, Mr Box,' said Phelps, 'to explain why the whole area around the Mithraeum is dangerous. The original burial vaults of that long-demolished church, although cleared of human remains in the seventeenth century, are still there, great empty spaces beneath the earth. Parts of them are represented by the basement area of Hatchard's, but there's another, unseen section, long sealed off. Nearby, but six feet lower down, is the Roman Mithraeum, another empty space.

'More important, though, is the presence now — I mean in September 1894 — of twelve vast empty sewer tunnels which are in a poor state of preservation. They had, in fact, been condemned for years by the Metropolitan Board of Works. The danger of collapse is very great, Mr Box, which is why the area of the Mithraeum will be shored up, filled in, and levelled as a public garden. There's talk, I believe, of turning that upper section of the site into a pleasant residential square. When the time comes, we'll tell Professor Ainsworth to remove his Roman monument to the British Museum.'

Box, looking at the young engineer, made

a sudden decision. The time to act in this matter of the so-called Mithraeum was now, and Mr Percy Phelps should play his part in this, the last stage of the murderous drama.

'Mr Phelps,' he said, 'I have already obtained a search warrant to investigate the premises in Catherine Lane, Clerkenwell, known as Hatchard's Furniture Repository. I can assemble my search-party within the hour, and my search would take us down beneath that mysterious flagstone marked in red on these plans. Would you agree to join the party as its specialist guide?'

The young man gave Box a broad smile. His eyes danced with excitement.

'I'd be delighted, Inspector Box,' he said. 'Myself — and the London County Council — are at your service!'

★ ★ ★

The morning of Saturday, 1 September, began with a bright mist, through which the sun's disc rose to assume that brazen hue so typical of those deceptively hot days that often presage the onset of autumn. Rising from the dining-room table, where he had breakfasted alone, Professor Roderick Ainsworth stepped out through the open French window and on to the rear terrace of Ashleigh Manor.

Zena would be in her studio by now, earnestly addressing the various challenges of kneading clay. He could hear Margery playing something slow and pensive on the Bechstein grand piano in the music room.

How horrible — damnable — those murders had been! At first, he had tried to rationalize his deeds by telling himself that fear of exposure as a fraud had temporarily unhinged him. But that was not true. As soon as Crale had told him of Wayneflete's attempts to have the mortars and the pigments analysed, he had yielded to an overwhelming surge of anger. This had been followed by a long period of deadly calm, during which he had meticulously and dispassionately plotted the destruction of the two men who had posed an immediate danger to his public reputation. With Crale's unwitting help, all had gone well.

Professor Ainsworth descended some steps that took him on to a sunken garden, where some late roses still bloomed valiantly in their well-tended beds. He lit a cigar, and walked thoughtfully along the paths.

Had Abraham Barnes ever done anything about those mortar samples? Certainly, nothing had been heard of them since Barnes's death. Perhaps his executors, or his family, had thrown them away? It was of no matter, now.

He hadn't minded about Barnes. For one thing, he had struck in the dark, and had seen little but an agitated shadow as his prey. There had been just enough light to do the devilish business with the mercury, and leave the lapis lazuli token behind . . . But young Gregory Walsh — that had been different.

He, Ainsworth, had arrived, unseen, at the Mithraeum, and concealed himself in the darkness of the vault. Walsh had come down the wooden steps, brisk and businesslike, just before seven o'clock. By that time, light was pouring down from the open entrance, and he could see the man quite clearly. Seeing Walsh's youthful face from his place of concealment, his determination had almost failed him. But then, Walsh had produced a spatula, and had begun to scrape the scarlet pigment off the figure of Mithras, pausing to wipe his hands on a handkerchief before turning his attention once again to his work of desecration by flaking some more paint off the monument with his fingernail. He had applied those specially chosen pigments carefully and subtly, to heighten the shadowy traces of the original, long faded over the countless centuries. And now, this philistine was destroying his work of restoration . . . A blinding anger had consumed him.

He had hurtled out of the darkness like a Fury, and had struck the young man dead with a single blow of the adze.

Spooning the honey into the dead man's mouth had almost driven him mad, but it had been necessary. How low he had sunk as a man and a scholar in that moment!

What was he to do? Could he bear the guilt much longer? Could he live with the ghosts of his innocent victims for ever present in his mind? Perhaps not. But at any rate, he would try to survive as long as he could. If the time came for confession, then he would seek out that young detective inspector, and confess to him. A remote possibility of escape through suicide he had dismissed with revulsion and contempt.

He'd never intended the Mithraeum to exist for more than a month or two. He knew that the fabric was unsound, and that the whole area was riddled with tunnels and chambers. After all, he had explored it all, at leisure and unseen, ever since he had discovered the Clerkenwell Treasure nearby, in 1887.

Within minutes of Walsh's death, so he had been told, a great stone slab had fallen from the roof of the crypt, forming a kind of canopy over the poor young man's dead body. Curse Wayneflete! Why couldn't he have curbed his jealous desire for revenge? What a mean, sneaking fellow he was! All this business was *his* fault.

He would go up to London now, this very day, and move slightly out of true some of the pit-props that supported the roof. There were already hidden cords attached to the bases, which he could pull from a concealed position beyond the Roman vault. If he could bring the roof down, then he could appear later with some of the site workmen, and remove the shattered remains of the reredos. The great image of Mithras could disappear for good, and with it all fear of exposure as a fraud.

Ainsworth found Zena in her studio. She was wearing a flowered smock, and her hair was tied back with a black ribbon. She paused, her hands caked with clay, and dragged her eyes away from the massive clay figure that she called *The Sleeper*.

'What is it, Ainsworth?' she asked. 'I'm frightfully busy this morning. I thought you were going to write up those new lecture notes?'

'I've changed my mind, Zena. I'm going up to London today, to have another look at the Mithraeum. I don't know when I'll be back. Have you seen Crale this morning?'

'Crale? Yes. I saw him hurrying down the drive towards the main road about half an hour ago. I assumed you'd sent him on an errand. That man Box was here, yesterday. He had quite a long chat with Crale, so Mason told me. Why, you've gone quite pale! You're liverish, that's what's the matter. It's those foul cigars. Goodbye, I'll see you this evening, I expect.'

When her husband had gone, Mrs Ainsworth — Zena Copley, the rising sculptress — returned to the serious business of *The Sleeper*. Her hands moved skilfully across the figure, kneading the clay, and giving physical form to what she had conceived as an image in her fertile mind.

She heard the crunch of the carriage wheels on the gravel, left her work, and crossed to the window. Her husband was climbing up into the vehicle, a stout canvas bag in his hand. There: the groom had closed the door, and the coachman was moving away along the drive that would take them to Epsom Station.

A sudden fear clutched at her heart. What was wrong? What had ailed the man for these last few weeks? He was moving away from her through the heavy haze of the late summer day, moving away from her . . . 'Goodbye', she'd said. Zena Copley stood motionless at the window, heedless of the clay drying on her hands. This house, and her husband's fortune would all pass to her if anything happened to Ainsworth. Margery had better settle upon which young man to marry, and do it as quickly as was decent . . .

What was the matter with her? Her husband would be back that evening. She gave her whole attention once more to *The Sleeper*.

★ ★ ★

Catherine Lane, cobbled and narrow, dozed in the strong late morning sun. Mr Gold's shop was closed and barred, and there was nobody about. Nobody, that is, except the stately, bearded figure of Sergeant Kenwright, who was standing guard at the narrow entrance to Miller's Alley.

In the derelict and doomed Miller's Court beyond, Arnold Box stood on the broken flags and surveyed the back wall of Hatchard's Furniture Repository. Nothing had changed since he'd first seen it on the day of the murders. The stout door, with its three mortise locks, was undisturbed. Whatever may have happened there during the past few weeks, no one had gained entrance to the building through that door. A discreet

329

examination of the front entrance in Catherine Lane had shown him that the locks there were stiff and free of oil.

This building, so Superintendent Mackharness had discovered, belonged to a company called The North-Eastern Storage Association, with an address in Sunderland. That company was ultimately owned by Professor Roderick Ainsworth. Had he used this building as a workshop, in which he had secretly assembled the five pieces of ancient stone from which he had concocted his fraudulent altar of Mithras? It seemed more than likely.

He would have needed an accomplice — no, that was too strong a word. He'd merely need a not very imaginative workman to assist him. Hadn't he shown a slide in which such a man had appeared? 'The indispensable Ruddock', he'd called him, 'now dead, alas!' Yes, no doubt the late Mr Ruddock had done the necessary heavy work for his master.

Arnold Box looked at his companions, Sergeant Knollys, silent and grim, a tempered steel cold chisel in one hand, and a compact steel hammer in the other; PC Gully, the local constable from 'G' Division, who had summoned them there on 16 August to investigate the death of Gregory Walsh;

Sergeant Kenwright, who had just joined them from Miller's Lane; and Percy Phelps, the council engineer, who would guide them through whatever labyrinth faced them beneath the floor of Hatchard's Furniture Repository. He had brought with him from Spring Gardens two powerful paraffin lanterns as his contribution to the coming search.

The time for talk and speculation was over. Only by breaching the guarded privacy of this enigmatic building would the full truth of Ainsworth's imposture be known. He turned to Sergeant Knollys.

'Break off the locks,' he said, and the massively strong sergeant began his assault upon the doors.

★   ★   ★

Their voices echoed in the vast warehouse. It was very clean, and well swept, but entirely empty. Light poured in from a number of skylights, and the atmosphere was warm and without any hint of the sinister. They had closed the doors, and secured them with a bolt.

'Remind me, PC Gully,' said Box, 'what did that old man tell you — the old man who once lived out there in Miller's Court?'

331

'Sir, he said that he remembered a pile of packing-cases being brought into the warehouse through the rear doors, soon after the discovery of the Clerkenwell Treasure. Other things went in, too: bags of cement, pots of paint, and so on. This old gaffer reckoned that the owners were going to do a bit of decoration.'

'I suppose they were, in a way, PC Gully,' said Box. 'But the man who brought those packing-cases in here was bent on decorating the truth, not the walls.'

Percy Phelps had crossed to a low door set into the left-hand wall of the warehouse. His voice came as a hollow echo across the empty floor.

'Mr Box,' said Phelps, 'this is the staircase leading down to the basement.' Box saw the young man produce a folded plan from his pocket, and shake it open impatiently.

'Yes,' he continued, 'the basement floor is six feet lower, and there's a decent iron staircase here. Isn't it time we went down?'

Yes, thought Box, it's time enough to plumb the depths — the depths of deceit which had led to the murders of two innocent men. Ainsworth's star had set.

'Will you take the lead, Mr Phelps?' said Box. 'Sergeant Kenwright, light those lanterns, and make sure they're burning at full power. I think it'll be very dark where we're going.'

They left the ground floor of the bright warehouse, and followed Phelps down a spiral staircase which brought them into the basement of the building, the floor of which had once formed the nave of old St Catherine's Church. The lanterns were very powerful, but they failed to penetrate the dark farther limits of the vast space. Phelps had commandeered Sergeant Kenwright, and Box watched the two men walk away in a pool of lantern light. Presently, Kenwright called out, and his voice came as a muffled echo through the chill gloom.

'Sir, there are some half-used sacks of cement here, and a work-bench. And there are two massive fragments of stone, with images carved on them. Perhaps they were pieces that wouldn't fit in to the final design.'

Box and the others had reached the spot where Kenwright stood, and looked down on what they were convinced was the evidence of Professor Ainsworth's engagement in an appalling fraud — appalling in its own right as a betrayal of scholarly integrity, and appalling because it had led to the violent murder of two innocent men.

'It's unbelievable, sir,' whispered Knollys. 'And it was this paltry fraud that led to murder. Do you think that man Crale was an accessory?'

'I let him believe I did, Sergeant,' Box replied, 'but I never really thought so. You see, Professor Ainsworth is too honourable a man to implicate a subordinate in a capital crime. I know it sounds paradoxical, Jack, but I think it's true enough.'

'Inspector!' Percy Phelps's voice came from somewhere in the darkness beyond the circle of lantern light. 'Here's the flagstone! The flagstone covering the entrance to the vaults of old St Catherine's Church. There are metal rings let into its surface. Get your two massive sergeants to raise it, and I'll guide you down.'

The stone flag rose easily. Knollys and Kenwright pulled it bodily to one side of the black pit that yawned beneath it. There was a stout wooden ladder lying against the wall of the warehouse, which was evidently used to gain access to the vault. They lowered it cautiously until it came to rest on a hidden pavement below. The burly Kenwright made as if to climb down immediately, but Percy Phelps placed a restraining hand on his arm.

'Just a brief word of warning, gentlemen,' he said. 'This cellar floor is safe enough, but once we descend into the old vaults of St Catherine's Church, we'll find ourselves in a world of empty, abandoned chambers, and decaying brick sewers. Tread carefully, and be ruled by me, because I know where all these ancient places lie with respect to the roads above.'

Percy Phelps stepped on to the ladder, and cautiously descended the six feet that took him to the floor of the vault. The others followed him, the two sergeants carrying the blazing lanterns. A cellar beneath a cellar . . . It was not a pleasant place to be, thought Box, twelve feet below ground level, where the topsoil gave way to the binding London clay, and they were dependent upon paraffin lanterns for illumination. The air smelt damp, and the stone walls were dank with moisture. Somewhere near them they could hear the running of water along a hidden conduit.

'This was the major burial vault of the old church before the Great Fire,' Phelps told them. 'All the human remains were removed when the site was levelled in 1668, and buried elsewhere.'

Percy Phelps stood still, squinting at his folding plan by the light of the lanterns, while the police officers searched the ancient crypt. They found a neatly folded tarpaulin, and a number of paint-brushes standing stiffly in an earthenware pot. There was also a wooden box containing candles and an old-fashioned tinder-box.

'Mr Box,' said Phelps, 'here is the door leading to the Roman vault. It's an ancient thing in its own right — oak, I'd say, strengthened with iron bands. It's medieval, of course: the clergy of St Catherine's would have used the old Roman chamber as an extra burial vault. Shall I open it? If my plan's correct, there will be a short passageway leading directly into the Mithraeum.'

'He must have arranged some kind of false wall at the back of the chamber,' said Box, half to himself. 'A kind of secret panel . . . Yes, Mr Phelps. Open it, by all means. Let's explore this business to the end.'

Phelps put his hand to the catch, and pushed open the door. They had just time to glimpse a short tunnel stretching ahead into the darkness when the pavement of the vault began to tremble, and a noise like a fast-approaching roll of thunder was heard. Phelps shouted a warning, and they rushed as a man towards the ladder that would take them up to the basement of the repository. There came a sudden scream of collapsing masonry, and a tornado of dust-laden air rushed at them from the tunnel that Phelps had exposed.

Half blinded, they scrambled up the ladder and into the empty basement. In less than a minute they had climbed the iron staircase, and were safe in the vast, sunlit warehouse, which rapidly filled with a kind of hot acrid mist. They heard shouts coming from Miller's Alley, and the shouts were followed by a frantic hammering on the bolted rear doors.

★　★　★

'Ainsworth? *Dead*? It's not possible!'

Arnold Box had found Sir Charles Wayneflete sitting on one side of the chess table in the study of his house in Lowndes Square. Major Baverstock, looking particularly pugnacious as he fought a losing battle against his opponent, seemed to freeze in surprise, one of his green malachite bishops still held in his right hand.

'He is dead, Sir Charles,' said Box. 'He was in the Clerkenwell Mithraeum this morning, engaged upon some private business of his own, when the whole site collapsed, burying him under tons of earth and masonry. He must have died instantly.'

'And you came here to tell me? Why did you do that, Mr Box? I'm more sorry than I can say. He and I were no friends, God knows, but I would never have wished that fate upon him.'

'Best thing that could have happened,

Charles.' Major Baverstock had finally relinquished his bishop, and was watching his old friend with interest. 'Don't forget that Mr Box here had proved Ainsworth to be a double murderer. He's lucky to have gone that way, though I expect the inspector is vexed that he's cheated the gallows.'

'Professor Ainsworth was never charged, Major,' said Box. 'But the warrants were already prepared, and I would have taken him up this coming Monday. As to why I came straight away to you, Sir Charles, it was because I feel you were mightily abused by Ainsworth, who publicly belittled your standing as a scholar in order to gloss over his own failings. I think he resented your honesty, and his constant sniping at your reputation may in the end have undermined your own self-confidence. Also, of course, he may have attempted to do you an injury. So I came here straight away to tell you that you can now breathe freely.'

Sir Charles glanced briefly at the chessboard, made as though to move a piece, and then thought better of it.

'That was very civil of you, Mr Box, and I thank you. Did you know that I'm selling the lease of this place, and moving out to a new house in Chiswick? Old Josh there — Major Baverstock — has persuaded me to make a fresh start. I'm minded to write a scholarly monograph on the Clerkenwell Treasure in collaboration with Father Brooks, with the idea of restoring its academic integrity. Oh, I'll give Ainsworth his due, but I'll set the record straight about those chalices.'

'I did a little research myself, sir,' said Box. 'At least, I asked a scholarly friend of mine, Miss Louise Whittaker, to undertake it for me. Professor Ainsworth said that he'd found out about the existence of the Mithraeum in an old manuscript called — I have it recorded here, in my notebook — Cotton Augustus Extra B vii. He said that the original had been destroyed in a fire, and that he'd bought a transcript of it at Sotheby's. He crowned his tale by declaring that this transcript was in turn destroyed by a fire in his own house.'

'And what did your friend find out?'

'She found out that Sotheby's had never sold such a manuscript, and that, in fact, no manuscript of that name had ever existed. The so-called 'Mithraeum', sir, was based upon an elaborate and impudent lie.'

'Well, well,' said Sir Charles Wayneflete, 'it's a wicked world, Inspector. Ainsworth was a greater rogue than I thought. Maybe Josh is right, and it's all for the best.'

His hand hovered over the chessboard for a few seconds, and then executed a series of rapid moves. 'Yes,' he repeated, 'perhaps it's all for the best. Check! And also mate!'

★   ★   ★

Superintendent Mackharness finished reading a report that he had picked up from his desk, and then looked at his audience. Box and Knollys waited to see what he would have to say about the previous Saturday's dramatic conclusion to the business of the Clerkenwell Mithraeum. It was the morning of Monday, 3 September.

'It would appear from this brief report from Superintendent Hunt, of 'G',' he said, 'which was kindly brought to me here at the Rents this morning, that Professor Roderick Ainsworth entered the Mithraeum from Priory Gate Street at the very moment that you and your colleagues had chosen to push open that subterranean door. We shall never know why he went to that place on Saturday, or what particular action it was that caused the sudden and total collapse of the site. However, when the body was finally unearthed, its right hand was found to be clutching a length of thin rope that was attached to the base of a splintered baulk of timber, one of several that had been used to support the ceiling of the chamber.'

Mackharness put down the report on his desk, and sighed.

'You'd been warned by Mr Phelps that the area was dangerous, and that cave-ins were likely,' he said, looking at Box. 'But in view of what I've just told you, I don't suppose you will see this sudden collapse as an accident?'

'I don't, sir,' Box replied. 'I thought all along that Ainsworth took fright, and went to the Mithraeum on Saturday in order to destroy the evidence of his fraud. He must have arranged some kind of apparatus to weaken the structure. I wondered, too, whether he'd planned to start a fire — we'll never know for certain. But I believe he was there for malign intent, and that either something went wrong with his apparatus, or events simply took their course, and the whole rotten site collapsed. It was an act of fate, sir, or Providence, to my way of thinking.'

'He fell into the pit that he had digged for others, as the Good Book says,' said Mackharness. 'Well, whatever the cause, Professor Roderick Ainsworth is dead, and beyond our earthly justice. He also remains unaccused in law. All this business of his frauds will cause an enormous public scandal. Do you think that side of the affair could be quietly forgotten?'

'No, sir, I don't,' said Box hotly. 'You and I

341

know well enough that Ainsworth cruelly murdered two innocent men, and tricked out their slaughters to look like ritual sacrifice. That truth, sir, must not be suppressed, and therefore his frauds — the cause of those murders — must not be suppressed either. Let all be known!'

'Well done, Box!' cried Mackharness. 'I admit I was tempting you there, in order to see what you'd say, though I knew what your answer would be. You're right, of course. Yes, let all be known.'

'Thank you, sir,' said Box. 'There's a gaggle of reporters outside, with Billy Fiske holding court among them. I'll go out to them now, sir, and make a brief statement. Then I'll meet them all in the Clarence Vaults in Victoria Street at two o'clock, and tell them the whole wicked story.'

'Tell them the *facts*, Box,' said Superintendent Mackharness, wagging a finger at Box, but smiling at the same time, 'no *tripe*, do you hear?'

'No tripe, sir!' said Inspector Box. He and Sergeant Knollys left their master's office, and made their way downstairs and out on to the steps, in front of which a crowd of eager reporters, notebooks and pencils at the ready, had assembled on the cobbles facing 2 King James's Rents.

We do hope that you have enjoyed reading this large print book.

Did you know that all of our titles are available for purchase?

We publish a wide range of high quality large print books including:
Romances, Mysteries, Classics
General Fiction
Non Fiction and Westerns

Special interest titles available in large print are:
The Little Oxford Dictionary
Music Book
Song Book
Hymn Book
Service Book

Also available from us courtesy of Oxford University Press:
Young Readers' Dictionary
(large print edition)
Young Readers' Thesaurus
(large print edition)

For further information or a free brochure, please contact us at:
Ulverscroft Large Print Books Ltd.,
The Green, Bradgate Road, Anstey,
Leicester, LE7 7FU, England.
Tel: (00 44) **0116 236 4325**
Fax: (00 44) **0116 234 0205**

Other titles published by
The House of Ulverscroft:

THE AQUILA PROJECT

Norman Russell

At the opening of Tower Bridge in June 1894, a would-be assassin, Anders Grunwalski, is rescued from police custody. Detective Inspector Arnold Box, working with Colonel Kershaw, Head of Secret Intelligence, uncovers a conspiracy to assassinate the Tsar and plunge Europe into war — The Aquila Project. When Box learns that Grunwalski is on his way to Russia, he and Kershaw pursue Grunwalski across Europe. In Poland, as an unwilling guest of the enigmatic Baron Augustyniak, Box realizes the true purpose of the Aquila Project. After a desperate race against time, he and Kershaw bring their mission to a breathtaking conclusion.